Kriegsmarine

Victorious

Part Two

By Kim Kerr

2019

Chapter One: Winter 1942

Shells burst below his aircraft. Kapitänleutnant Hans-Joachim Marseille led his Rotte of four fighters over the coast at three thousand meters. For once there were large masses of clouds towering into the sky, well above the German flight. The British were wasting ammunition, he thought; a foolish decision when their supplies must be limited. The enemy had received some relief when the fast supply ship HMS Glengyle snuck into Valletta harbour. The vessel was still down there, attracting the attention of the Stukas and Ju 88s from Sicily and high level attacks from the Regia Aeronautica. As the dive-bombers fell upon the lone ship, flying through a wall of anti-aircraft fire, Marseille watched for the British fighter response. It wasn't long in coming.

Six Hurricanes emerged from the immense cloud before rolling over to attack the Stukas.

"Alright boys, here we go," yelled Marseille.

The He 112s dived after the enemy machines, catching them over the harbour. Marseille picked out a machine that was chasing a dive-bomber.

"Stay with me Clade!" he ordered.

His wingman Leutnant zur See Emil Clade acknowledged and Marseille relaxed, knowing that someone was watching his tail.

Small red dots flew from the Stuka's rear gunner at the approaching Hurricane, however the British pilot held his fire, not wanting to waste a single round. Marseille admired the man's discipline but understood it gave him a second longer to save the German dive-bomber. He was right behind the enemy machine so there was no need for any deflection shooting. He slowly depressed the firing button and watched as his 20mm shells tore into the Hurricane's wings and tail. The enemy pilot threw his aircraft into a tight turn but the damaged plane staggered and went into a spin. Somehow the machine recovered, however now his wingman lined up on the crippled plane and finished it off with a quick burst of fire, shattering the cockpit and engine.

Marseille had already moved on and was chasing another British plane away from the coast. He felt for the British pilot as he tried to climb and then dive away from him. The fact was the He 112C outperformed the Hurricane in nearly every way. It was faster by fifteen miles an hour, could out climb the British fighter, and turned just as tightly on both the horizontal and vertical plains. There wasn't even much difference in the armaments, with most He 112s having three 20mm cannons to the Hurricane's four. Marseille however, was flying the lighter German fighter which had swapped its two wing cannon for heavy 13mm machine guns, making the plane a little more manoeuvrable and slightly faster.

He let the speed bleed away as he spiralled downwards, slowly cutting inside the enemy pilot's turns. Marseille caught the British plane just above the blue water of the ocean and destroyed

5

it with a single burst which sent the Hurricane plummeting into the waves. A massive plume of spray marked the demise of another man and he couldn't help feeling a twinge of guilt.

"That's your one hundredth victim, skipper," yelled Emil.

"No, my ninety ninth. I'm giving the shared kill to you, because it will be your fifth," said Marseille.

"But you did most of the work, skipper."

"It would have got away Emil, if you hadn't finished it."

He knew he shouldn't chat over the radio and his commanding officer wouldn't approve of first names, but Marseille was never one to follow the rules.

The Stukas hit the British ship twice and even one of the high flying Savoia-Marchetti 81s (SM.81) scored. The merchant vessel caught fire and was later re-floated and scuttled outside the harbour as its engines were wrecked. The Kriegsmarine bombers lost three planes to flak and four Hurricanes were shot down without loss to the He 112 section.

6

The airstrip at Pantelleria was concrete and set against the side of a steep hill. The landing area was three kilometers from the main village as the crow flies, but much further by road. Most of the island had been cleared of civilians and there was little to do there except swim or watch the odd movie, and it was too cold now to do the former.

Since the death of his sister at the hands of her jealous lover, Marseille spent a lot of time writing to his mother. The sudden disappearance of Inge from his world left a hole that was immeasurably deep. With his father still stuck in Russia trying to save his command from destruction in the snow before Moscow his mother had been left to deal with her grief alone. Not that the old man would have been much help even if he had been around, as the pair had been separated since Marseille was a child.

His mother needed him, but the navy only gave him three weeks compassionate leave, then flew him back to Sicily before moving his Staffel out to share the Italian air base on Pantelleria. At least he had spent Christmas with her. While he'd been at home in Berlin, Marseille hadn't visited the clubs or drinking halls. He had stayed at home with his mother, reading to her or sitting around listening to the radio in the evenings. He used his connections in the Kriegsmarine to get extra food supplies, and more coal and wood for the fire. It was a bitterly cold winter in Germany and he could only imagine the suffering of the troops in Russia.

It had all been too brief, and now the time with his mother felt like an ancient memory. Yet, paradoxically, the death of his sister was still raw and fresh. Marseille supposed he would heal in time, that's if he didn't die first. Meanwhile, the war dragged on.

Sharing an air base with the Italians was a strange experience. They had different ways of doing things and a more relaxed attitude to life. Marseille wondered if he liked their national mindset more than the German one, but doubted it suited the business of war. They certainly seemed to have a better appreciation of jazz. Macchi 202s sat in rows next to a few Reggiane Re.2001s. Both aircraft looked similar, though the 202s seemed a little lighter. Flak guns ringed the airfield, which was itself a well-constructed affair with both a large east-west and a smaller north-south runway. The accommodation was comfortable and lack of distractions on the small island kept Marseille concentrating on flying.

The Staffel was called to the main briefing room early the following morning. A German and Italian officer stood on a slightly raised platform, and behind them hung a map of the central Mediterranean. The Italian spoke first, then the German naval officer translated.

"The British are sending two convoys toward Malta, each containing two freighters escorted by a large number of destroyers and cruisers. With the Afrika Korps having retreated to the area just east of Tripoli, the British are able to provide fighter cover from the area of Benghazi. That's where we come in. Stukas and Ju 88s will fly from bases in Sicily; we will meet them en route and escort them to the target. Our Italian friends will fly to Malta to distract any Hurricanes that might want to get involved, and they will also attack the convoy with torpedo planes. We need to be careful as there may be Italian cruisers in the area, but these should be north of our target. They are screening a convoy of four ships taking supplies and equipment to the Afrika Korps," said the older man.

The rest of the briefing related to speeds, fuel consumption and the projected point at which they would meet the Kriegsmarine bombers. They were warned there might even be British attack aircraft in the area, and Marseille thought the airspace over the Mediterranean was sounding as though it may become very busy.

Twelve Macchi 202s carrying drop tanks took off first, followed by the Re.2001s. The latter had been fitted with bombs and were to attack airstrips around Malta. The He 112s were the last to become airborne and flew to a position above the Italian aircraft. The route to the British convoy went past Malta so the formation flew together for the first two hundred kilometers, with the Macchis and Re.2001s turning north when the island came into sight.

At first Marseille was concerned his Staffel might not find the Stukas and Ju 88s as the weather was still cloudy with showers sweeping over the ocean, however the further east they flew, the better the conditions became. Eventually the sky cleared and Marseille spotted the bombers approaching from the north-west. He was surprised to see six He 111 torpedo bombers with the formation. He had heard the naval air contingent of the Kriegsmarine was to receive reinforcements due to the losses they had incurred, but thought none were due until February. The extra planes would be an unpleasant surprise for the British.

The British convoy was thought to be about one hundred kilometers from the German formation's position when other planes were spotted. These aircraft flew at a lower altitude and seemed to be twin-engined machines.

"British bombers and attack aircraft; probably after our ships," said Marseille over the radio.

"Take your Rotte after them Marseille. We'll get our bombers through," ordered Kapitän zur See Fredrick Muller, the Staffel commander.

"Yes, sir."

Four He 112s peeled off from the main group of fighters and dived after the British aircraft. They'd been warned that such a meeting might occur and the Staffel commander had been given the choice of ignoring enemy bombers or attacking them, as long as some of the Kriegsmarine escort planes stayed with the main force. Now four German aircraft opened their throttles and gave chase.

The British planes had probably come from Benghazi and were following directions from reconnaissance aircraft. As Marseille got closer he realised the enemy formation was made up of Bristol Beaufighters and Beauforts. Six Tomahawk single-engined fighters which hadn't been spotted earlier, also accompanied the twin-engined planes.

"That's a lot of aircraft, skipper," said Leutnant zur See Emil Clade.

"I count twenty four," said Marseille. "Alright, this is what we'll do. Emil and I will attack the fighters. Anton One, you and your wingman will go after the torpedo bombers. The Beaufighters are not to be attacked head on. They are both escort and flak supressing aircraft, though they may carry bombs. The Beauforts are the most important target. As soon as we scatter the British single-engined fighters, we will come down and help you. Good hunting."

They had the advantage of altitude and speed, though the enemy saw them and turned to attack. Marseille was able to veer inside the Tomahawks and shoot down a machine painted with a mouth of sharp teeth over the engine. The fuel tank caught fire and the pilot bailed out immediately. The rest of the formation went into a defensive circle. Marseille dived in from above, firing a quick burst at a British machine. Pieces flew from the aircraft and it dropped out of formation, black smoke spewing from its engine.

13

Diving through the circle, he pulled up quickly, firing another burst at a plane on the other side. The Tomahawk shuddered and a tongue of flame shot from behind the engine before it rolled on its side and fell toward the sea.

The British defensive circle fell apart and his wingman, who had lost him in all the violent maneuvers, latched onto another fighter and shot it down as it tried to climb away. But Marseille didn't see this as he was already diving down to the battle between the Beaufighters and his other Rotte.

"Emil, go after the bombers," he ordered.

His wingman rolled over and headed toward the British machines which had opened a gap between the two groups of opposing planes. Marseille dropped down into the swirling dogfight and found himself behind a Beaufighter at a range of only two hundred meters. The rear gunner fired his rifle calibre machine gun at the He 112 but Marseille ignored the bullets. Two bursts from his cannons set the British aircraft's engines alight, and the plane turned and fell into the ocean only one thousand meters below. The enemy machines were slower and less manoeuvrable on both the horizontal and vertical axes; their only advantage being the very heavy armament they carried, as the pilot flying Anton Two discovered when he turned in front of an enemy plane. The cone of 20mm shells and machine gun bullets tore the He 112 to pieces. Marseille cursed at the sight and turned inside one of the twin-engined fighters, destroying it by shooting its port engine apart at close range. The British planes began dumping their bomb load at this point and Marseille smiled as some turned in the direction of North Africa. With Anton One he dived after his wingman who had taken on the Beauforts by himself.

His wingman was darting in for what looked like his second attack, just as one of the British bombers had broken formation and was flying south with smoke streaming from an engine.

"Shall I finish him, sir?" asked the pilot of Anton One.

"No, he isn't a threat to the convoy anymore. We need to convince his friends to do the same thing," said Marseille.

They came up behind the tight British formation and saw why Emil was firing from a range of four hundred meters. The concentrated fire of the rear gunners made it impossible to get any closer without risking being shot down.

"Anton One, assist my wingman," Marseille ordered. He remembered the method he had used to attack Wellington bombers earlier in the war and flew to the flank of the enemy formation. Coming in from side on he had to allow the right amount of lead in front of his target, predicting where the plane would be when his bullets reached it. Marseille was now an expert marksman and knew the speed the bombers were travelling. He needed to fire about an aircraft and a half-length in front of the target. Marseille flew out to the side of the formation and then rolled over to come in quickly from the flank. The enemy gunners didn't cover this zone of approach and he was able to line up the first Beaufort with little pressure. His cannon shells raked the bomber from one end to the other, shattering the cockpit, destroying an engine, and killing the pilot. The plane went into a spin briefly before crashing into the water. He flew over the British formation, rolled his aircraft up and over in a loop, and then came back and repeated the method, from the opposite flank. This time his target exploded violently, throwing pieces of aircraft in all directions. The British formation had closed up to provide mutual support, so when the bomber blew up, its engine hit the plane flying next to it, taking the entire wing off.

"Two for the price of one, skipper," yelled Emil.

At this point, the enemy dropped their torpedos, turned, and fled. They descended to wave top height but Anton One still shot down another machine and Marseille damaged a bomber before they let the remaining planes go. The He 112s were low on fuel and ammunition so the German fighters didn't pursue. Marseille found out later, when news of his exploits reached Germany, he was to be awarded the Oak Leaves to his Knight's Cross for shooting down seven aircraft in a single engagement and preventing an attack on a critical convoy. All of the ships reached Tripoli and unloaded their cargo of fuel, ammunition, trucks, seventy Panzer IIIs and forty half-tracks for the Afrika Korps.

Rommel sent a personal note of thanks to Marseille for protecting the convoy, and he was invited to Berlin to receive the medal from Adolf Hitler himself.

V

The Ju 290 was an easy aircraft to fly but KapitänHelmut Bruck missed the old Do 19. He now commanded the Staffel and his crew were the first to try the new aircraft. The story was that Grossadmiral Wever had pushed the aircraft's development, having convinced Reichsmarschal Kesselring of the dual role the plane could take as both a transport aircraft and a marine reconnaissance machine. Originally it wasn't supposed to be ready until August, but with the project fast tracked by the head of the navy, the first Ju 290 were now ready to fly in February. This version carried a 20mm gun in the nose and one in the tail, and two heavy calibre machine guns in a gondola beneath the main fuselage. Stronger defensive armaments were proposed, but in order to get the plane into action, the lighter weaponry was all that was available for the moment. Bruck thought even this was an improvement over the carrying capacity of the Do 19.

The main advantage of the new aircraft was its range. At six thousand kilometers, it was far beyond anything any other reconnaissance machine could accomplish. Even the Do 24 seaplane could only fly half as far. Flying from Iceland took the new aircraft out as far as Spain to the south and Newfoundland to the west. Bruck wished he was flying from the air bases in southern France but another Staffel had been assigned there. He wanted to be warm and drink fine wine, but the bases in Iceland allowed the Ju 290 to reach the Canadian coast; those flying from France could only reach a little past the mid-Atlantic.

His crew was new, with most of Bruck's original companions in either administrative roles or training new gunners, navigators or pilots at the air bases on Rugen Island. This plane carried seven men, including himself.

The wind blew from the north, causing Bruck to wrap his scarf more firmly around his face. The weather was bitterly cold but he supposed that was to be expected at this time of year in Reykjavik. At least the sky was partially clear.

"Another beautiful day on our island paradise, sir," said Matrose Helmut Khole, the rear gunner.

"Positively balmy," answered Bruck.

The little Berliner smiled and gave him the thumbs up as he climbed in through the rear hatch. He followed and made his way forward to where he found Oberfähnrich zur See Hals Bruner conducting pre-flight checks.

"She's good to go skipper, though we'll only be carrying two five hundred kilo bombs," said Bruner.

"Why is that?"

"There's a shortage it seems and we are waiting on more to arrive on one of those giant submarines we got off the French."

"Well, it will have to be enough, though I hope we won't be using them. Our job today is finding enemy convoys."

20

"I thought all the U-boat boys were off the coast of America picking off the unescorted tankers."

"That's just the long range boats. The type VII variety can't make it that far and are still trying to find vessels to sink in the mid-Atlantic."

"We find them and they somehow slip around the waiting patrol line of submarines. I don't know how those U-boat commanders keep missing them."

"They're not all getting past, but you're right, it's becoming a real problem. The British have become very good at dodging our U-boats. Anyway, let's get our new mount in the air and see what she can do. The few flights across the island really haven't shown me what the Ju 290 is capable of. "

"Those cannons certainly make me feel a little more secure."

"If the British protect their convoys with more of those little carriers, we might find ourselves meeting Hurricanes or Wildcat fighters. Now that the Americans are in the war who knows what we might run into."

They took off a little after breakfast and flew southwest toward the tip of Greenland before heading due south. Cloud cover increased until the plane reached a position two hundred kilometers north of St Johns, then the sky cleared and Bruck and his crew could see the ocean clearly. They flew to a position due east of the fishing port before turning for home. It was then that Matrose Henrik Beck, in the ventral gunner's position, spotted the convoy.

"Looks like about thirty ships, skipper; quite a few tankers among them."

"Escorts?" asked Bruck.

"Two corvettes, a minesweeper, and one of those four stacker destroyers."

"Hmm, more might meet them at sea, but call it in Klein."

The radio operator Bootsman Hans Klein could be heard speaking to the command centre in Iceland while Bruck thought about bombing

22

one of the ships. There were a few stragglers at the rear of the convoy though they weren't tankers. He took the aircraft around in a gentle turn, when he saw the flash of a rocket.

"CAM ship," yelled Matrose Beck.

"I've seen it," said Bruck.

One of the convoy had a Hurricane which took off on a rocket-assisted catapult and attacked German patrol aircraft before landing in the sea, where the pilot would hopefully be rescued. They were desperate attempts to protect British ships but Bruck admired the pilots who volunteered for these dangerous assignments.

"We are too low to run so get ready to fight. Gunners, is the enemy aircraft cannon armed?" asked Bruck.

"Too far away to tell, skipper," said the rear gunner Matrose Khole.

"Right, the enemy have never faced a Ju 290 and won't know about the 20mm in the tail. Khole, it's up to you."

"I've got this, sir," said the Berliner.

Bruck smiled, he knew the little gunner had been first in marksmanship in his course but it was always different when someone was shooting back.

The Hurricane climbed rapidly toward them and Bruck dumped his bombs over the convoy knowing there was little chance of hitting anything. He then turned the big aircraft north and increased his airspeed.

"He's coming up fast behind us, skipper," said Khole. "Do you want me to tell you when to turn?"

"If he doesn't have cannons I was thinking of letting you get a good shot at it," said Bruck.

"It's an old type one Hurricane, so rifle calibre machine guns only," said the gunner.

"Right then, I'm going straight and level if he keeps coming from behind. Let me know if the enemy pilot changes his angle of approach."

24

"No change, sir. He's almost in range, coming up slowly from below. Must think we haven't seen him."

"The Do 19 only had one light machine gun in the tail," said Bruck.

Seconds ticked by and Bruck heard the chatter of distant machine guns. Bruck realised the British pilot had opened fire too soon; a common mistake when shooting at a large aircraft for the first time. Bruck wondered if the enemy pilot had ever experienced combat before (Pilot officer Conway had only ever flown against Bf 109s over France on two occasions, without success). The slower thud of the 20mm cannon came two seconds later. Two short bursts were followed by one longer barrage of fire and a yell from the rear gunner.

"He is hit, skipper. Smoke's pouring from the engine," said Khole.

"Good shooting," said Bruck.

"Piece of cake, sir."

Bruck laughed and watched as the enemy aircraft flew west toward Newfoundland. There was a chance the pilot might make it, as the coast was only one hundred kilometers away, though the question was whether the Hurricane would stay airborne for another twenty minutes. Perhaps the plane would crash into the sea close to the coast and somebody would fish the British flier out of the water. Bruck hoped the man would make it, as even though he wasn't a great tactician, the enemy pilot was still exceptionally brave.

v

Convoy HX173 was caught by three type VII U-boats two nights later and five ships were sunk, one of those being CAM ship the Empire Ray, the other four were freighters. Two stragglers, the six thousand GRT Evita and Havprins at eight thousand GRT were discovered and attacked by Do 24s and Ju 290s over the next few days and also sunk. A second attack by U-751 destroyed the tanker Skaraas, originally from Norway, and damaged the cargo ship Pacific Enterprise. After that, winter storms hid the convoy from view and the surviving ships safely made it into port at Liverpool.

26

The office of the commander of the 9th U-boat flotilla was well heated and had a pleasant view of Reykjavik harbour. Newly promoted Fregattenkapitän Hans-Gerrit von Stockhausen sat behind his desk and read reports on the attacks on convoy HX 173. He was glad not to be out in the Northern Atlantic, fighting his way through storms and dodging depth charges any more. He stood and stretched his back, aware that the wounds he had suffered whilst fighting against British commandos on the Faroes needed more time to heal. Still, he was fit enough and had insisted on returning to his post before someone else could take the position.

Looking out his window, he could see the Prince Eugen aground, just offshore. The cruiser would probably never move again, or at least not until the war was over. Its anti-aircraft batteries and the eight-inch guns provided a much needed boost to the defence of the capital of Iceland, though Stockhausen guessed the Grossadmirald would much prefer to have the heavy cruiser at sea.

Overhead a helicopter buzzed, flying to patrol the coastline. The Fa 223 Drache was a new addition on the island and its ability to move small amounts of cargo or a few troops to different locations quickly had proved to be of immediate benefit. In some ways, it helped to alleviate the shortage of motor transport on the island. The air contingent on the island was nearly all from the Kriegsmarine with the only Luftwaffe aircraft being the Ju 52 and brand new Ju 252 transport aircraft, the latter plane being able to make the round trip back to Norway without refuelling (as long as they landed on the new air base on the east coast).

Stockhausen was still getting over the size of Iceland. Being just over four kilometers long and nearly three hundred wide, the area was larger than Belgium and Holland together. The countryside was unlike anything in Europe, being made up of grassland, barren rock and glaciers. The population mainly lived near the coast and even then, it was sparsely settled. With the removal of many of the children and married women, as well as the elderly, the density of people was even further reduced.

Over the previous autumn, the 56th Infantry Division, which had fought in France and Russia, had replaced the mountain units on the island. Unfortunately the unit still wasn't back up to its nominal strength of thirteen thousand men and lacked some of its heavy equipment. There were probably about five thousand Kriegsmarine personnel on Iceland, mostly service troops and gunners and a few security troops. There was also a fast response group, or reinforced reconnaissance battalion, made up of half-tracks, light four wheeled armoured cars, a few eight wheeled cars, some French Somua S 35 tanks and twelve Panzer IVs. A few Panzer IIIs were due to arrive soon on a fast destroyer, to further strengthen the group.

Most of the movement around the island was done by horse and cart with Icelandic ponies proving to be very useful in pulling small wagons. The food supply was worse than earlier in the war due to the need to supply the German Army in Russia, however there was still plenty of fish and fast transport vessels kept Iceland fed. British submarines were always a danger but the winter months allowed the German occupying forces to build up a two-month reserve of food and a one-month reserve of fuel.

A knock at the door interrupted his thoughts.

"Enter," he said.

A young woman with red-gold hair set in a bun stuck her head around the doorway.   "Coffee, sir?" asked Matrose Mila Roth.

"Is it real?"

"No, sir. We haven't had proper coffee for months. This is made from chicory, rye and acorns." She smiled apologetically.

Stockhausen wrinkled his nose and then sighed. "Better than nothing I suppose. Thank you Mila," he said.

The young woman left and he sighed again. Mila was very pretty but she was the girlfriend of one of the fighter pilots. Stockhausen believed he flew one of the few Bf 110s on Iceland. He longed for decent female company and didn't like visiting the local dancers or prostitutes that had been flown in from Germany. The unmarried

30

local girls generally kept their distance and anyway, he found the women in Iceland too forceful for his tastes. German women knew their place but those around Reykjavik held strong opinions and didn't like being told what to do.

Oh well, he had work to do, so best not to think about what he couldn't control.

"Mila, have you typed up the roster for sailors who are to go out on the fishing boats?" he yelled through the door.

The young woman appeared with his hot drink and a folder containing a number of sheets of paper.

"This will last to the end of the month when the fuel situation will be reassessed, sir. You said it might be difficult to put more than a dozen boats into the waters north of the island this summer," she said

"True enough. It all depends on supplies," he said.

"I've heard some of the locals are eating horse meat, sir."

"There are a lot of ponies on Iceland so it doesn't surprise me. Still, I thought it hadn't come to that yet."

"Plenty of fish to be had sir, and bread, but not a lot of red meat, that's all."

"I know. I'd kill for a steak or a nice pork chop."

"When we win we'll be able to eat whatever we want, sir."

He nodded, and Mila smiled and left.

The problem with his secretary's last comment was they probably wouldn't win. The best Germany could hope for, Stockhausen thought, was a well-fought draw. Already the Americans were flying over the island from a base they had carved out in Greenland at Narsarsuaq, the very southern tip of that frozen land mass. B-17Fs had attacked once and the wreck of one which had been shot down still rested just outside the docks in a field. American Liberator bombers often made reconnaissance flights over western Iceland and their Catalina flying boats prowled off the coast. Stockhausen knew this was only the beginning. The USA had more cars per head of population than any other country in the world before the war, and if that production capacity was turned to items of war then Germany was in a lot of trouble. The fact the Americans faced enemies in two oceans wouldn't bother them.

Then there were the recent defeats in Russia. He had friends in the Soviet Union and knew of the casualties. Perhaps they would get another chance to win in the east, but he doubted it. What they could do is bleed the Russian bear until it agreed to end the war. In the meantime, they needed to keep Britain and America at arm's length. It could be done, but it would mean a much longer war. Another reason to be thankful he wasn't somewhere out in the Atlantic.

At night, he would lie awake and feel guilty for reporting on a fellow Kriegsmarine officer to get his position. Stockhausen felt like a fraud. He often considered throwing his medals into the sea and admitting his sins to the SS. He knew he was being ridiculous and they'd probably just give him another U-boat and send him back out to die. Then there were the dreams. He awoke feeling like he couldn't breathe, that he was drowning as his boat filled with cold water. Then he would wake up gasping for air and wouldn't sleep again for the rest of the night. His feelings were in conflict between the fear he'd be discovered as an imposter, and relief that he didn't have to guide a U-boat through the heart of an enemy convoy ever again.

"Sir, U-216 has returned," said Mila through the door.

"Good; call for my motorcycle and driver. I'll head down and see them," he said.

Stockhausen was lucky to have transportation. The motorcycle and sidecar combination allowed him to visit various facilities around the island, as his command reached beyond the 9th flotilla to coordination of the Kriegsmarine Staffel as well as various supply units.

A Matrose was found to take him down to the wharf and he arrived just as U-216 was tying up. The boat was a minelaying type and he had ordered the deadly cargo laid inside the Saint Lawrence waterway. He wanted to know how great the risks had been.

Stockhausen would never have asked a crew to attempt such a feat

in summer but believed the storms and fog that dominated the

Canadian coast in winter could hide a U-boat. The fact the U-216

had returned was an excellent sign, although as he got out of the

sidecar and walked toward the dock, he noted battle damage. The

deck gun was turned slightly on its side and some of the metal

plates around the conning tower were buckled.

Oberleutnant zur See Karl-Otto Schultz looked like a young

priest, his long face serious and clean-shaven, something very

difficult to achieve on a U-boat due to the lack of fresh water. He

wore his Iron Cross around his neck and gave the stiff-armed Nazi

salute, followed with a Heil Hitler. Stockhausen responded in kind.

"It looks like you hit a few problems Oberleutnant?" asked

Stockhausen.

"Yes sir, it was a rough trip and I don't think the old girl will

be ready for another operation anytime soon," answered Schultz.

"I'll probably have to send the boat back to Germany for repairs but at least it will give you a chance to have some leave. Care to tell me what happened?"

"May I see to my crew first, sir?"

"Of course, and then clean up a little and meet me at my office. I'll leave the bike and its driver for you and walk back. I need the exercise."

"It's a bit cold, sir. You could wait at the guard house if you like."

Stockhausen glanced at the sky. It was grey but not threatening snow and there was little wind. "I'm well wrapped; it'll do me good," he said and started walking.

He returned to his office, his toes and fingers almost numb. Stockhausen now realised that the Icelandic weather was more challenging than he realised. Kassel, his hometown in central Germany, could become very cold in winter, but not like this. He was glad of the heat the pipes gave off as he stood in the outer office. Geothermal energy was harnessed from the many hot springs in the area and piped into the city's houses. Mila smiled at him and continued typing. Stockhausen found the tapping somehow soothing and allowed the noise to drown out all other thoughts, until Oberleutnant zur See Karl-Otto Schultz arrived on the motorcycle. He asked Mila to make them both a hot drink and took the young officer into his room.

"Well, what did all the damage Shultz? Destroyer or aircraft?" he asked.

"Mainly corvettes, sir. Though we were hit so many times it's hard to tell. I didn't think we would make it back," said Schultz.

Stockhausen remembered that feeling. The crushing despair of thinking your boat wouldn't survive the pounding it received. He could still hear the depth charges exploding and the sound the metal skin of the submarine made as it flexed and buckled. He shook it away.

"When did it start?"

"The attacks? Soon after we reported in. We surfaced just a little west and north of Corner Brook on Newfoundland as ordered."

"So you were inside the waterway?"

"Yes, sir. We came in through the gap between the mainland and the northern end of the island and continued south, intending to lay our mines between Anticosti Island and New Brunswick but never got the chance. Soon after we sent the radio message enemy ships seemed to come from everywhere."

"Their radio detection finding equipment must have improved."

"I'd agree sir, except this is the third time it's happened and the last time we were well offshore. We sent a signal and almost a day later two destroyers appeared in our area. On the other occasion it was an aircraft showing up out of nowhere. Sometimes I think the British are reading our mail."

"Enigma is uncrackable. That's what all the experts keep telling us."

"Then we need to stop using our radios at sea because the enemy must be able to detect them from a few hundred kilometers. Anyway, when we surface we dumped the mines because there were still enemy ships in the area, and this part was strange, some of them were minesweepers. I understand the British picking up our signals and using them to pinpoint our location, but how did they know we were carrying mines, sir?"

"You make an excellent point."

"Sir, there were at least three corvettes and possibly a couple of destroyers hunting us. They were very confident we were there."

Stockhausen thanked the U-boat commander and promised to expedite temporary repair of his submarine so it could return to Germany. He then thought about why the mine-laying submarine had been discovered. Of course there were many possible reasons, but the arrival of the mine sweepers was very interesting. It was doubtful the enemy knew these vessels had been spotted by the Germans and perhaps they were rushed to the area to help find the U-boat. It was still a coincidence, and one that Stockhausen found hard to ignore. He decide to write a report to his superiors in Berlin recommending investigating the possibility that the German codes were broken.

V

Another British convoy was trying to fight its way through to Malta. Fregattenkapitän Bernhard Jope led the eight Ju 88s toward the North African coast at an altitude of four thousand meters. The previous night an Italian fleet had attacked the convoy but withdrew due to British torpedo attacks. Jope shook his head. He was stunned that a few destroyers and light cruisers could hold off a fleet consisting of a battleship and at least two heavy cruisers. If the Italians had possessed radar then perhaps the attack would have turned out differently. Now though, the enemy was within fighter range of Malta. The escort of He 112s from Pantelleria had just joined them, as had a Staffel of Macchi 202s. Jope felt a little safer with the fighters flying above him but knew the British interceptors would soon arrive.

"Skipper, there are He 111s coming in from the north, and they're with Bf 110s," said Bootsmann Walter Herkner, his co-pilot.

"The 110s won't be much help," muttered Jope.

He knew the big twin-engined fighters would enter a defensive circle at the first sign of a British single-engined fighter, and leave the bombers to fend for themselves.

"There's the convoy," Werkner added.

"Well maybe we won't have to worry about Hurricanes," said Jope.

He put the plane into a shallow dive and radioed the other eight aircraft to follow him down. The He111 torpedo planes were already losing altitude. The anti-aircraft fire wasn't fierce and Jope wondered how much ammunition the British had used fighting off air attacks on the previous day.

41

"Fighters skipper, six o'clock high, moving quickly," reported the pilot of Bruno one, the leader of Second Flight.

"Dive for the deck, leave them to the escort," ordered Jope.

As the enemy ships loomed larger below him he heard the leader of the He 112 Staffel radio a warning to the bombers. "Enemy fighters are Spitfires. We won't get to them in time Anton leader."

Shit, thought Jope and he pushed the throttle wide open. He understood the Spitfire to be at least forty miles per hour faster than the Hurricanes they usually faced. Now he confronted a dilemma. You couldn't skip bomb at this speed, and if they did, nearly all of the missiles would bury themselves in the waves or bounce right over the enemy ships.

"Drop your bombs directly on the enemy ships, and only dump speed if you can. Your lives and the aircraft are more important than getting a hit at this stage," he said over the radio.

He wondered if his commanding officers would see it that way but they weren't here.

HMS Cleopatra was a Dido class light cruiser which had only been commissioned in November of the previous year. She was low on ammunition and had suffered a hit in the previous day's engagement with the Italian fleet, with her radar and wireless station destroyed by a six-inch shell. Jope approached her at high speed from the stern, firing his four 20mm cannons and two machine guns down the length of the ship. As he lifted the aircraft's nose, Jope pushed the release. Four 500kg bombs fell from an altitude of two hundred meters, landing on either side of the vessel and almost lifting it out of the water with the combined blasts. The propellers of the ship were damaged and many of the anti-aircraft positions knocked out by the cannon fire. Anton Four hit the slowing cruiser with two bombs which blew a thirty meter hole in the ship's bow and knocked out B turret.

"Break right," yelled Jope's rear gunner and a Spitfire shot past them, firing at Anton Two. The Ju 88 was hit in the port engine and along the wing, causing pieces of metal to fly loose. A trail of thick smoke streamed from the engine as the plane tried to gain a little height. A second Spitfire came in behind the stricken aircraft and fired again, causing the starboard engine to explode in flames. Jope watched as the Ju 88 wobbled and fell into the sea near one of the British destroyers. He threw his plane around in a tight turn and saw four He 111s in the distance, dropping their torpedoes. The weapons hit the water and sped onwards, hitting a merchant vessel twice. Jope could see at least two other ships on fire and formed the opinion the torpedo bombers had been able to attack almost uncontested. His Staffel though, was hit hard. At least another two other aircraft from Bruno flight were missing and a second damaged.

He 112s and Italian fighters were chasing British Spitfires above the convoy, twisting and turning as each side tried to gain the advantage. He saw one German fighter loop behind an enemy machine and shoot it down with a quick burst. The plane had a blue tail and a dolphin painted on the nose, so he knew who the pilot was. Marseille was here and adding to his score. The sky was full of smoke and flames with aircraft hurtling past in all directions. He saw a Macchi 202 fly through a cloud billowing from a burning freighter, to collide head on with a Spitfire flying in the other direction. Both aircraft blew apart hurtling metal and burning fuel in all directions. Jope dropped the nose of his plane and ordered the remains of his Staffel to head home. A destroyer sailed at high speed in front of him and he strafed it with cannons before flying over it with meters to spare. Behind him, the remains of the British convoy struggled onward.

One freighter made it to Malta where the Luftwaffe and Stukas from the Regia Aeronautica hammered it until it was scrap. HMS Cleopatra sank twenty kilometers from the southern coast of the island as did HMS Carlisle. Five destroyers were sunk but over forty aircraft from across the different German services were lost. No supplies made it to Malta. As Jope landed at his airfield on Sardinia he noted a group of new Ju 88s and a few Ju 252 lining the southern end of the runway. Finally some replacements had arrived. He landed and went straight to the Intelligence Officer where he learned about the casualties his Staffel had suffered. The reports of the attack on the convoy were positive but he knew the naval air arm of the Kriegsmarine couldn't sustain losses like these forever. His Staffel would have been down to four airworthy planes if the replacements hadn't arrived. The stress of commanding was keeping him awake and he mourned the loss of every single man.

There was also the distress of reading Emma's letters. Her suffering was tangible in every word she wrote. It seemed that conditions at Ravensbruck Concentration Camp had changed completely in the last few months with the number of Jews arriving increasing substantially. His fiancée spoke of the difficulty in keeping everyone fed and the problems with housing and the increasing death toll. She understood the enemies of Germany needed to be punished, however spoke of her confusion when the penalties seemed so random.

It was impossible to know what to say in way of a reply. Jope managed to write back but found all he could manage was a string of platitudes. He told Emma her job was critical to keeping Germany safe and the SS wouldn't send people to Ravensbruck who didn't deserve to be there. However, he wasn't sure if he believed his own words. Jope remembered Ingrid's incarceration and her statements about the corruption of Germany's morality. He recalled the bruises and lacerations on her body and knew Emma had helped put them there. This type of physical brutality was something his future wife said was now a daily occurrence. Jope shook the uncomfortable thoughts away as he needed to focus on the problem of staying alive while flying over the Mediterranean.

There was a knock and a young Matrose stuck his head in the door. "Leutnant zur See Wolfgang Lang's plane is in trouble, sir," said the sandy haired man.

Ingrid's brother still hadn't forgiven him for becoming involved with one of her jailers and Jope was still trying to repair their friendship. Now his comrade flew back from the attack on the British convoy with a single engine.

"Are the crash crews ready?" Jope asked.

"Yes, sir. Fire trucks are standing by," said the Matrose.

The Cagliari-Elmas base had a hard surfaced runway and good facilities by Italian standards. Jope looked across an open area dotted with planes and hangars toward the sea. In the distance a speck appeared, trailing a long plume of dark smoke. It grew in size and he could hear the laboured sound of the engine and saw the wheels were down.

"Are there any wounded on board?"

"The tower told me they can't raise him. They think his radio is out. I don't think they'll be able to go around again if we signal him not to land, sir."

The young man was right. Looking at the plane through binoculars Jope wondered how it was still airborne. The port wing was riddled with holes and the cockpit area heavily damaged. The smoke pouring from the engine was thick and dark and hinted that the wing might start burning at any moment.   As he watched, the plane banked slightly and lined up on the runway.

"Why haven't you bailed out, Wolfgang?" he said out loud.

There were probably injured men on the plane and he knew his friend would never abandon his crew. He watched as the Ju 88 dropped lower but Jope understood Wolfgang's chances were poor. Jope watched as the plane landed, almost perfectly, until the left wheel blew out and the undercarriage collapsed. Then the wing dipped and dug into the ground. The aircraft slewed sideways and the nose hit the runway with sickening force. Jope closed his eyes and heard the plane cartwheel along the concrete, tearing itself apart, before finally exploding in a ball of flames. The fire engine raced to the scene of the crash but Jope knew nobody could have survived. He wondered how he would tell Ingrid what had occurred, and in the back of his mind he speculated about when it would happen to him.

v

American merchant losses had been extremely heavy, yet Gross Admiral Walther Wever doubted they would be enough to slow the build-up of allied merchant fleet. He was pleased the convoys to Malta had been destroyed or turned back, but worried about the losses his forces had taken. Already there was a shortage of pilots and navigators, and the shortening of the training courses was only helping marginally. It also meant the quality of the new pilots wasn't what it once would have been. He tried to ensure these new crews went to Norway or into the small reserve he was trying to build but this wasn't always possible. Only a week ago he'd sent twenty undertrained crews to the Mediterranean to take on the British Navy.

At least now the Bismarck and Scharnhorst were back in service and the Graf Zeppelin would be ready in a month. He had heavy cruiser Moltke in Narvik but the Graf Spee was in dry dock receiving a much-needed overhaul. Repairing the large ships had been made a priority by the Führer, thanks to Heydrich's support, but it had slowed the production of U-boats temporarily. The only heavy ship now under construction was a new Jade class carrier, being created from the ocean liner SS Potsdam. Wever wasn't happy with the project as the ship was going to be far too slow for the role it was slated to undertake. The other ships under construction were five powerful type 36B destroyers and a single light cruiser.

Wever's greatest concerns, however, were not centred on the Kriegsmarine. The news from Russia was disturbing in more ways than one. It was true the Soviet offensive had been halted, at great cost, and that German success in the Mediterranean was promising, but Wever was privy to information that was forbidden to be disclosed to ordinary Germany citizens. He understood how thinly spread his country's resources were. The competing interests of the SS and the army were creating a myriad of problems in the armament industry, with different panzer designs and tank destroyer projects all fighting for recognition, making the situation even worse.

At least the air industry was in better shape with both Wever and Kesselring agreeing to the need for the streamlining of production and concentrating on the most promising and practical designs. That was why the Fw 190 was the basis for the new single-engined torpedo bomber, and the Bf 109 and Fw 190 competed for the role of naval fighter. The Ju 290 would be both bomber, transport aircraft and reconnaissance platform, and the Luftwaffe wouldn't be tempted to produce a multitude of different types of aircraft. Albert Speer's promotion to the role of head of production was already showing early signs of improving the output of planes, though some said he was only building on the earlier work of Doctor Fritz Todt. Still, the projected output for the year of seven thousand bombers, five thousand fighters, one thousand ground attack, two hundred floatplanes and seven hundred transport aircraft wasn't going to be enough.

Wever knew there were many in the German high command who saw him as a pessimist, but he believed the entry of the USA and the failure to defeat Russia before the winter of 1941 had sealed Germany's fate. Now, from what Admiral Wilhelm Canaris was telling him, his country didn't deserve to win the war. The grey headed commander of the Abwehr was waiting for him in the study and Wever dreaded what he was about to hear. He poured himself a large whisky and swirled some around in his mouth before swallowing. Taking a deep breath, he opened the door and walked into the small room. Books lined one wall and coals glowed in a small fireplace. Canaris stood near the window and turned as he entered, saluting and then reaching to shake Wever's hand.

The Grossadmiral gestured at a leather chair and both men sat down. Between them, on a small table, was a thick grey file of loose-leaf paper. Canaris gestured at the folder and frowned.

"It's all in there, the treatment of the Russian prisoners of war and the order to execute all British Commandos. Our Führer didn't take kindly to the raid on the Faroes, though I suspect he would have issued such an instruction eventually. Then there is the instruction from your friend Heydrich to Martin Luther, asking for administrative assistance in the eradication of all Jews in Germany and the occupied territories."

"So the conference at Wannsee wasn't a myth?" asked Wever.

"No, it's real enough but the radicalisation of policy toward the Jews started back in September last year."

"It's monstrous! The killing of a whole group of people as government policy, using bureaucratic methods is chilling."

"That's only the beginning of the plan. If Hitler wins, he intends to cleanse the world of intellectuals, Slavs, and the clergy."

"The clergy?"

"One must only worship Germany or its leader. I think the chicken farmer, Himmler, wants to return us all to the age of the Viking, where we can all live in some Wagnerian opera."

"Are they all insane? Even logically, this doesn't make sense! We can't afford to be using all these resources in order to kill innocent people. It's wrong on so many different levels."

"The question is what are we going to do about it?" said Canaris.

Wever stared at his drink. He had some idea about what was happening in Russia but the plan to systematically destroy an entire group of people rocked him to his very core. He didn't know what action he could take.

"I want to get these papers to the Allies," said Canaris.

It took Wever a moment to understand what the Admiral was saying. His eyes went wide and he stared at his friend. "You're suggesting we commit treason?"

"We need to let the world know about this. Maybe they'll shame us into abandoning this disgusting policy, or perhaps they'll bomb the camps. I don't know, but we need to take some sort of action."

Wever glanced at the folder and then looked away. "Is this what Hitler and his cronies force us into?" he muttered.

"I'm being watched and my association with you may put you under suspicion. I think it's become necessary for us to put some distance between us. I'll find a method of contacting you that's safer and I suggest you do everything to appear as loyal to the Führer as possible for the time being. Unfortunately it's too dangerous for me to attempt to get those papers to the British."

Wever hesitated but finally turned back to his friend. "Leave them with me and I'll think about what we should do."

Canaris smiled. "I didn't know if you would help."

"This is very difficult for me. I've always loved my country but what our leadership plans will stain us all for centuries. If I do this, I need to take precautions. I have no doubt that if the SS think I'm about to betray my country then my whole family is at risk."

"In the meantime I will seek out other like-minded individuals. Please be assured I will not mention your name."

"And I will do likewise," said Wever.

Chapter Two: Spring 1942

The fighters met the He 111s and Ju 88s about three

hundred kilometers west-southwest of Sardinia. Kapitänleutnant

Hans-Joachim Marseille led twelve He 112s and eight Bf 110s.

Twelve Macchi 202s were loaded, carrying one hundred liter drop

tanks; with their eighty liter auxiliary tanks filled, they would

accompany the formation as far as they could, but the enemy fleet

was over five hundred kilometers from their base. The best the

Germans could hope from the Italians was ten minutes of combat

before they were forced to turn for home. Intelligence had the two

enemy carriers due north of Algiers, steaming at high speed toward

Malta. There was no doubt the enemy planned to fly more Spitfires

to the island, however the carriers were bound to have air cover.

Fifty-eight British fighters were to fly from the USS Wasp

and the HMS Indomitable. These planes had faulty radios and the

external fuel tanks leaked badly, forcing the carriers to get closer to

Malta before launching the Spitfires. The Luftwaffe and Regia

Aeronautica planned to attack the British planes as soon as they arrived, but the opportunity to sink two carriers, especially an American one, was too big an opportunity to miss. This vessel with its wooden deck was vulnerable to heavy bombs, or so it was believed.

"Skipper, we have bandits inbound at four o'clock high. Not sure of the type," said his wingman Leutnant zur See Emil Clade.

Marseille glanced at the approaching machines and guessed they lacked the air-cooled engine of a Hurricane or a Spitfire. "I think they might be Martlets, otherwise known as Wildcats," he said over the radio.

"What do we know about them, sir?"

"Not much, and now's not the time to talk about it."

"The Macchis are going after them, skipper," said Clade.

"Good, then they will be able to fight for longer. We are still forty kilometers from the position of the carriers."

They weren't; it was more like sixty and it left Marseille with the impression that American radar must have a longer range than the Germans were used to.

"More fighter skipper, but these are at the same height, coming in from three o'clock," said the pilot of Bruno One.

"Right, keep them off the bombers, the Bf 110s need to look after themselves," said Marseille.

The Wildcats turned toward them and held course, Marseille's Staffel did the same and the two formations flashed through each other at a combined speed of almost eight hundred miles per hour. He saw the sparkling lights on the wings of the enemy fighters and watched as the traces flashed past his cockpit. His quick burst smashed into the engine and cockpit of the leading machine, causing it drop suddenly with black smoke pouring from the fuselage. At least one of the He 112s was hit and two opposing fighters collided head on resulting in a massive explosion that tore both planes apart. Marseille pulled his aircraft up and around in an Immelmann climbing turn that gave him extra altitude and had him facing back in the direction he had come from. Most of his Staffel performed the same maneuver but found the Wildcats had dived away toward the Bf 110s.

"Go after them," ordered Marseille as he pushed the nose of his aircraft down.

He wasn't to know the American pilots had mistaken the twin-engined heavy fighters as bombers and were trying to destroy the wrong aircraft. The US Navy pilots hadn't fought against German or Italian forces until now, so it was an understandable mistake to make. He saw two of the Bf 110s fall out of formation, their engines spewing smoke and fire, while the rest of the twin-engined aircraft tried to form a defensive circle. Marseille's aircraft picked up speed as it dived to assist.

The Wildcats noticed the He 112s coming and turned to face them. Marseille was now wary of the six heavy machine guns in the wings of the stubby little fighters and even though the armament of the He 112 possessed four similar guns as well as a cannon, he didn't want his Staffel to suffer any more casualties. They had drawn the Wildcats away from the Bf 110s and that was enough. Instead, he ordered his pilots to use the speed they had gathered in the dive to loop over the top and stay above the Americans. He intended to keep the US Navy pilots looking up, then the bombers could slip past underneath them.

As one, the Wildcats turned back and again savaged the German heavy fighters. Marseille cursed and dived once more. Enough with the cat and mouse game, he thought. This time the Americans didn't have enough time to turn and face the He 112s and were forced to fly in an arch across the sights of the German machines. Deflection shooting is difficult at the best of times and though Marseille's Staffel managed to shoot at the enemy, the robust structure of the Wildcats meant most of the Americans flew away damaged, but not crippled. All except for Marseille's target. His cannon shells shattered the engine of an enemy machine, causing the pilot to bail out as burning fuel flowed into his cockpit. The man's feet and hands were burnt but the thick gloves and boots saved the pilot from worse injuries.

Ahead, Marseille saw flak exploding above the enemy fleet. The Ju 88s and He 111s had dropped down to wave height and made their run at the carriers and cruisers. It was hard to see what happened but at least one carrier was burning and another ship was sinking by the stern. German planes exploded or splashed into the ocean as the Wildcats dived toward them. Marseille chased the US fighters, but the enemy turned away after shooting down a damaged He 111 and flew back to their own depleted fleet. He guessed they were low on ammunition.

v

Back on Pantelleria Marseille received the news that an American carrier was heavily damaged and had withdrawn from the area. A cruiser had also been sunk, though intelligence wasn't sure if it was a heavy variety or the lighter version of the vessel. Marseille also learnt that he was to fly to Berlin. He was to receive the Oak Leaves to his Knight's Cross, flying to Germany the following day. That night his Staffel managed to find a quantity of Italian wine and Marseille bordered the Ju 90 an hour before dawn, very much the worse for wear. When he arrived in Rome after a four-hour flight, the first thing he did was vomit on the tarmac. The German and Italian officers who were there to meet him didn't look impressed. Photographers were chased away and Marseille taken to a hotel where he slept then showered before slipping out late in the afternoon and heading to a local jazz club.

It took two days to sober him up, for him to be in a suitable condition to send back to Berlin. Even then, a disgruntled Luftwaffe Major was assigned to escort him.

When he arrived at Templehof Airport Oberst Adolf Galland was waiting for him. The man's dark eyes twinkled as they shook hands.

"You're a hard man to pin down," said Galland.

"I got a little distracted in Italy; too many women, too much wine." said Marseille.

The dark haired man laughed and smoothed back his hair.

"Why is the Luftwaffe sending one of its finest to meet a navy boy, sir?" asked Marseille.

"They didn't, it was my decision. I have an offer to make while you're here and no need to call me, sir. We are both pilots as far as I'm concerned."

"You don't want me to transfer services?"

"No, no, I just want your opinion on a new aircraft I've got my eye on."

"I'm interested, especially when someone with your reputation approaches me."

"You have outscored me Marseille, first Lion of the North, then the Star of Africa."

"If you hadn't been promoted out of combat I'm sure you would be in the lead."

"Who says I don't occasionally sneak in a little combat flying? Anyway, we can talk more about this over a few drinks."

"I thought I was to proceed straight to Naval Headquarters. The High Command are a little annoyed that I'm late."

Galland raised an eyebrow. "And since when has that ever worried you."

Marseille grinned. "Good point. I see my reputation precedes me."

"The stories of your parties, flying, and drinking have travelled well beyond naval circles. Let's just say you're a man after my own heart."

Marseille laughed again. "Lead the way," he said.

The night passed in a blur of faces and alcohol. Marseille met a lot of important people in the Luftwaffe, as well as some of the most important designers such as Willy Messerschmitt and Kurt Tank. Both men were keen to speak to him and he noted they wanted his ideas on what sort of fighter should take the place of the He 112. He admitted he preferred the idea of centre lined cannon and pointed out it needed to be a balanced machine.

Marseille said the hitting power of his present fighter was excellent and though he thought the Bf 109 F a better aircraft in many ways, it lacked a decent armament and was too fragile for his liking. The range was also short and naval fighters needed to be able to fly long distances. Both men then quoted the statistics for their respective designs; Tank, the Fw 190 T and Messerschmitt, his Me 155. The speed range and cannons of both aircraft sounded very similar, though the latter had a better rate of climb and was more manoeuvrable. However, the Fw 190 T was sturdy and not easily shot down, similar to the designs the Americans favoured.

Later, Marseille started to relax when Galland brought him an ice-cold beer and dragged him away to meet some of the women in the room.

. "Messerschmitt has invited you to play at a party in a few days. The Führer will be there, as well as some of Germany's highest ranking generals. Your Grossadmiral should be there as well," he said.

"Women, wine?"

66

Galland laughed. "By the truck load, but just wait until the Führer leaves before you get too rowdy. He usually doesn't stay long as he always has a conference to attend or a briefing he has to listen to."

"I receive my medal from him the previous day, so we will be old friends by then."

Galland's face became serious. "He has no friends, just people who want to use him."

"You sound like you feel sorry for our leader."

"Leading Germany in this war is a massive responsibility and I'm not sure if he always listens to the right people, especially where the Luftwaffe is concerned."

"What about the other stuff?"

Galland looked away and didn't speak for a moment. When he did his eyes failed to meet Marseille's "I don't listen to rumours," he said.

After two wonderful days with his mother, sleeping late and generally recovering, Marseille tried to contact Heidi, but his former lover wasn't in Berlin. So he read and ate home cooked meals, while purchasing lamb and coal from the black market. He also collected timber from some of the wrecked houses destroyed by the bombing. There were less of these now as air raids had dropped away to almost nothing, with most night attacks by the British being directed at Germany's ports. He helped his mother around the house, feeding the rabbits, or planting seeds in the small vegetable garden in the rear yard, and even digging up the very small front area and planting it with potatoes.

His mother smiled at him as they worked, and spoke of the neighbours or rumours about the Eastern Front. They never talked about Inge or the pain they both felt at her absence. Marseille knew her murderer had been found guilty and was sentenced to hang, but Marseille found no joy in this. It didn't bring back his smiling, happy sister so she could chastise or tease him. His father still served with his men in Russia, not that he helped when he did get leave, as the old man had another family now, and they took priority over his eldest son and ex-wife.

One evening, after listening to the radio together, his mother leaned toward him and took his hand. "We only have each other now," she whispered as though frightened to break the peace of the small room.

"I know," he said, swallowing the lump in his throat.

"Every day you're away I worry. If you go, then I'm completely alone."

He couldn't answer. They both knew any promises would be a lie. Marseille flew a high performance aircraft at the limit of its abilities. Combat, a mechanical problem, flak or even flying through a flock of sea gulls may kill him.

"If the worst happens, you must go and stay with your sister at Erding. It is a small town without any factories so you should be safe there."

"I hate the south and Bavaria is so uncouth."

"Aunty Hanna's husband is a kind man who has always treated us well when we visit. You will have my pension and you won't be alone."

His mother's eyes filled up and she angrily tried to wipe away the tears. "Why did we even start this war?" she growled.

"According to the Führer, they started it"

"We all know that's bullshit."

Marseille blurted out a laugh. "Mother! You never swear."

"The situation we find ourselves in makes me angry. I know we are winning the war and it will soon be over, but think of how many people have died."

"Now the Americans are involved, victory is less assured."

"But if we beat Russia, then surely they will give up."

He didn't want to worry his mother anymore and the prospect of Germany winning the war was the one piece of hope she was holding on to. "You are probably correct," he said.

v

His medal presentation was over quickly and Marseille was surprised at how short the Führer was. The man was unimpressive on many levels, except for his eyes. Those blue eyes pierced him with their intensity, boring into Marseille as if imploring, do you understand what must be done? Then, the moment Hitler looked away, it was as if Marseille no longer existed. There was a little forced small talk between the two of them and Marseille stayed formal and followed Galland's advice of not offering too much detail on the front line. He found this easy as his main preoccupation was escaping and getting back to his mother. Marseille thought the German leader odd and a little frightening, but after leaving the ceremony he returned to his mother's house and forgot about his Führer.

v

The Goebbels family attended the party, as well as Grossadmiral Wever and Adolf Galland. As he walked into the room, he noted there were a number of attractive women, but one
71

immediately grabbed his attention. This one was blonde and tall. She stood in a long dress, her hair piled above her head, exposing her neck. She smiled at him and her eyes sparkled, but before he could make his way across the room to her Galland swept him over to the Führer, and introduced him to the other important people in the room. Suddenly he found himself in front of Grossadmiral Wever. The man had a sharp face and a high forehead, and regarded Marseille with thoughtful eyes.

"I've heard a lot about you, young man," said the Grossadmiral.

"Thank you, sir," said Marseille.

"Not all of it good."

Marseille froze and waited, only relaxing slightly when he saw the corner of the Grossadmiral's mouth turn up in a grin.

"You drove some of my staff insane. They just couldn't seem to get you on that plane in Rome."

"The capital city of our ally has many distractions, sir," said Marseille.

Wever's grin grew wider. "I dare say it has. Anyway, you are here now. I believe you'll be playing for the Führer later?"

"Yes, Beethoven."

"I heard a rumour that you prefer jazz?"

Marseille's eyes went wide. "That would be un-German, sir."

"Pity," said the older man. "I like jazz."

Marseille's eyes glowed and he smiled.

Later he sat with a couple of SS men near a small bar and drank beer while listening to the buzz of conversation. The older individual at the bar was speaking to a younger man about something, and Marseille's ears pricked up when he heard the word 'Jews.'

Out of curiosity, he eased himself a little closer to the two men and tried to hear what they were saying.

"So, Obergruppenführer, you are saying Madagascar is no longer an option," said the younger man.

"No, it has been decided we have to eradicate them. It's the only way we can get rid of them and keep Germany safe in the future. Once the war has been won they would remain a threat," said the older man.

"Do we know how many Jews there are?"

"Estimates vary, but it's thought there are between four to seven million of them. We will need to build the facilities to hold them, and then ultimately dispose of the useless mouths. Those that are fit enough, will work for Germany until the war is over."

"A grim business."

"Yes, however those who undertake it are heroes. Germany's enemies need to be destroyed and this is an important role in securing the Reich's future."

"Well, I'm back at the front in a few days. My leave is up," said the younger man.

"It's still cold there?"

"Its spring, so there is mud everywhere. There's talk of my division being sent west to refit. We lost heavily before Moscow."

Marseille lost interest in the conversation and drifted away from the bar. He later learned that the older man was Obergruppenführer Hans Lammers and the younger man was Standartenführer Christian Tychsen, a member of the 2nd SS Division. Lammers worked closely with many German leaders, being in the Führer's cabinet. Marseille knew in his heart what he had heard about the Jews was true. He watched men speak to the leader of his country with respect and wanted to vomit. It was then that Willy Messerschmitt invited him to play.

"Stick to Beethoven and you can't go wrong," said the German aircraft designer.

Marseille walked to the piano in a daze. He looked at the keyboard for a moment, not knowing what to do. In front of him was the music to Für Elise. His fingers started to move and the music flowed. He always thought this piece had the quality of a gently bubbling brook and he let his hands dance over the keys. Around him the room went quiet and he increased the volume of the piece enjoying the sensation it created in him. Then he played the Moonlight Sonata, however as he did so he felt the sadness of the music and his feelings started to change. Rage grew. Marseille needed to make a statement, something that showed he didn't support the monsters in this room. He was brought into this world by a Jew and had been nursed through serious illness by the same man. The leadership of his country even said his favourite music was degenerate. Marseille's smile grew and he thought of what the Grossadmiral had mentioned earlier. As he finished the piece, he moved swiftly to Summertime by George Gershwin, a Jew living in America. He sang in English and noticed when the Führer stood suddenly and left the room. Marseille kept playing, moving to Ragtime, and noticed the Grossadmiral tapping his feet to Crazy People by the Boswell Sisters. Now there was a man he could fight for, he thought.

Marseille didn't care that he'd insulted the German leader. He drank heavily for the rest of the party until Grossadmiral Wever crossed the room and stared at him.

"You've had too much to drink," he said.

Marseille looked up at him through bloodshot eyes. He didn't care anymore; these people were murderers. "Did you know?" he slurred.

"Know what?" said the Grossadmiral.

"About the Jews?"

Wever's eyes went wide and he glanced around the room. He signalled a junior officer and the man approached quickly.

"Please take our young hero to his mother's and ignore everything he says," said Wever to the man. Then he turned back to Marseille. "When you sober up we will talk about this, but for now I order you to shut up."

Even in his drunken state Marseille understood that an order from the head of the German Navy should be obeyed. His mouth snapped closed, and he was escorted to the door and bundled into the back of a large car, where he soon fell asleep.

V

"What can you tell me about him?" Grossadmiral Wever asked the white haired man.

Admiral Wilhelm Canaris looked at the file in front of him and shook his head. "The man is a hot head. An amazingly gifted pilot who has trained himself with a variety of exercises and reaction activities to become probably the best in his field," said Canaris.

"You said his family had a strong connection with the Jews?"

"They knew a doctor well, and Marseille had a number of Jewish friends. He is also interested in American culture, through his love of jazz."

"I saw that yesterday. It took bravery to play banned music in front of the Führer."

"Or madness."

78

"The SS were at Messerschmitt's place in force and I think he overheard something about the recent decision to destroy the Jews."

"We should call it what it is, mass murder."

"Indeed," said Wever, though he felt uncomfortable with the statement. "Anyway, I put/planted the seed in his head but I never thought he'd play the music of a Jew!"

"It was a risky thing to do."

"I'm not sure if anyone realised who composed the song. It probably won't be long before someone works it out, however we could be lucky, that particular song has been performed by many different people."

"You know this music?" asked Canaris.

"I didn't lie when I said I liked jazz. It's up-tempo and I enjoy that. Gets the feet tapping."

"If you say so," said Canaris, grinning..

"Anyway, do we reach out to him?"

"If you do, he must be warned against excessive drinking and opening his mouth."

"Fair point. I've sent a car for him, though he still might have a sore head. I wanted to speak with him again."

"Do you want me here?"

"No. If he joins us, we all need to keep our connections at arm's length. After today, if he agrees to become part of our group, I won't speak to him again. We'll need a conduit who is not easily traced to either of us."

"Leave that with me. It's what I do best," said Canaris.

There was a knock at the door and Wever's secretary, a young man with a pronounced limp, stuck his head around the door. "Kapitänleutnant Hans-Joachim Marseille to see you, sir," said the junior officer.

"Send him in," said Wever.

Canaris left through a side door seconds before the bleary-eyed ace stepped into his office and saluted, in the old style; no Heil Hitler's from this young man.

"Sit down and relax Marseille. I can see you probably need to," said Wever.

"Thank you, sir." the young man sat heavily in a high backed chair.

"Yesterday you asked me about the Jews."

Marseille shuffled his feet and looked out the window, then sighed and met the Grossadmiral's gaze. "Yes sir, I did."

"I played no part in that decision, but yes, I have heard. What do you think of the policy?"

"Is that what it's being called, sir? A policy?"

"Yes, The Final Solution to the Jewish Question."

Marseille's face screwed up like he had just swallowed a bug, then his skin flushed red.

"You don't like the program of our Führer?"

The young man refused to answer and stared at a spot on the wall, his mouth now a hard line.

"I can see from your demeanour you're less than pleased with the plan to destroy the Jews. Well, truth be told, neither am I, though if you repeat that outside this room I'll have you shot."

Marseille's eyes nearly popped out of his head. His mouth dropped open and he gaped at his Commander and Chief. "Sir, the idea of killing all of the Jews disgusts me."

"And for me, the question is, what can we do about it?"

Marseille's eyes narrowed. "I suspect sir, that's why you have invited me here."

Wever chuckled. "You are absolutely correct. If you agree with my proposal then some may say you have committed treason. I, however, think we are doing Germany a service by trying to stop this madness."

The young man thought for a moment and then nodded. "Of course I'll help sir, it just needs to be in such a way that it doesn't put my mother at risk."

"Naturally. At the moment plans are still being formulated, allies gathered. With Germany doing well in the war it's hard to get too many people interested, especially as every approach has to be made very carefully."

"Yes, sir."

"In future somebody who can't be traced to me will contact you. He or she will indicate that they are your contact in a way that's yet to be determined."

"Understood, sir."

"Until then try to stay alive, lead your men. Nothing changes until you hear from us. Also, watch your mouth and don't drink too much. I meant it when I said I'd have you shot if you even hint at this conversation."

"Yes, sir."

Marseille left and Wever relaxed. The popular air ace could be a powerful ally and if utilised in the right way might prove to be very useful. The Grossadmiral knew he was now officially a conspirator and not only risking his life but probably the lives of those he loved, yet he couldn't sit by and do nothing. He needed to do something to stop the madness that was taking over his country.

V

The Staffel consisted of four planes that were airworthy. Only seven pilots and their crews remained to fly the Ju 88 Cs. Fregattenkapitän Bernhard Jope watched as the three Ju 90s landed and his men walked down the dusty runway toward them. They were leaving their aircraft and returning to Germany to reform and reequip. He was exhausted and struggled to focus on the numerous tasks needed to move the Staffel. His men climbed slowly into the aircraft before the transport planes taxied to the runway and took off to fly over southern France and back to Rugen Island.

The last attack on a British attempt to ferry Spitfires to Malta had been a disaster for his command, with British anti-aircraft fire destroying at least four planes. The carrier, HMS Eagle was damaged by a single bomb from a Stuka, but the enemy fighters had flown off and some landed on the island safely. Another British cruiser went down after being struck by two torpedoes, however, the Royal Navy seemed to have an unlimited supply of these vessels.

Still, no merchant ships had reached Malta since December the previous year and the situation on the island had to be getting desperate. Jope certainly hoped it was as the cost to his Staffel had been calamitous. The Luftwaffe and Regia Aeronautica bombed Malta day and night, and everyone speculated whether there would be an invasion. Jope wanted the island to surrender so that he could rest and spend some time with Emma. He hadn't received a letter from her for at least a month and wondered why she had gone quiet. As soon as he settled his men into their new barracks in Germany, Jope planned to visit her and perhaps accelerate his plans to marry her.

The flight north was bumpy but otherwise uneventful as the route was far from any allied airfields. They landed on the concrete strip on Rugen late in the day and were escorted to a series of prefabricated wooden huts heated by large stoves. The weather was improving as spring progressed, but it was still a lot cooler next to the North Sea than it had been in the Mediterranean. Later, the commander of the base introduced him to a number of young pilots and informed him that twelve Ju 88 and a new aircraft called the Ju 188 would be allocated to his Staffel. The last plane was still being tested but the navy wanted some feedback on the machine. Jope liked the look of the aircraft but thought it was suited to being a torpedo bomber rather than a low-level attack aircraft. He liked the heavy cannon in the nose of his Ju 88Cs and this new plane had gone back to a glass nose with a single gun. He hoped the Kriegsmarine would look at the Ju 188 as a replacement for the aging He 111s rather than as a skip bomber.

The following day, as the weather closed in, Jope borrowed a car and drove south to Ravensbruck. He travelled through showers of rain to the concentration camp and parked outside the main administration block. As he walked up the steps of the brick building, Jope noticed the smell. An odour of ash and burnt animal hung in the air, as well as the foul smell of sewage. Glancing beyond the wire, he saw a large number of women walking between different compounds and the camp seemed to be overcrowded. In the letters Emma had sent him she said the number of inmates had increased dramatically and the camps were clogged with Jews. Now he understood. No wonder his future wife felt under pressure.

Jope waited in the outer office of the large building for what seemed like an age. When Emma first walked in, shaking the rain from her clothes, he felt his heart clench. Her hair was plastered to her head accentuating the tightness of her skin. Her clothes hung on her like sheets on a clothes line, showing that she had lost weight. Emma's eyes seemed too large for her head and her skin looked stretched like the cover of a drum. He tried to keep the shock from his face but she noticed and her mouth twisted.

"If I'd known you were coming I could have at least attempted to disguise the changes," she said.

"I wanted to surprise you," said Jope.

Emma glanced around and noticed other guards staring. "I'm working but my shift finishes at six, unless they extend it again."

"I can wait. This weather is forecast to last another day so I should be able to get permission to stay overnight."

Emma's eye remained flat. She hadn't attempted to kiss or even touch him. He moved toward her but she stiffened and drew back. "I'll meet you here soon after I finish. That should give you enough time to find somewhere to stay," she said.

He nodded slowly and she frowned before turning and plunging back into the rain.

Showers continued to fall as Jope sat in the front office. He'd found a small hotel just north of the town and received permission to keep the car until the following afternoon. Emma entered the area through a side door and walked over to him, smiling tentatively.

"I just need to get changed and have a quick shower," she said.

Jope smiled back, relieved at the renewed sparkle in her eyes. His face lit up and he walked over and took her hands in his. "I've missed you," he said.

Emma's eyes filled with tears, she pulled him tight for a hug, and he felt the moisture on her coat. "And I you. So much has changed since you have been gone," she said.

"I noticed when I got here."

She shook her head. "Let's not talk about that yet. I want to work on making myself beautiful for you. The stink of the camp is on me and I need to get rid of it."

"Don't worry too much. I'm just glad to see you."

"Bernhard, I need to do it as much for me as for you."

He nodded slowly at her, not really understanding.

She didn't meet him at the car for another forty minutes and Jope started to worry that something was wrong. When Emma appeared, her hair was piled on her head and she wore a knee length green dress. She frowned while walking toward the vehicle and as he opened the door, she looked at him. "I still can't get rid of the odour, sorry," she said.

He took a deep breath. "All I can smell is perfume and soap," he said honestly.

She gave him a flat stare and then shrugged. "If you say so."

The drive to a local restaurant was short and quiet. As they walked from the short distance from the car Jope held the umbrella over both of them as the rain had increased, coming down in bursts that caused the gutters to overflow like small rivers. They went inside and the warmth enveloped them. A fire glowed in a small grate against the wall and an old man greeted them, sitting the couple near a bay window overlooking the drenched street. Jope checked his ration book to check he had the appropriate coupons for the meal, and smiled when he realised he could get enough meat for both of them. He told Emma this but her gaze remained on the scene outside the window.

"I know something is troubling you," Jope said gently.

The corner of Emma's mouth twitched, however that was the only sign she had heard him speak.

"Your letters speak of difficulties at the camp," he pressed.

She turned to him, eyes flat like those of a shark. "Are we still people?" she asked.   "What do you mean?"

Emma's gaze went back to the street. "I know these are desperate times and I would do anything for my country but is there a line that shouldn't be crossed, one that turns us from human beings to animals?"

Jope's mouth went dry. "What have they asked you to do?"

"It's best we don't speak of it. I'm not supposed to anyway, but all the guards do. You can't participate in these activities and just push it down and forget it. The women are all affected in one way or another."

"Alright. Let's order and talk of happier things."

They did so, finding that only chicken and pork were available. They ate and Jope shared stories about Italy and the Island of Sardinia. He spoke of the dust and heat but also the wine, rock lobster and flat breads.

"The water is clear and at this time of year and we swim whenever we have a spare moment and lie in the sun to dry. I'll take you there after the war," said Jope.

Emma stared out the window and he tried to swallow his frustration. She didn't seem to be listening and it was though her mind had taken her somewhere else.

"Will the war ever end?" she asked.

"It must," he answered.

"Britain still fights and now the USA have joined them. Russia stopped our armies outside Moscow where many of our boys froze."

"America is corrupt and will not be able to stomach any setbacks.   We didn't break in Russia and will soon attack once more and the British are on the ropes down in Africa. Rommel is only sixty miles from Tobruk and though it's quiet at the moment, the Royal Navy has taken a pounding, losing many ships. We will starve Malta into submission and then the situation will change."

Emma sighed. "I know you are right it's just that I'm so tired and the work is so…" she struggled to find the right word. "Confronting."

"Do you want me to take you back to your room?" Jope asked.

Emma smiled for the first time. "No," she said.

Their lovemaking was passionate, though Jope thought he detected a level of desperation in Emma. It was as though she was trying to drive something out of her body. When they collapsed exhausted into the twisted sheets he held her close and stroked her hair.

"I want to marry you sooner rather than later," he said.

She stiffened in his arms and he wondered if the question was premature. "I thought we were going to wait until the war was over?" she said.

He ran his fingers over the bones of her shoulder, noticing the tightness of the flesh. "Why wait? Let's take what pleasure we can."

She rolled away from him. "When you find out... the world will discover what I have done..." Emma couldn't seem to finish her sentence.

"It won't matter. Anything you do at the camp is in the service of Germany and you're not responsible."

Emma chuckled but the sound held no joy. "The whole country seems to think that, yet is it true? We better win this war or the guilt will be with us forever."

"What guilt? You are destroying Germany's enemies."

She turned back to him. "We experiment on women, break their limbs so the bone shows and then wait until they are infected so we can test new drugs on them. The screams when the hammer snaps the bone..." She stopped again and her eyes filled with tears. "You can't understand what it's like."

His mouth fell open. Jope understood punishment and the need to lock up the enemies of the state. He could even understand why some might need to be executed, yet this was barbaric. His Germany wasn't one of the uncivilised nations of the east. It was a shining light of culture and strength, but it was experimenting on women. Emma stared at him and nodded.

"Maybe you do have an idea of what I mean. I've worked on farms and helped prepare animals for the table. This is worse than how we would treat a pig. Some of these girls are barely eighteen. And do you know what I need to do next week? I've got to select ten women to become prostitutes for male prisoners. How does that fit with the Führer's view of women and the morality of our country? I'm sure he doesn't know; but still, it feels wrong."

Jope pulled Emma to him. "I'm sorry, I didn't know."

"Nobody does. I thought my role would be protecting Germany from enemies and even though I understand the Poles, Jews and gypsies are less than us, to treat them worse than a pig is disturbing. And they look and sound like us. Bernhard, it confuses me."

"The Führer mustn't know. His attention is probably focused on the war and when it ends he will stop this treatment and bring the camps back to their original purpose."

Emma shook her head. "By the time the war ends there won't be any Jews, or gypsies. Darling, we are gassing them. Not at

Ravensbruck, at least not yet. We send them to some place called Auschwitz in eastern Germany."

Jope wasn't sure how he felt about that. The Jews started the war and had tried to destroy Germany for years, yet to kill them all including the women and children seemed excessive.

"I don't know what to say."

"There is nothing you can say that will make any difference. There's only one request I would make of you. Shoot me if I turn into a monster."

"What!"

"There are guards who enjoy what we do. For me it's necessary to protect Germany, well some of it is. But for them, they like it. If I become like Irma or Maria then you should shoot me like the mad dog I would have become."

"That will never happen."

"You don't know that! The pressure to show you hate the inmates is constant. The strange thing is that when I started, I did.

97

Now though, I can't help but notice their suffering. Surely there's a better way of safeguarding our country."

Jope couldn't think of an answer. He held Emma close for the night, barely sleeping. She relaxed and managed to snore gently for most of the evening and he wondered if sharing her burden helped in some way. He couldn't imagine what her life was like and wanted to find a way to save her, but Emma had made it clear she wasn't going to resign until she had saved enough money. Besides, part of her still believed what she did was important, it was just the system that had become corrupted. Jope hoped she was right and that his future wife wouldn't carry the scars of what she had seen to her death.

Chapter Three: Summer 1942

He was just about to turn the four- aircraft around when he spotted the ships. Kapitän Helmut Bruck eased the Ju 290 in a curving path to the south and peered through the front window out over the northern Atlantic. There were at least thirty vessels further to the southeast, and a large number of these appeared to be warships.

"Where are they going?" asked Oberfähnrich zur See Hals Bruner.

"With their present course and speed, it looks as though the destination is the Faroes, and they will be there tomorrow morning," said Bruck.

"We are lucky to have spotted them in this weather," said Bruner.

"Yes, but the forecast is for continual improvement, and the enemy will know that."

"I can see at least one battleship, three or four cruisers, and a swarm of destroyers."

"Keep your eyes open for fighters. We probably haven't been intercepted yet due to the weather. I'm heading for home," said Bruck.

"Skipper, a large four-engined plane, six o'clock high," yelled Matrose Helmut Khole.

"Shit, I'm heading for the clouds however the enemy radar can keep directing their aircraft at us until we get out of range, so stay alert," said Bruck.

He realised the British must have gathered their fleet off the western Scottish coast and probably expected their ships wouldn't be discovered until close to the shores of the Faroes. His warning would give the island a day to prepare, and he hoped it would make a difference.

Air activity over both Iceland and the Faroes had increased in recent weeks with American B17 bombers attacking from a new base on Greenland, and also making the shorter run from Scotland. So far, these planes had only come in groups of thirty or forty but they had hit the German airfields hard on at least two occasions. He didn't know at that very moment both his home base and the Faroes were being attacked by large numbers of enemy aircraft.

"It's a Liberator, skipper," said Khole.

"We will have to fight it then. They are faster than we are. I'll try a maneuver to put us in a position where we can use the cannon," said Bruck.

The big American plane dived from above and he waited until it was a kilometer behind them when he turned and attempted to dive under the enemy machine. The liberator put its nose down and followed the Ju 290, and Khole fired at its tail. The American plane closed the distance and its single point five-calibre machine gun in the nose started shooting. Then the enemy machine was under them and Bruck could hear the rattle, as bullets hit the belly of his plane. Someone screamed over the radio and Khole yelled for the plane to turn hard to port. Bruck hauled the aircraft around and heard both the tail cannon and the dorsal turret shooting at the enemy.

Both of the machines hammered each other like two heavy weight boxers circling, and trading blows. Bullets scoured the fuselage of the Ju 290, ripping through metal and flesh, but the cannon shells did more damage to the American aircraft. Eventually the Liberator headed north, smoke pouring from two engines. The damaged machine made it to the coast of Scotland where uninjured crew men were ordered to bail out. The Liberator then tried to land in a field but hit a hidden ditch and flipped over, exploding and killing the captain and two wounded men.

Bruck nursed his damaged aircraft north. He thought of heading to the Faroes as they were closer, but was advised it was under heavy air attack. With little choice he flew north and eventually landed his crippled machine at the emergency German airfield near Breiodalsvik in Iceland. He lost one crew member to a stomach wound and another had a shattered shoulder. The plane would be out of action for at least a week, yet Bruck knew that he was lucky to be alive.

v

The British had amassed a large number of planes in Scotland, and moved them north the previous day to airfields that had been supplied with extra, fuel, bombs, and mechanics. Beaufighters, Halifaxes as well as naval Martlets and Fairey Albacores

hammered facilities on the Faroes, while fifty-two B17s pounded Iceland's eastern airfields. The British had camouflaged everything carefully, and all instructions outlining the attack had been hand delivered to the ships while in port. The Germans were caught completely by surprise; not that the Kriegsmarine could have done much to stop the attacks. Their air component was stretched thin due to the demands of the siege of Malta, and the large heavy naval units didn't want to venture too close to the Scottish coast.

The truth was that the Faroes were always untenable and were only taken early in the war as a stepping-stone to Iceland. If the war had ended quickly, then perhaps taking the Faroes would have proven worthwhile. That was what the German High Command had hoped, but now the war was in its third year and didn't look like ending anytime soon, at least not in the west. Being three hundred and fifty kilometers from the Shetland Isles and just over four hundred from mainland England made the German bases on the Faroes vulnerable when the focus of the struggle moved elsewhere. The Kriegsmarine just didn't have the resources to contest the islands anymore.

The navy could charge south with the Bismarck, Scharnhorst and Graf Zeppelin, but this would place them in range of British land based aircraft. This was what the Kriegsmarine had done in May the previous year when Ju 88s and He 111s from Iceland had attacked the Royal Navy. Now, however, most of the Kriegsmarine's attack aircraft were in the Mediterranean attempting to stop the enemy resupplying Malta. Those aircraft they did have were pinned to the ground by air attacks, or busy holding off much larger allied air groups. This didn't mean the Germans were defenceless. Over Iceland the Americans found the B17s suffered at the hands of the Kriegsmarine's heavy fighters. The small number of Bf 110s shot down six machines in two days and the He 112s another four, bringing US losses to almost fifteen percent of their attacking force. Over the Faroes, Beaufighters tangled with single-engined German fighters and lost four of their number, while three bombers were destroyed in air combat and another two by flak.

Yet the defences were swamped and the Kriegsmarine struggled to attack the Royal Navy's invasion force. He 111s and Ju 88s tried to strike from Norway, but were intercepted just north of the Shetland Isles. A small number of He 112s attempted to protect the bombers, however Spitfires directed by radar on the island swept the meagre escort aside and shattered the attempt. Eight Kriegsmarine aircraft were lost and only a single Spitfire went down.

In the end the Graf Zeppelin tried to intervene from a position three hundred and fifty kilometers north of the Faroes. This was a risky venture and though Stukas managed to sink a transport and a destroyer, and Fi 167s damaged a cruiser, it was at the cost of damage to both the Bismarck and the German carrier. The British launched raids with every bomber they could find and though some couldn't locate the German naval targets and others were shot down by the combat air patrols, enough got through to put a bomb into the Graf Zeppelin and two torpedoes into the German battleship. Twenty-two Beaufighters, Beauforts, Wellingtons and other bombers were shot down or lost to accidents. Only three He 112s went down in response. Yet the damage to the two German capital ships again crippled the Kriegsmarine's ability to put an effective fleet into the northern Atlantic.

The main British invasion forces landed on Vagar Island and Sandoy Island. There was no doubt that the airfield on Vagar was the main target as paratroopers dropped into the field a little after the main landing force assaulted the town of Sandavagur. The infantry came ashore at the mouth of the Stora River. A German battery of five-inch guns at the Witches Finger, protecting the entrance to the fjord, were knocked out by the guns of the heavy cruiser Sussex, fresh from a long refit. The German guns had been attacked by Wellington bombers, and then Beaufighters, before being blasted by eight-inch guns. The town itself was smothered with heavy shellfire as the landing vessels steamed toward the shore. Landing Craft Assault boats, or LCAs, brought the men of the 3rd Infantry Division ashore where they ran into heavy fire from the remains of a number of German mountain companies. British destroyers supported the assault and though one was sunk by Stukas later in the day and another hit by a mine, they managed to strike at the Germans, allowing the British to take the town with relatively few casualties.

The same couldn't be said for the paratroopers who dropped in a shallow valley north of the airfield. Here enemy flak couldn't reach them, as the planes dropped the men from only nine hundred meters. Unfortunately strong cross winds blew many of the paratroopers into the rocky hillside, where many broke legs and arms (as well as a few deaths). The British force was scattered and took some time to come together around an unwounded Major John Frost. Two companies moved overland but ran into German reinforcements travelling east from Sorvagur. This allowed the 3rd Division to take the town without having to confront the extra troops, but caused the lightly armed paratroopers many casualties.

Once ashore, the British overwhelmed the Germans and took the airstrip. The battle was over by the end of the day, despite the attacks from enemy aircraft. Once the airfield was taken, supplies were flown in and soon the remaining German mountain troops were forced to surrender. Only a few pilots and aircrew managed to escape, flying out just before the airfield fell. The Führer was furious, but really there was little the Kriegsmarine could do to change the situation.

v

His eyes bulged and he slammed the table with the palm of his hand. "We cannot just allow the British to walk in and take the islands from us," screamed the Führer.

"There is little we can do about it without pulling most of planes away from Malta," said Wever.

"The navy has been made a fool of by the enemy, and your lack of judgement reflects badly on the whole nation!"

"With respect my Führer, we did what we could. My forces are stretched thin across four different seas. The battle for Malta is reaching a climax and we will soon replace the loss of one island with the capture of another."

The German leader glanced up and his shoulders relaxed, yet he wasn't prepared to entirely let the matter go.

"Rommel says we don't need Malta anymore now that Tobruk has fallen. The amount of supplies he captured will see him through to July."

"And after that? If he fails or gets held up, then what? The British will not give up Egypt and more importantly the Suez Canal, without a fight. Besides, the capture of Malta will increase the prestige of our nation."

Wever knew the German leader was wavering on the invasion of Malta. The losses incurred at Crete the previous year had made him wary of large scale paratrooper operations, but the British capture of the Faroes had pricked his nationalist pride.

"You are right. We must strike back and Malta is the place to do it. The British still haven't managed to reinforce the island's air defences?"

"No, my Führer. Since the damage to the US carrier Wasp, and the crippling of the Eagle, they have given up trying to fly Spitfires to Malta. Their air defences rely totally on anti-aircraft guns, and even their ammunition is running low."

"Then Rommel will have to wait. We will respond to the British attack with one of our own, then I will bring the prisoners to Berlin and march them through the streets."

"My Führer, Iceland needs its defences strengthened now that the Faroes are gone."

"You just told me the navy has nothing to spare!"

"Yes, but the Luftwaffe has. The Reichsmarschall has agreed to transfer ZG 1 with its Bf 110s to Iceland. This will add another twenty to thirty aircraft to the defence. US bombing raids from Greenland have increased recently and now we expect British attacks from the Faroes."

"These planes are needed in Russia."

"The unit is being reformed at the moment near Berlin. It was to become part of the reserve. It wasn't supposed to go to the east."

The German leader frowned and then gave a single nod. "I don't want to lose Iceland as well. Send the twin-engine fighters, though they won't help you if the enemy send ships against the island."

"We are taking the short term measure of basing the Stukas from the Graf Zeppelin at Reykjavik. This adds another eighteen attack aircraft to the defence."

"What are the numbers of the twin-engined planes?"

"Fourteen Ju 88s and twenty six He 111s are operational, as well as eight He 112s and five Bf 110s."

"It will have to be enough. Iceland must hold. What is the supply situation like?"

"This is the most difficult time of the year to get supplies in, with the long days and calmer weather. However, four destroyers recently used a spring storm to run out a critical fuel delivery and the giant ex-French submarine the Serpent, took out extra food last week. We've had to cut the use of fishing trawlers right back but there's enough fuel to last until the end of August. Losses of the fast merchants to British submarines has restricted their use but two are sitting ready and will charge west to Iceland as soon as bad weather closes in."

"Do you have any heavy units in the Baltic?"

"Just the Graf Spee."

"She isn't needed there. You can move her out to the Norwegian Sea if it helps."

"Thank you, my Führer."

"Now was there anything else?"

"I wanted to ask about the stories I've heard regarding the treatment of the Jews."

The Führer stiffened and his eyes narrowed. "This is none of your concern. The navy should keep its eyes on the ocean and leave these affairs to the SS."

"It's just I worry that these tales might affect Germany's reputation with our allies."

"They don't know what is happening and you shouldn't either. I will not speak of this with you and don't want to hear any more questions on the subject."

Wever remembered what Canaris had said to him about not losing the Führer's ear, yet he felt some conformation was needed that the German leader knew what was happening to the Jews before he took any action. This discussion was all he needed to show him that the Führer was well aware of what was being done to the Jews.

"I will never speak of it again," he said.

The German leader stared at him with his intense blue eyes for a moment, before relaxing and signalling he leave.

On the drive back to his headquarters on Rugen Island, Wever considered his next move. He would do his best to see that Malta fell and Iceland was reinforced but his main preoccupation was getting the file on the Final Solution to the British and Americans. Perhaps they would do something to stop the wholesale murder of a people, though Wever couldn't think how they could intervene. He needed to contact the flier Marseille to find out what the man was prepared to do to assist, and reassure him that his mother would be protected. Given Marseille's father was an avowed Nazi and had little to do with his son, he should be safe, and even if he wasn't that was just too bad.

The problem was that Germany was still riding high on a series of victories, such as the capture of Tobruk and the defeat of the Russian spring offensive. British night bombing was now aimed at German ports and did some damage but it was not a threat as yet. The Japanese had conquered vast areas of the Pacific, however they had recently been defeated at Midway Island and their advance in Papua New Guinea and the Solomon Islands had slowed. The USA was still ramping up its war effort and the only sign of its presence was the increased supply of their tanks to the British, the use of the carrier Wasp to try and run Spitfires to Malta, and the increasing appearances of their destroyers in the Atlantic. Wever understood the reluctance of anybody in Germany to even consider opposing the Führer.

But Russia still fought on, the British grew stronger at sea, despite their losses, and the Americans would soon become a force to be reckoned with. If one of Germany's enemies wasn't knocked out of the war by the end of the year, then the Third Reich would be in danger. Wever didn't want his country to lose the war. He was still committed to victory, yet not with the current leader. Something needed to be done to regain Germany's honour, he just didn't know what it was.

v

The July convoy had been defeated even though it had almost gutted the Regia Aeronautica and caused the naval air arm of the Kriegsmarine to lose a dozen more aircraft. Yet the British failed to get any supplies through to the besieged island. Two British destroyers, an anti-aircraft cruiser and the merchant Welshman were all sunk. Fregattenkapitän Bernhard Jope had missed these battles as his Staffel was reequipping in Germany.

Now they were back on Sardinia and ready to assist in the defeat of the Royal Navy. Sixteen brand new Ju 88 Cs with their heavy cannons and bombs would help the Stukas and He 111s destroy the enemy.

There was also an aircraft on the runway he'd never seen before. The Fw 205 torpedo bomber was a single-engined plane built around the Fw 190 fighter used by the Luftwaffe. It was a twin seater with a gunner operating a 13mm machine gun from the rear position and the pilot able to fire two forward firing rifle calibre guns which were mounted above the engine. Yet it was the speed and robust nature of the new aircraft that made it so promising. This version flew at two hundred and ninety miles an hour when fully loaded and could travel another forty miles an hour faster after its torpedo had been dropped. Jope understood the plane was still being modified for carrier operations and the version which would fly from the Graf Zeppelin would have longer and wider wings and be at least ten miles an hour slower. Still, it was a vast improvement over the Fi 167.

There were at least eighty attack aircraft at the base and another forty watching the approaches to Malta from the Eastern Mediterranean. The Luftwaffe had even added twenty of its own Stukas to the attack force, basing them on Crete. With the British now forced back as far as El Alamein they had no fighters with the range to protect their ships beyond Tobruk. Everyone expected the main enemy effort to come from Gibraltar, though nobody knew if the enemy would risk any more carriers, especially as the British had lost two capital ships to the Japanese and their bases at Ceylon were now under threat. There were rumours however, of a number of smaller carriers capable of carrying up to twenty aircraft, and there was at least one Royal Navy fleet carrier at Gibraltar with another two somewhere else.

Jope had been told that the Luftwaffe had also reinforced units on Sicily and the Italians had pulled in planes from southern Russia as well as Greece. The Royal Navy would be sailing into a whirlwind of fire.

Thoughts of Emma and their final parting played out in his mind. He could still see her standing by the side of the road as he drove away, tears streaming in silent rivers down her cheeks. She refused to set a date for their wedding and her mood swung wildly every time he saw her. Jope considered speaking with Emma's commanding officer but wondered if that would do more harm than good. Her reaction to his departure was the most normal response he'd experienced from her during his visits, yet he was still concerned about her mental state. In the end he decided not to do anything as he thought the shame of her weakness toward the enemies of Germany might cause her comrades to distrust and ridicule her. He told her the war would soon be over, at which time she could leave her position at Ravensbruck with honour. She just looked at him with that flat faraway stare he was used to seeing on her face.

The news that the British were steaming east arrived the following day. A U-boat had torpedoed a cruiser before slipping away, and had radioed the enemy strength at two battleships, a number of cruisers, at least thirty destroyers, fourteen merchant vessels, one fleet carrier (probably HMS Victorious) and two smaller escort carriers (HMS Archer and HMS Biter). Jope thought this would give the enemy at least fifty fighter aircraft, and his guess was fairly accurate. A fourth carrier, HMS Battler, travelled with a smaller escort further back from the main fleet and was to fly thirty Spitfires to Malta as replacements at some stage during the battle. The whole affair was building up to be one of the greatest confrontations between naval and airpower the world had ever seen.

His Staffel took off soon after dawn and met with the He 111s and the Stukas. Jope could see the He 112s and Bf 110s forming up above them and the entire force then flew southwest to meet the enemy. What he didn't know was the Italians attacked half an hour before them, after leaving from a different Sardinian base with thirty-five SM 84 torpedo bombers escorted by twenty Re 2001s. This attack was met by twenty Sea Hurricanes and four Martlets and was largely ineffective, however it did disrupt the enemy's defences enough that when the Kriegsmarine aircraft arrived, only fourteen fighters were airborne to meet them. The Bf 110s and He 112s swept them aside and the German naval aircraft attacked.

Jope ordered his men to concentrate on the merchants, especially the tankers, and he led the Staffel down through the thin clouds toward the rear of the convoy. The flak was intense with the sky almost black from exploding shells. Immediately, a Ju 88 was hit, exploding as a shell detonated under the engine. To Jope, the plane appeared to come apart, as though a giant hand ripped it apart in the sky.

"Stay steady boy, this will be rough, so remember your training," he said over the radio.

For at least two thirds of the Staffel this was the first time they would have seen action. Jope led the way, slowing his approach as he lined up on the refrigerated freighter, Melbourne Star. He ignored the shells buffeting the plane, and kept his approach at the recommended speed for skip bombing, releasing his ordinance at just the correct moment. All four bombs slammed into the vessel, ripping it apart and sending debris high into the air. Jope raced away, pushing the throttle forward and keeping the plane at wave top height. Eventually he climbed above the convoy and watched as the other aircraft attacked. The He 111s dropped their torpedoes at too great a range and the rest of his Staffel only succeeded in hitting a second freighter, which was sinking by the stern.

The new Fw 205 torpedo planes were more successful, hitting the battleship HMS Nelson with a single weapon and HMS Archer twice. The light carrier rocked with the blows, exploding in flames. An hour later, internal detonations tore the ship apart and the carrier rolled over and sank within minutes, taking two thirds of crew to the bottom. The results from Jope's Staffel were disappointing with many of his younger pilots attacking at high speed and skipping their bombs over the British ships. The Ju 87s sunk another freighter but the Stukas lost four planes in the effort, while the He 111s and Jope's Staffel only lost three aircraft. He believed that was because the rookie pilots hadn't pressed home their attacks and this was something he couldn't tolerate.

That night he called a meeting in the mess hall and stood at the front of the room. All eyes were on him and he tried to keep his face neutral.

"Today you let Germany and the Führer down. Attacks weren't pressed home and bombs were dropped at a speed that ensured they would never hit their targets. Why?"

The aircrew looked at their feet though some frowned, clearly insult by his statement.

"Did you think this would be easy? You've all done the training and know what speed the ordinance needs to be released at, yet you attacked at high speed then fled the area. Some of you look annoyed, thinking, how could he accuse us of this? Well, give me another explanation?"

Now everybody was looking away. He understood if they truly examined their actions, they would see that they were rattled by the amount of flak the enemy threw at them. Jope blamed the shortened trained schedule. He knew losses meant the pilots and their crews were being rushed into action before they were ready, but he couldn't allow that to become an excuse.

"Tomorrow we will attack again. The enemy convoy will be in the Sicilian Narrows and the only fighters we might meet are those that were flown off to Malta. All of the British carriers have now turned back and we think they managed to get thirty fighters to the island, though six have already been shot down and more damaged. However, these aircraft are nearly all Spitfires. The Luftwaffe will be over Malta in strength tomorrow so I don't think any of them will get to us. I expect attacks to be carried out at the correct speeds and aircraft to press home their attacks. Don't let Germany down again! Dismissed."

With that he walked from the room. Jope thought of Emma and the work she was doing for her country. She had undertaken a role that was destroying her in ways his aircrew would never understand. If she could keep going day after day, serving her country, then it was the least his men could do.

That night the Italians attacked with three heavy cruisers, two light cruisers and twelve destroyers. In a confused night action the British managed to accidently sink two of their own ships: HMS Laforey and HMS Lookout. They also lost a light cruiser to a volley of torpedoes, and the cruiser HMS Phoebe was hit by four eight-inch shells, heavily damaging the ship. Then the destroyer HMS Matchless blew up when a six-inch shell detonated in her forward magazine. The Italian losses were catastrophic with all of the heavy cruisers being sunk and one of the light cruisers crippled. After the initial surprise, British radar had ruled the night and the remains of the Italian force chased north.

Fourteen Ju 88s and ten He 111s caught the convoy in the morning as it was trying to reform. The escort had scattered during the night as it fought the Italian cruisers and destroyers in the early hours of the morning, and were still picking up survivors and taking position around the merchants when the aircraft arrived out of the rising sun. There was high cloud building from the north and the wind came up, creating white capes which dotted the ocean with small specks. Eight He 112s escorted the group at an altitude of three thousand meters.

Flak started bursting around the naval aircraft as they came down to wave top level, yet Jope noticed it was lighter than the previous day. The British battleship had turned back with the carriers, however another cruiser and two destroyers had joined the escort. This didn't make up for the loss of the Nelson's flak guns or compensate for the amount of ammunition the British ships had expended. He led his planes straight toward the merchant vessels, determined to sink every last one of them. The He 111s flew in from the north, trying to divide the enemy's fire between Jope's Staffel and theirs. The British fire, though lessened, was accurate and soon a Ju 88 was riddled with shrapnel and fell into the sea while another just blew apart as it was hit by a three point seven-inch shell. Then the merchant ships were in front of them and Jope had to pick a target. He searched for a tanker but all he could see were freighters. The ship in front of his plane was the Dorset, a large freighter carrying food and other supplies for Malta. The ship grew in his sights as Jope adjusted his speed and waited until the range was perfect. He released his bombs and pulled up over the bow of the vessel, opening the throttles and continuing in a shallow climb.

"Two hits, skipper!" reported the pilot of Bruno Four.

The bombs ripped apart the stern of the vessel, causing sea water to flood in through two large holes. Further damage occurred when his wingman hit the ship with a bomb which detonated amidships. He turned back over the convoy, ready to strafe any British destroyers that appeared. That's when he saw Bruno flight attack the tanker, the Ohio. The vessel was protected by two destroyers which poured fire at the approaching aircraft. Jope saw one plane dip as its wings were shredded by 20mm cannon fire. The Ju 88 ploughed into the sea, summersaulting after a wing clipped the ocean. Then a second plane was hit, seemingly coming apart as if someone had opened a zipper down the fuselage. One aircraft turned away at that point but the final plane continued, even as machine gun bullets and cannon fire tore into the wings and tail. Both engines caught fire but the aircraft continued on until it slammed straight into the tanker. Both disappeared in an explosion that seemed to lift the ship out of the water. The explosion threw an expanding dark cloud high into the sky and planes were buffeted by the blast.

Jope watched with a sense of awe. He felt as though his Staffel had just stuck an important blow but wasn't sure. Then his rear gunner yelled a warning.

"Skipper, twin-engined fighters diving on the survivor of Bruno flight."

The final aircraft of the group of four which had attacked the tanker had tried to hit a fast moving destroyer and was now climbing away from the ocean. They had pressed home their attack and damaged the British vessel but were now in danger. Jope dropped the nose of the Ju 88 and dived to assist. As his plane picked up speed he radioed a warning to Bruno Two but the pilot didn't respond. He noted smoke coming from one of the engines and realised the aircraft was damaged. Then the British Beaufighter opened fire. The first burst went high so the enemy pilot adjusted and four 20mm cannons smashed into the Ju 88's port wing. There was an explosion and the plane was falling. It hit the sea and disappeared in a fountain of water, disappearing as though it had never existed.

Enraged, Jope went after the enemy formation. They hadn't noticed him with all the flak and smoke, and he managed to slip in behind the last British aircraft and open fire from below. His own cannon sliced off the Beaufighter's wing as cleanly as if he had used a carving knife and the plane tumbled end over end before splashing into the sea. As he continued after the two remaining aircraft, his airspeed built up and he overshot the next target. Both the enemy machines turned hard away from him and flew at his aircraft from different directions. He looked around for assistance and discovered the convoy was now behind him and he was alone.

The remaining English twin engined fighters came at him from each flank. Making a split second decision he turned toward the closest one and flew at it head on. Both planes started firing at approximately the same moment and Jope could hear the thump of his aircraft's cannon and the chatter of its heavy machine guns. He watched as the enemy's tracers raced at his plane and then felt the Ju 88 shudder as the British fire tore into the wing. His own cannon ripped through his opponent's cockpit and peeled away the Beaufighter's fuselage. The enemy plane fell away trailing smoke and flame.

"Skipper, the port engine's on fire," yelled the rear gunner.

Glancing out the side window he noted the thick smoke billowing from holes in the wing and around the propeller. Jope quickly shut down the engine and dived the plane back toward the Sicilian coast. Then he heard the rear machine gun shooting at an unseen target.

"Where is he, gunner?" he called but was answered by a scream as bullets lashed his plane.

Jope threw the aircraft into a tight turn and watched as the enemy fighter bomber overshot. He was in no position to fire at the British plane and watched as it turned back.

"He'll try and hit us if we keep heading toward Italy," Jope muttered.

His plane was flying like a drunken duck, pulling one way and then the other. The controls were sloppy and his lateral control was nominal. Then a He 112 climbed into his view. The single engined fighter had a blue tail and a dolphin painted beneath the cockpit. Jope realised this was the second combat he'd seen the great ace Marseille participate in and this time the man's presence would save his life. The He 112 looped over the top, turned inside the Beaufighter, and shot it down with two quick bursts, both fired from impossible angles. Jope had never seen marksmanship of that quality and he thanked his lucky stars as he continued to wrestle with the controls. Glancing back he saw two parachutes drifting down and realised the British airmen had both survived. He wasn't sure how he felt about that as he knew their fire had probably killed one of his men.

Marseille brought his aircraft close to Jope's bomber and he saw the other pilot frown. He flew his fighter under the Ju 88 and then around to the other side. Shaking his head the ace pointed

northeast and Jope nodded. He didn't know if he'd be able to nurse

his aircraft that far but there was no way the bomber would make it

back to Sardinia. The rear gunner was dead but his ventral gunner

was uninjured. Marseille slowly climbed to about five hundred

meters above the Ju 88 and escorted the wounded plane as it flew

northeast. Eventually, after fifteen minutes, Jope saw the coast. He

breathed a sigh of relief and dropped the nose slightly,

endeavouring to build up speed. Just then his starboard engine

started to cough and splutter. Jope couldn't see any hits on that

side of the aircraft and wondered if the fuel lines had been hit. He

couldn't ask Marseille if his plane was leaking fuel as the radio was

wrecked. Jope supposed it didn't matter. The bomber wasn't going

to stay in the air much longer.

"Time to bail out Stephan, before we get too low," he said to

the gunner, who was now standing behind him leaning forward to

peer at the controls.

"The wind's from the south, skipper. It will blow us over Sicily, I hope," said Matrose Rosen.

"It doesn't matter if it doesn't, we have no choice. Check your parachute and then jump."

The man nodded and disappeared into the rear of the plane. Jope tried the autopilot and found it wasn't functioning, so he tied the stick in position and wedged a flare pistol to hold the rudders in place. As it was, as soon as he left the pilot's seat the plane started to pull around to the north. Jope moved quickly, hoping his gunner had already left the aircraft. He moved to the hatch near the plane's belly and found it already open. Good, Stephan had jumped. Just as he reached the hatch the Ju 88 started to increase its roll and Jope found himself looking through the opening at the Sicilian countryside, as though he was peering through a window. He threw himself forward before the plane rolled over completely and the plane turned upside down. The hurried maneuver caused him to bang his ankle painfully against the door as the plane continued to roll.

Then the aircraft flashed past him and wind roared in his ears. He felt a moment of panic and wildly felt for the release handle on the parachute. His body spun at crazy angles and he thought he would die when his fingers found the metal ring and he pulled. There was a loud cracking sound and the silk billowed out above his head, his body jerking in the harness. He looked around and saw his plane falling toward the sea, trailing a line of dark smoke. Behind and below him another parachute floated on a gentle southerly breeze. The sudden loss of noise, except for the wind in the canopy, was almost surreal and it left Jope feeling disorientated. Before he felt prepared, the ground was rushing up to reach him and he was scrambling to ready himself for impact. He landed in shallow water only ten meters from the beach, the parachute quickly filling and sinking below the surface. Italian soldiers ran toward him, cutting his guide ropes away and assisting him on to dry land. Jope fell to his knees on the sand and laughed. He was still alive.

v

The battle with the British convoy continued all the way to Valletta harbour. Not a single merchant vessel survived, except for a small badly damaged freighter that was then swamped by Luftwaffe bombers as it tried to unload. In the end only a little of the food and some rifle ammunition made it onto the docks. During the second night S boats and Italian motor torpedo boats attacked the convoy, sinking another cruiser and damaging more of the merchant shipping. Italian submarines also tried to destroy the British vessels but were driven off, only managing a single torpedo hit. The following day however, the full force of the Luftwaffe, Regia Aeronautica and aircraft of the Kriegsmarine all struck the convoy in a rolling series of attacks. In the end the defeat for the British was both tactical and strategic. People on Malta started to run out of food and the twenty remaining Spitfires managed to fly only two more missions before their tanks ran dry.

Fourteen days later, German and Italian paratroopers landed on the island, followed by the 22nd Airlanding Division. Italian troops were put ashore from barges and other vessels during the day. By nightfall the garrison was in disarray, with ammunition supplies running low and hungry troops surrendering in large numbers. The battle dragged on for another two days but the result was never in doubt. The Royal Navy provided some support with a mixed force of cruisers and destroyers, and even managed to evacuate a few thousand troops, but lost three ships to air attacks in the process. The invasion, coming at the end of summer, was too late to help Rommel's attack at El Alamein. His panzer force was ground down by relentless air bombardment and his attack veered off its course and crashed into a group of dug-in six pounder anti-tank guns. He was well supplied with fuel so was able to withdraw in good order, and the arrival of thirty new Panzer IVs and twelve Marder IIs helped. He also received the support of a Gruppe of Ju 88s and a lot more fuel. Rommel blamed the invasion for the failure of his attack, but most military experts, both in Germany and the west, believed that the capture of Malta had improved the situation of the Afrika Corps, especially their supply situation.

Rommel received more reinforcements and his fuel situation

was now adequate, however the British were building up their

forces and soon would outnumber the exhausted Germans and

Italians. In the end, a massive set piece battle in January of the

following year would force Rommel to retreat in good order to

Tobruk. The battered British 8th Army slowly followed the retreating

Afrika Corps and both sides would then renew the battle as the

Allies landed in French North Africa that same spring. Before then

however, the Americans and British would unleash another

surprise; one which would set the North Atlantic aflame.

Chapter Four: Autumn 1942

The Staffel was back in Germany reequipping after the swirling air campaign above Malta had finished. Work on the Me 155 had begun in 1941 as the Kriegsmarine leadership realised that the He 112 was too small for further development. For a while it looked as though the Fw 190 would be modified for carrier operations and take its place. Then the Me 155 came along. Kapitänleutnant Hans-Joachim Marseille liked the new plane and appreciated the centre line cannon. The flutter problem had been solved by thinning the wings, though this led to the loss of the other cannons. However, there was still room for a pair of 13mm heavy machine guns so the firepower of the plane remained about the same as his present mount. The speed of the new fighter was a drastic increase over that of the He 112, as was the rate of climb, and Marseille looked forward to using the new aircraft against the newest Spitfires and also against American fighter pilots.

At the moment there were only twelve early production models available and the Kriegsmarine was running them through their paces, looking for any possible flaws or weaknesses. Marseille's Staffel was to be the first to receive the new machines, after which the Graf Zeppelin's fighter pilots would take delivery of theirs. All of the training and flying was interspersed with leave, of which Marseille took full advantage. He spent as much time as possible with his mother in Berlin and also visited a number of underground jazz clubs. He didn't drink as much as in the past, preferring to enjoy the music and wake up relatively clear headed in the morning.

Marseille read the paper and listened to the radio in the evenings, trying to work out what was really going on in the east. The army seemed to have advanced quickly across the Caucasus until they reached the mountains, and then the advance ran out of steam. The same seemed to have happened around a city called Stalingrad, where progress was now measured in meters, not kilometers. The newspaper 'Das Reich' continually wrote that the

Soviets were on their last legs, yet a breakthrough on the Volga seemed slow in coming. Marseille knew the Russians weren't receiving any supplies via the Atlantic, yet a friend had mentioned that the Americans were pouring war material into Russia through Persia, and even via the Far East where the Japanese left Russian shipping alone as it sailed into US ports. He shook his head and wondered at the true state of play.

On the third night of his leave there was a knock at the door of his mother's house. He walked to the door holding a mug of fake coffee in his left hand, and opened it to find a woman wearing a Kriegshelferinnen uniform. She had sandy blonde hair and cool blue eyes which seemed to weigh him up.

"Can I help you?" Marseille asked.

"I was sent here for piano lessons," said the woman. "My name is Unteroffiziere ohne Portepee Charlotte Hartmann."

Marseille blinked a few times before he remembered something said to him by the Grossadmiral. "Ahhh, yes, it's come back to me," he said.

"Can I come in?" asked the woman.

"Of course. Would you like some very poor coffee? I just made some."

"No, thank you," said Charlotte as she followed him down the hallway. He led her into a small sitting room that overlooked the rear garden. Outside, various vegetables grew; the main crop being potatoes, with a few sweet corn and a lot of peas.

"Are we alone?" Charlotte asked.

"My mother is out at a friend's place but will be home in an hour or so," said Marseille.

"Good, I have a lot to tell you. First is about our cover story: I am your lover. From what I've been told, this fits with the narrative of your life so far and will be easily believed."

"Alright. I have no problem with that." Marseille couldn't hide his smile; after all, Charlotte was a very attractive woman, with her small upturned nose and dimples.

"This is fiction only so don't get any ideas. I'm here to discuss how certain documents will be transported to Sweden."

Marseille frowned and then closed the door. "I can't just fly over the Baltic; there'd be repercussions for my mother."

"We are aware of this and are trying to find a solution. At first we thought she could disappear but that would show you weren't working alone and our enemies might instigate an investigation, which we would rather avoid."

"We?"

"You won't hear any names from me. This isn't a game. From now on, your life and everybody else's who is involved in this operation, is in danger, including your mother's. You agreed to help. Has that changed?"

"No. The world needs to know what these monsters are up to."

For the first time Charlotte smiled. "Good. Then listen. There is a package waiting for you at the local post office in a box with this number." She handed him a key. "As far as we can ascertain you aren't being followed so it will be easy for you to retrieve the package. Hide it somewhere here and keep it dry. We will give you more details when we have them. Oh, and keep a low profile when you collect the package. Try not to be recognised as that will help avoid suspicion when you disappear."

"I understand," said Marseille. He turned the key over in his hand seeing the number 73. It was a simple brass affair, dull with age. "Any idea how you will protect my mother?"

"Not yet."

"So I wait? And collect the package?"

"Yes, but you also need to give me a piano lesson, just in case anybody gets suspicious. It's unlikely, however we don't want to take chances."

"Is there a risk you were followed?"

The blonde woman shook her head, dislodging a strand which had been tied into a bun. "Very unlikely. Still, it's best to be sure."

"I don't know the first thing about teaching the piano. Are you sure we couldn't do anything else instead?"

Charlotte's eyes went flat. "No. You play quite well from what I have heard, and I'm not a rank beginner."

"I'll be teaching you jazz after you've got the basics, but I probably won't be very good at it."

"We'll see."

In the end Charlotte was a better player than she'd led him to believe. He took her through her scales and they played some simple tunes, which she picked up easily. Marseille enjoyed the close contact with her as they shared the piano stool. The corner of her mouth turned up in the imitation of a smile a few times as he leaned in, however she always inclined away from him.

His mother arrived home as they finished up and he gave Charlotte some sheet music to take with her. The blonde woman introduced herself to his mother in formal language which caused the old woman to raise an eyebrow.

After Charlotte was gone she turned to her son. "Not your usual taste, I must say."

Marseille shrugged. "It's a piano lesson only Mother. I'm doing a favour for a friend."

"I saw the way you looked at her."

He glanced away; however he didn't answer.

"Could it be there's a member of the opposite sex who is immune to your charms?"

Marseille couldn't help but laugh at his mother's teasing. "Early days, Mother early days."

The helicopter flew low over the icefield toward Reykjavik.

Fregattenkapitän Hans-Gerrit von Stockhausen could feel the cold

as he leaned back in his seat. The Fa 223 Drache skimmed low and

then dipped as it approached the coast. Moving at one hundred

miles an hour he found the experience exhilarating. The fishing

harbour at Hofn held four S-Boats and a minesweeper, as well as a

number of fishing vessels. There was also a battery of 88mm guns

on the flat ground to the south of the warehouses and diesel tanks.

A small garrison of only fifty men held the area, with the rest of the

company kept further back at Hornafjordur airstrip. Because of the

narrow entrance and the mud banks in the area, and the ice fields

and nearby mountains, the area was an unlikely target. Any

invasion was more likely to occur closer to the capital city. Still, it

was part of his job to check the battery, its condition and the

morale of the men manning the 88mm guns.

The helicopter flew over a river that ran grey with the

sediment of the glaciers, and continued until the machine touched down near a well-protected harbour. He climbed out, ducking low under the swinging rotors and walked to a tall man standing with a Matrose near the edge of the helipad.

"Welcome to Hofn, sir," said the Ober-matt.

"Thank you, Steiner, isn't it?"

"Yes, sir."

They walked to a car which was obviously a local vehicle that had been seconded for service.

"What the hell is that?" Stockhausen asked.

"An Austin twelve-six, sir. A British car that was owned by the local mayor. We use it as the main communication vehicle around this area, though a lot of the time riders on horseback are sent from the airstrip to save fuel. I've got to return it to the company commander tonight, then I'll catch a cart back to the village."

Stockhausen grunted. He knew motor transport and fuel was in short supply and supposed he should be grateful that he didn't have to ride to the battery. The supply situation had always been tight on Iceland but had become worse since the loss of the Faroes. Now British aircraft flew far out into the Norwegian Sea looking for German ships. Even the fast destroyers weren't safe as Beaufighters hunted them in the grey northern waters. Bf 110s escorted the Kriegsmarine vessels when they could, and sometimes He 112s stood watch for the final stretch of the journey. Dog fights between the heavy fighters occurred over the Atlantic with sixteen Beaufighters being shot down with exactly the same number of Bf 110s also being destroyed. However, there were times when German shipping was vulnerable and two destroyers had been sunk running supplies to Reykjavik. Once a vessel was to the north of the island, it was generally safe from air attack but not from British submarines. Three fast transports had been destroyed earlier in the year and even one of the captured Norwegian destroyers lost its bow to a torpedo; the ship just managing to run aground near the village of Raufarhofn where most of the supplies were salvaged.

One of the huge French cruiser submarines had disappeared without a trace on a journey from Bergen to Iceland in July, and it wasn't until after the war it was discovered she had been sunk by the submarine HMS Thrasher. All the personnel and supplies were lost. It wasn't that provisions weren't getting through and the air bridge picked up some of the slack, but these aircraft were needed elsewhere. The summer months were always the hardest to get the necessary ammunition, fuel and food through due to the long hours of daylight and the improved weather. Fast supply ships only left Trondheim when storms blew down from the North Pole. This could still occur during summer and one did in late July, allowing a small fast tanker of 5000grt to make the journey, as well as two freighters of slightly higher tonnage. Unfortunately all of the vessels were damaged by the British on the return journey, with one of the freighters sinking just off the Norwegian coast.

The drive to the gun emplacements only took a few minutes and Stockhausen found everything in order. Then he visited the harbour and inspected the S-boats and the minesweeper, the

Kamerun. The ship had been captured in Norway and only had a crew of twenty-five. It carried a single 88mm gun and a few machine guns, but it did important work along the coast finding and destroying mines. Everything appeared fine except one of the S-boats had engine problems that prevented her from moving at faster than ten knots. Stockhausen promised to see about the necessary parts which had been promised but hadn't arrived.

He was heading back to the car when the helicopter buzzed overhead before landing in a nearby parking lot. The pilot clambered out and ran toward him, a deep frown on his face.

"Sir, you are needed back in Reykjavik immediately," said the man.

"Any idea about the source of urgency?" asked Stockhausen.

"They didn't say sir, just that they want you back now."

He saluted the Ober-matt and climbed into the helicopter which immediately took off and turned west. They flew along the coast so the machine could refuel at the small village of Vik, and then continued on to the capital city. As he climbed out of the helicopter Stockhausen fought off waves of fatigue. He'd been in the air for over six hours, the planned overnight stay at Hofn a distant memory. The airstrip was a hive of activity and Stockhausen found a car waiting for him. This time the vehicle was German and had a machine gun mounted on the passenger side. He was driven into town and ushered straight into army headquarters. A major from the 56th Infantry Division met him in the foyer of the National Library building. The man introduced himself as Herman Graf, attached to the headquarter staff and responsible to Lieutenant General Karl von Oven.

"We heard you were inspecting troops further to the east?" said Graf.

"That's right. I got the message to hurry back sir," answered Stockhausen.

"Yes, a fleet is coming our way. A Ju 290 spotted it this morning and radioed in before disappearing. U 409 confirmed the sighting as did a Do 24, which is also missing. They definitely saw transport vessels."

"Has the High Command been informed?"

"Yes, we are expecting reinforcements tomorrow, mainly in the form of aircraft. Extra fuel and ammunition is coming on Ju 252s and three modified Me 323s are bringing Marder IIs."

"I didn't know we had a transport that could carry a small tank."

"They're very new and only have an eight hundred kilometer range. They'll carry extra fuel and strip out their guns and radios. It's risky but we lack armour. The plan is to bring over six of the assault guns and use them to bolster the Panzer IIIs and French Somuas."

"I thought I saw a Panzer IV recently?"

"We have four, making it thirty-eight running panzers in total."

"And the Allies will be bringing more than that."

"The general wants to know what the Kriegsmarine can add to our forces."

Stockhausen nodded and started to run through the possibilities in his head. Of course he wasn't responsible for the naval air Staffels but he did oversee the batteries, as well as commanding the 9th U-boat flotilla. Then there were various groups that could be formed into naval infantry. He thought through this as he walked up the stairs, into what would have been the main library room.

"Ah, Stockhausen," said General Karl von Oven. "We've been talking about what your command can add. Maybe you can enlighten us."

The man before him was tall and slightly stooped. His head was shaved and his nose large and straight. A Knight's Cross hung around his neck.

"Certainly, sir. I can form two companies from the clerical staff as well as another one from various service troops. The mechanics and other technicians can probably form two more. I wouldn't use these troops for anything but defence as they are not trained to operate with armour or in cooperation with artillery," said Stockhausen.

"We will use them to hold ground. I expect you'll command them?"

Stockhausen's gut clenched and he struggled to keep his expression neutral. "Yes, sir."

The General's face twitched as he picked up something in Stockhausen's demeanour. "You are alright with that?"

"Yes, sir, I'm just trying to get my head around commanding what will basically be an infantry battalion. It's not something I trained for back in Germany."

"Good point. I'll appoint an officer from my staff to assist you and place a few NCOs to help at the company level. You'll need radios. Make sure they are on the same frequency as the army, and use the men I give you to liaise with the artillery."

"Yes, sir."

"Then there's the batteries. Are they ready to engage enemy ships and defend the beaches?"

"Yes, sir. It all depends on where the enemy lands but if there are guns in the area, they'll hit back."

"Good, good. Well, I won't hold you up. You'll need to form these units quickly. We expect the first raids by their carrier planes tomorrow and the landings soon after that. It depends if they spend time softening us up, or land as soon as their shipping is in place. Dismissed."

Stockhausen barely slept that night as he called junior officers together and directed them to form companies. He armed the men with what he could find in the armoury, finding there was a mixture of guns from a dozen countries. French MAS-38 submachine guns sat next to Danish Masden light machine guns. There was plenty of ammunition for the latter but little for the former. Standard German rifles and pistols were in short supply, with there being only enough to equip one man in two, so Danish Krag-Jorgensen rifles made up the shortfall. Luckily someone had thought to bring enough ammunition to keep the weapons operational for a few days of fighting. The ad hoc companies had little in the way of mortars or heavy machine guns (though a few of the latter were found), so Stockhausen attached some 20mm guns to the battalion and organised vehicles to tow them.

He collapsed into a chair around four o'clock in the morning and fell asleep. A Matrose woke him around eight with a hot drink. Standing at the young man's shoulder was a Hauptmann of medium build wearing glasses. He had a hooked nose and dark hair and Stockhausen though he looked like a Jew. Shaking off the initial impression he stood and wiped the sleep from his eyes.

"Sorry Hauptmann, it's been a busy night," said Stockhausen.

"For all of us, sir."

He glanced at the man, trying to see if there was a hidden rebuke in the words. "I've organised five companies, all armed with an assortment of weapons. There is a 20mm cannon attached to each one and they are organising their platoons and commanders as we speak."

"Do we have radios?"

"I'm sorry, I don't think I caught your name, and you need to address me as sir."

The expression on the man's face didn't change. "Of course. I'm Hauptmann Ritter, sir. I was attached to the general's staff, and now I'm to advise you."

"Good. As for the radios, I've delegated the task and expect a report soon on whether we have found what we need."

"Have second-in-commands been appointed sir, and so on down the line, as replacements in case officers become casualties?"

"Not yet. We've been flat out equipping the men. I hope they won't ask us to move very far."

"Hard to tell sir, though I did hear that all efforts will be made to avoid using your troops as an attacking force."

Just then an air siren went and everybody ran to the slit trenches in the street. Stockhausen watched the sky as single-engined aircraft dived toward the port. Guns thundered and flak fired from the roof of a nearby building. The sky filled with balls of black smoke but the planes continued their downward spiral. Stockhausen realised these had to be carrier aircraft from American or British flat tops. He recognised Wildcat fighters and bi-planes which were either Albacores or Fairey Swordfish attack aircraft. He saw a plane become a fireball and another come apart and crash into the town. He wondered where the Kriegsmarine fighters were and decided they had probably intercepted the enemy force out over the sea. They would be scattered far and wide, waiting for a chance to land and refuel.

The attack lasted only ten minutes and the all clear was signalled a little later. Smoke poured from the Prince Eugen and at least one of the destroyers, the Karl Galster, was hit and smouldered where it lay at its moorings. Stockhausen was just climbing from his trench when the sirens sounded again. This time high flying B 17s rained bombs on the airstrip with a few taking the time to attack the harbour. An explosion tore apart a section of the road and Stockhausen felt the ground move. A familiar emotion crept over him and he started to shake. Turning away from the men who sheltered with him, he fought to control his hands by shoving them into his pockets. He then closed his eyes and tried to focus his thoughts on a scene from his youth. He'd used this technique before and it usually helped.

He imagined his home town of Kassel in winter and saw himself throwing snow balls at his sister. Slowly the shaking eased and he was able to open his eyes. The American bombers had moved away and all he could hear was the crackle of flames. Nearby, a warehouse burned and in the distance smoke drifted from the location of the airfield. He wondered if the German planes would be able to land.

V

"We hit them hard sir, but our naval attack force was almost destroyed in the process," said Vice Admiral Herbert Schmundt. The man had large pouches of flesh under his eyes and sported a goatee

beard. Schmundt was old navy and absolutely loyal to the

Kriegsmarine and to Germany, but he wasn't a Nazi and was

extremely brave, as shown by the Knight's Cross resting around his

throat.

"Five carriers! I don't know where the Allies found them all,"

said Grossadmiral Wever.

"Some are fleet carriers, such as the Victorious and

Illustrious. Others are what are being called escort carriers, or baby

carriers, and only hold fifteen to twenty-five planes. We sank one of

them. It seems they're not well armoured. However, they were

loaded up with Wildcats and Sea Hurricanes and are providing both

air cover and ground attack services. The fleet carriers are carrying

their normal complement of planes. Then of course, there are all

the battleship and cruisers, including some American ships."

"We threw everything we had at them and only sank four

ships?"

"One baby carrier, a transport and two light cruisers."

"How many planes do we have left?"

"Five Ju 88s, eight He 111s, three Stukas, four of the new FW 205 torpedo planes and a dozen fighters. We are flying out reinforcements but that's only another twelve Ju 88s and the same number of He 112s," said Schmundt, reading from a list. "Most of the Luftwaffe's Bf 110s were destroyed, some in the air and a few at the airfield. The survivors were withdrawn to the eastern airstrips. We think eight can still fly."

"I want contingency plans to rescue all the pilots and aircrew if this falls apart," said Wever. "They are too valuable to lose."

"I'll issue the orders, sir."

"In the meantime what's available from the surface fleet?"

"The Bismarck, Scharnhorst and Graf Spee. The Graf Zeppelin is still being repaired and having its radar upgraded."

"We will need to risk them. Air cover can be provided from Norway and whatever's left of the fighters on Iceland."

"It will be risky sir, our pilots are under extreme pressure as it is."

"The Führer will expect it; however, the ships need to be ready to fall back if it looks as though their air cover is compromised. Have those transports arrived yet? The big Me 323s?"

"Yes sir, though one crashed at the eastern airstrip and its cargo was destroyed."

"This is not good. If we had a couple of carriers and weren't in the process of rebuilding after Malta we would have more of a chance. We have few reserves."

Later, Grossadmiral Wever repeated what he knew to the Führer.

"I'm not willing to risk the Bismarck unless it can attack the transports," said the German leader, as he leaned over a map of the northern Atlantic.

"We cannot guarantee that our fleet will get close enough to hit the invasion force. The enemy are escorted by at least two battleships, with another travelling with the transports," said Wever.

"I don't want to lose Iceland, but at the same time the Bismarck is the only battleship we have," said Hitler.

Wever didn't say anything and waited for the German leader's decision. "I'll order Kesselring to send more support. We'll transfer fighters from Jagdgeschwader (JG) 5 to Iceland and I'll start moving units from the 22nd Air Landing Division there as well."

"We will have to move quickly my Führer, the enemy might land any day now."

"Another failure of the intelligence services. Your friend Canaris needs to try harder to give us warning of these attacks."

Wever knew he needed to distance himself from the Admiral. "We don't see eye to eye anymore. He has let me down too often and his failures cost German lives."

"Well to be fair, he has little in the way of resources in America and I have no doubt that is where the invasion force gathered."

"You are generous, my Führer."

The German leader nodded and then stroked his moustache. "I'll issue the orders immediately and give them the highest priority. You have permission to use the fleet but be careful with it. If we can't cover it from the air, withdraw it; if it faces superior forces, bring it back. Those are my orders."

Wever nodded and left the conference room in Berlin slightly relieved. He had a measure of freedom and intended to use it wisely.

V

The British sailed past Reykjavik and landed the 4th Infantry Division at Isafjordur, Bolungarvik, Sudureyri and Flateyri in the northwest of the island. The Vestfirdir peninsula had been chosen by the Allies as the area to land, due to its protected beaches, sheltered waters, and small harbours. Isafjordur also had an airstrip that had been built by the Germans just outside of the village. It only consisted of a single emergency strip, but it was enough to hold thirty or forty fighters and attack aircraft. It was also an area where the Kriegsmarine had struggled to find enough costal guns to protect the area. A battery of four 127mm guns sat at the entrance to Isafjardardjup, the long stretch of water that almost cut the peninsula in two. However Sudureyri and Flateyri were only protected by batteries of freestanding 105mm guns. These weapons were only protected by earthworks, while the 127mm battery was surrounded by concrete as well as sandbags.

The batteries were swamped with shells from allied cruisers and destroyers. USS Strong and HMS Musketeer were both sunk, and the light cruiser USS Trenton heavily damaged, all the German guns were destroyed and the 10th 11th and 12th Brigades of the 4th Division managed to land most of their troops without casualties. Paratroopers from the 2nd and 3rd battalions of the 1st Airborne Division dropped in a valley to the south of Flateyri and on the flat open country blocking the crossroad to Holavik and to Burdardalur. The landings near the village of Flateyri were successful as there were no German troops of any number in the area. This was just as well, as strong winds and poor preparation led to the paratroopers being scattered over a wide area with many breaking limbs in the rough terrain.

The same conditions faced the 3rd Battalion at the crossroads though they landed on flat grounded dotted with many small shallow lakes. The flight from the Faroes had been long and the planes carrying the men became strung out on the strong winds. Fortunately the first troops to land immediately set small fires and fired flares, which guided the other aircraft to their location. However, the 3rd Battalion's problems were just beginning. Two planes had developed engine problems over the southern coast of Iceland forcing their passengers to jump early. Unfortunately, one of these contained Brigadier George Fredrick and his headquarter staff. These men fought around the small village of Hof on the southern coast until their capture three days later. They would be rescued when the island eventually fell.

Without its commanding officer the unit coalesced around Captain Roger Bennet. German troops came up the road in company strength meeting the paratroopers in a fire fight which sent the men of the 171st Infantry Regiment scurrying away. The paratroopers then scraped shallow trenches for themselves in the stony soil and waited. Early the following morning they had to sit and endure a bombardment from four ex-French Somua tanks which fired at them for over an hour. The vehicles' 47mm guns killed eight men and wounded ten, while the British soldiers hugged the earth.

When the German infantry attacked a second time it was with the support of armour, as well as a battery of heavy mortars. Despite these advantages the paratroopers held until their ammunition ran out. They fled into the surrounding countryside, however many were captured. By the time the Germans were in possession of the crossroads, the British were ashore in numbers, with a reinforced battalion charging away from Isafjardardjup to meet them.

The landings had swept aside the scattered German companies in the area, using eight Covenanter tanks equipped with either three-inch howitzers or two-pound anti-tank guns. These accompanied a group of Universal Bren carriers and a few trucks as they hurried to relieve the paratroopers. The landing craft tank (LCTs) made the dangerous journey from Greenland carrying only half of their usual complement of tanks. Even using the bigger LCT Mark 3s, one sunk with all of its cargo and crew in heavy seas, one hundred kilometers from the coast. Only twelve made the crossing with all other vehicles having to be laboriously unloaded from transport ships at the small fishing port of Sudavik. There were no German forces on the northern side of the large fjord that could threaten the landings, except for some S-boats. These fast boats were blown up before they could attack, by a group of allied destroyers and the British 4th Division had three quarters of its strength ashore by the end of the day.

At sea the Kriegsmarine struck hard at the carriers and other ships guarding the landing forces. A second escort carrier was wrecked, having to be towed back to Halifax in Canada, and a supply ship sunk, yet the cost for the Germans was high. The plan to fly more fighters to Iceland was slowed by the range of the aircraft used by JG 5. The Fw 190s and Bf 109 Gs could fly eight hundred and fifty kilometers on internal fuel, and even with a drop tank the Messerschmitt couldn't make it to Iceland. The Fw 190 could, but there were only twenty drop tanks available at Trondheim for them to use. As it was, four planes flew into a storm and were never seen again, with the other aircraft arriving the day after the invasion.

So fourteen Fw 190 A3s joined eight He 112s and four Bf 110s to protect the German surface fleet as it moved forward to attack the following day.

The Battle of Jan Mayen is named after the island sitting between Norway and northern Greenland. It is sometimes known as the Second Battle of the Denmark Straights. Both names don't accurately describe the location of the clash between the

Kriegsmarine and the Allies though, as the action took place roughly halfway between the small volcanic island and the coast of Iceland (a little closer to the latter if properly measured). The Royal Navy had landed many of its aircraft on the small captured airstrip at Isafjordur and most of their planes had been damaged or destroyed in the ongoing raids against German positions in and around Reykjavik. P-38Fs were also flown from Greenland to the small airstrip, though three were lost en route, whilst another fourteen arrived safely; however, none of these planes participated in the battle of Jan Mayen.

The approach of the German fleet was noted first by scout planes from HMS Victorious. Both British carriers then collected twenty-four planes to attack the German surface fleet. Four Bf 110s and eight Fw 190s guarded the Bismarck, Scharnhorst, Hipper and Graf Spee. The raid was escorted by ten Wildcat fighters however these were no match for the Fw 190s and easily swept aside. This allowed the Bf 110s to attack the slower moving Fairey Albacores. There were no dive bombers involved in the attack so the defenders weren't forced to divide their fire, and the few torpedo bombers that made it past the fighters, found themselves facing a wall of flak. Every British attack aircraft was shot down except for one heavily damaged plane which struggled back to north eastern Iceland where it landed on a straight stretch of road. The raid incurred the highest percentage loss of the war.

British and American warships steamed north to attack the German fleet and met heavy weather as storms blew down from the north. In the early stages of the battle German helicopters managed to become airborne, while British and American spotter aircraft failed. The German fleet contained one battleship, one battle cruiser, one armoured cruiser (also known as a pocket battleship) and a heavy cruiser. It was escorted by the two ex-French super destroyers and four German destroyers. The Allies had the battleships, USS Washington and the HMS Howe, as well as the heavy cruisers San Diego and HMS Sussex. Eight destroyers also accompanied them; two of them being Fletcher-class US ships, the other all smaller British Tribal class vessels.

The battle started as the Germans tried to take advantage of their spotter helicopters, while sending the destroyers forward. This took the lighter forces out of the battle as they duelled between the giants, the heavy vessels drifting southeast, away from the fight between the destroyers, though the San Diego, with her smaller 127mm guns also stayed to assist. Admiral John Cunningham was concerned that the ex-French super destroyers would overpower his light forces, as the German ships were almost as powerful as light cruisers. In this encounter the Germans lost one of the ex-French destroyers, as well as two of their own destroyers. The San Diego was hit by two torpedoes and sunk later in the day and three other destroyers were badly damaged, with another sinking while trying to make it back to the allied landing zone.

In the meantime, the long range duel between the battleships continued, with HMS Howe being struck three times. Her B turret was jammed when a fifteen-inch shell landed next to it and another struck the starboard side compass room, killing most of the personnel working there. Another penetrated below the waterline, exploding in the aft boiler room. The British battleship lost speed at this point and the USS Washington continued on alone. The weather now deteriorated and the German helicopters struggled to stay airborne. One crashed into the sea and the other struggled on to disappear into the waves one hundred and fifty kilometers from the coast of Iceland. The pilot luckily managed to inflate his raft, and heavy winds blew him ashore three days later.

Now the integrated radar system directing the fire of Washington's sixteen-inch guns held the advantage. The Bismarck was struck twice; once on the forecastle, above the water line, whilst the other shell hit the torpedo bulkhead and flooded the turbo generating room and an adjacent boiler room. Another shell struck the ship's superstructure but failed to explode. There was enough reserve power to keep the battleship moving forward at twenty-eight knots, though the increasing height of the waves made this difficult. By now Admiral Ciliax had abandoned any hope of attacking the British landing forces and decided to turn back toward Norway. First though he would give the Americans a parting gift. All three German ships curved back to close the distance, a move that took Rear Admiral Giffen by surprise. The Scharnhorst, which had played little part in the fight up until this point, being further to the north, straddled the Washington. Slightly further east the Hipper and the Graf Spee attacked HMS Sussex. The German admiral was aware the British battleship wasn't out of the fight and would be able to join the fray in minutes, so he wanted to strike quickly and run.

The Sussex was hit by five eleven-inch shells and two eight-inch shells, effectively knocking the ship from the fight. Her engine rooms were disabled, the forward magazines flooded and the bridge damaged. She struck the Hipper twice in return, one of these strikes knocking out the heavy cruiser's Anton turret. The Scharnhorst hit the Washington with her third salvo, striking the bridge with a single shell that failed to explode but still killed three men, and another slamming down into the stern of the ship, penetrating all the way to the port propeller shaft where it exploded. The great battleship immediately slowed and veered off course as sea water flooded the rear of the ship. However, she kept firing, using her radar to hit the Bismarck for the last time, this shell striking behind the main funnel, between the rear superstructure and one of the smaller twin five point nine-inch turrets. The explosion created a large fire and killed the crew manning the secondary guns.

The Scharnhorst struck again; this time hitting just in front of the forward turret, the shell plunging through the ship to explode just as it exited the hull. A huge twenty meter hole was torn in the ship's bottom and the Washington was forced to slow further, to protect the hull from ripping open. At this point HMS Howe arrived on the scene, and though moving at a reduced speed it managed to straddle the Scharnhorst. Admiral Ciliax then thought he'd pressed his luck enough and ordered all his ships to break off.

Though a tactical victory for the Germans, with two battleships and a cruiser very heavily damaged, the mighty Bismarck was also injured and the British weren't finished with the German fleet yet. Three days later the new T class submarine HMS

Thunderbolt fired a spread of eight torpedoes at the Graf Spee, four hitting along the length of the ship and she sunk later in the day with the loss of fifty of her crew. In the end the Kriegsmarine maintained its honour, although its intervention failed to prevent the Allies landing more supplies and men on Iceland.

V

The British had broken through. Holmavik had fallen and the Allies now held all of the Westfjords region. Enemy armour was advancing on Budardalur while mechanised infantry pushed along the northern coast toward Stadur. Fregattenkapitän Hans-Gerrit von Stockhausen stood surveying the shallow valley in front of him. Hauptmann Ritter looked through his 6 x 30 Dienstglas binoculars at the landscape and clucked his tongue.

"Not a lot of cover sir," said the dark haired man. Behind him Stockhausen's ad hoc battalion rested.

"If we are to hold this valley shouldn't we get some men on the high ground?" he asked.

"The peaks are a kilometer away and any troops we put on them will have to send a runner to tell us what they see. Still, it's probably worth it."

"What about the 20mm guns?"

The Hauptmann turned to look at the weapons and his eyes went wide. "Why aren't they manned? Where are their crews?"

"Resting, I suppose."

"We don't have air superiority. The enemy could attack at any moment."

Stockhausen thought the man was panicking. He watched as the Hauptmann waddled down the slope, yelling at the sailors who lay in groups on the grassy embankments. How this man could command anything more than a squad was beyond Stockhausen. He certainly didn't embody the physical attributes of the Nordic race. Then he heard the drone of aircraft engines.

Four Wildcat fighters dived through scattered cloud, growing in size as they approached. The battalion watched in horror as the aircraft came toward them and it took the screaming of the Hauptmann to galvanise them into action. Some of the men started firing at the planes, while others scattered. Only one of the 20mm guns opened fire and by then it was too late. The machine guns of the four aircraft raked the valley, throwing up clods of earth as the bullets tore into the ground. Men were cut down as they ran, while a few threw themselves to the ground clawing the soil in an effort to escape. There was nowhere to hide and men fell and screamed as the heavy slugs tore their bodies apart.

Hauptmann Ritter made his way to one of the 20mm guns and directed the crew. He made them hold their fire until the fighters turned for another run. Some of his men ran toward smaller side ravines while others found dips in the ground to shelter in, however a lot of men were still in the open. The two light anti-aircraft guns started shooting as the Wildcats came back down the valley. Some of the sailors opened up with Madsen light machine guns and someone was firing an MG 34 from a tripod at the Wildcats. The weight of fire threw the enemy fighters off and they pulled out of their attacks early, with only one opening fire at an effective range. More men fell and the machine gun team was scythed down like wheat, yet the plane pulled away trailing grey smoke.

Stockhausen made his way down to the bespectacled Hauptmann, reassessing the man's worth as he advanced. He could hear the cry of the wounded and see the shattered bodies of the dead. Ritter turned at his approach and wiped his brow.

"That was a shambles, sir. The guns must always be manned." The short man looked around and shook his head before continuing. "At least they didn't run. The first taste of combat can often break a man, but your sailors didn't flee, I'll give them that."

"I think this is the narrowest point in this valley. Should we dig in here?" asked Stockhausen.

"This is a good place, sir. I'll get the radio working and see if we'll have artillery support. We could really do with a few anti-tank guns." The man shrugged. "But wishing won't help."

179

"I'll leave you to it then to get the men organised. The wounded will have to be carried back to Budardalur."

"That's over thirty kilometers away. I'll try and find some transport to meet them on the way. There's a small aid station being set up at the crossroads eight kilometers from here. They might be able to get the badly wounded back to the hospital in Reykjavik."

"What about the helicopters? They could move the wounded more quickly," said Stockhausen.

Ritter nodded. "That's a good idea. I'll ask," he said.

Stockhausen watched as the wounded were carried south. To the north he heard artillery fire and soon German troops appeared on the road in front of him. Men from the 52nd Infantry Division's 171st Regiment marched past, carrying rifles and machine guns. Stockhausen could hear the Saxon accents and eventually found a young officer sporting a bandage around his right arm.

"What's happening Leutnant?" Stockhausen asked.

Then man stopped and adjusted the MP 40 on his shoulder. Two Unterfeldwebels halted with him but kept their eyes on the sky.

"We are withdrawing back to the creek just north of Budardalur. Armour and fresh troops are supposed to join us there. As it is, the 171st has lost about half its strength," said the Leutnant.

"Then why were we ordered here?" asked Stockhausen.

"I don't know, sir," said the man, but he looked away and shuffled his feet.

Then it hit him. His battalion was to be sacrificed so General Karl von Oven could concentrate enough of his forces to launch a counterattack. The fjords to the west were still covered by German costal artillery, so the British couldn't use the guns on their remaining battleship or heavy cruisers to support their army. The enemy would probably try and swat his battalion aside and race for the crossroads at Budardalur. A little further south from the small village was a second road which allowed the British access to the interior of the island. Then the Allies would no longer be penned up in the Westfjords Region and be free of the peninsula.

Perhaps he shouldn't care. The attack by the British carrier aircraft had shown him how dangerous the front line was and now armour was coming in his direction. He wanted to run and hide in his office back in Reykjavik, and wondered what Mila would be doing. His last image of her was when she wiped her eyes clear after learning of her boyfriend's death while attacking the allied fleet. She was then transferred to help out at the Landspitali Hospital to prepare for the expected surge in casualties. Already the Icelandic and German nurses had their hands full dealing with the wounded from the air raids which had struck the capital. Yet he couldn't leave, not without being disgraced and court marshalled.

In the meantime he would do what he could to survive.

"Leutnant, I see some of your men are dragging anti-tank weapons south. They are to stay here with us," he said.

"Sir, my orders are to take these men south."

At this point Hauptmann Ritter approached. "Young man, without those guns, this battalion is little more than a speed bump to the British armour. Fregattenkapitän Gerrit von Stockhausen outranks you and we need those guns."

"Hauptmann, I have my orders."

"Can I see them?" Ritter put out his hand and the Leutnant frowned.

"They were given to me verbally over the radio," said the young officer.

"Can you confirm this?" asked Ritter.

"The radio was smashed in an air attack," said the Leutnant. Both the Unterfeldwebels stepped closer to their officer and eyed Ritter with hostility.

Stockhausen stepped toward the man. "We need those guns or we won't stop the British."

"You can't stop them sir, only slow them," said the young officer. "And you won't even do that without those 50mm pieces. Alright boys, I'm staying with the anti-tank battery."

Stockhausen breathed a sigh of relief and noted the tension drain from Ritter's frame.

"I'll stay too, sir," said one of the Unterfeldwebels, a tall man with freckles who looked as though he'd just finished school.

"Danke, Kurt. See if you can find those two surviving mortars. If we are going to make a stand here, we might as well do it properly."

"I'll stay as well, sir," said the shorter Unterfeldwebel.

"No Hans, leave your MG but take what's left of the battalion to Budardalur. If the 192nd Regiment aren't in place the panzer boys will need your help. The armour must have infantry support if it's going to be successful," said the young Leutnant.

The other man grimaced but nodded. He handed his MG 42 to the taller Untefeldwebel and barked orders at a few men to leave extra boxes of ammunition.

"The name's Leutnant Paul Schaefer, sir," said the officer as he saluted Ritter and Stockhausen. "May I see to the positioning of the anti-tank guns?"

"Yes, see to it, Leutnant," said Ritter.

As he walked down toward the teams dragging the anti-tank weapons, the Hauptmann turned to Stockhausen. "That man is a veteran of Russia. He wears an Infantry Assault Badge and a Tank Destruction Badge. He also wears the Eastern Front Medal."

"Just the soldier we need then?"

"Yes. I served in Poland but we mainly collected Polish stragglers and fought in a few skirmishes. Not like that man, he's come up through the ranks is my guess."

The battalion dug in and everyone listened as the sound of the guns grew louder. Then there was a flurry of retreating infantry and silence. For a while everyone watched the entrance to the valley, but after a short time some of the men started eating or brewing up hot water to make ersatz coffee. A plane flew overhead but at fairly high altitude and everyone relaxed a little. Then there was the sudden whistle of shells.

"Mortars, take cover," yelled Ritter.

Stockhausen felt a familiar tightening in his bowels and jumped into a fox hole which had been dug in the stony soil of the valley. Ritter and Schaefer had positioned the battalion on the forward side of a slight slope, facing a choke point on the road. The eastern flank was protected by a steep ravine and a high, steep hill sat not far to the west. Both of the infantry officers believed it would be a difficult location to flank, with steep ground running out to the sides of the battalion's trenches for at least a kilometer. If the British spent time infiltrating around the battalion then they would have achieved their goal of slowing the enemy anyway. The only problem was that there was no way to hit back at the enemy's artillery as the mortars that Schaefer had looked for hadn't been located.

They obviously know we are here, thought Stockhausen. The Wildcats, or perhaps the higher flying plane had probably reported their location. He knew enough about artillery to realise that the British were firing blind. He watched as the mortar rounds rolled up the valley before plastering both slopes. The men were well dug in and only two sailors were lightly wounded by shrapnel. Then the bombardment stopped and he wondered what the enemy would do next.

When he heard the sound of tank tracks he started to shake. By this time Stockhausen had moved to a longer trench where the radio was situated. The headquarters group gathered in the wide trench, peering out over the top of a thin layer of sand bags. Tanks appeared on the road with infantry walking in groups behind them. The Convenanter tanks weren't used in the desert because the piping from the engine to the radiators heated the fighting compartments. In Iceland this wasn't a problem. The leading vehicle carried a two-pound gun. Stockhausen didn't realise this meant it had no high explosive capacity. The British had close support

Convenanter tanks but many of them had been used to drive the Germans from Holmavik. These vehicles were now moving down the coastal road toward Bordeyri where another ad hoc naval battalion blocked the British advance at a crossroads just north of the town. This force at least had a battery of four 88mm guns to support it.

The British tanks continued for some distance past the cutting and Stockhausen started to think that Schaefer wasn't going to open fire. Then the crack of 50mm guns sounded above the tank engines and the lead vehicle swerved off the road into a shallow ditch filled with water. He was amazed to see the neat hole in the tank, right in front of the driver's viewing slit. Men spilled from the vehicle as smoke started to pour from the hatches. British infantry ran to either side of the tank and dropped to the ground as German machine guns opened fire. A 20mm gun fired short bursts at the enemy, killing some and driving others back. Then a second tank was hit, but this one burst into flames. Three Universal Bren carriers shot from the rear of the column and sprayed fire from their light machine guns at the German trenches, allowing their infantry to retreat. The 20mm cannons caught one of these vehicles as it attempted to turn and retreat down the road. The carrier's 7mm armour wasn't immune to the light German anti-aircraft weapon and its shells split the small vehicle apart like a can opener. Men fell from the wreck to be shot by rifles or light machine guns.

Then the enemy were gone and all that was left was the crackle of flames and the screaming of the wounded. Ritter immediately sent men to bring in the injured British soldiers, though this had to stop when the enemy started dropping mortar shells into the valley again. Stockhausen felt his body relax, despite the odd shell dropping nearby. He'd survived, as had his command. Maybe they'd be allowed to retreat soon and the army would take over and begin their counterattack. He asked Ritter if there were any new orders, but the man shook his head.

"I've called for more ammunition, but all we will receive are rounds for the German guns. All the other Scandinavian equipment will be useless after the next attack," said the Hauptmann.

"We will go through it that quickly?" asked Stockhausen.

"The enemy has only probed us. Now they will attempt to soften us up and then there will be a full assault. The British did our battalion a favour by giving us this small victory as it will help the morale of the men. They have a better chance of holding now they've been exposed to combat gradually."

Stockhausen felt his muscles tighten again. Ritter obviously thought the battle was far from of over. He watched as the Hauptmann went over to find Leutnant Schaefer. The two men conferred near the 50mm guns for a while before Ritter returned.

"Our young officer thinks the enemy will hit us from the air and that we should expect a bombardment just before there's another attack," said Ritter.

Sure enough, almost as soon as the words were out of the Hauptmann's mouth, four aircraft appeared on the horizon. These machines had two engines and Stockhausen thought they might be Bf 110s until he noted the twin fuselages.

"What are they?" he muttered.

"I don't know, but they're not ours," said Ritter.

The planes were P-38s that had flown all the way from Greenland the previous day. Second Lieutenant Elza Shahan of the 27th Fighter Squadron had already shot down a Bf 110 and was now leading his flight on a sweep toward Reykjavik. The order to attack troop concentration and other targets of opportunity was only radioed to the aircraft once they were airborne. The P-38s came down and strafed at high speed, making it difficult for the 20mm guns to track them. Each plane lashed the trenches with their four 12.7mm guns and single cannons. Most of the German sailors dived into shelter and weren't hit, however one of the light flak guns caught a full burst from the P-38's guns and was smashed with the crew torn apart, the cannon twisted like rope.

Then the dive bombers arrived. The Douglas Dauntless had been purchased by the Royal Navy to replace the Skua in 1941, however so far only eighty were serving on different British carriers. Twelve had been flown to the strip at Isafjordur where they joined the P-38s and a number of Sea Hurricanes. Now six of them fell from the sky, screaming down on German positions. Hitting a soldier hiding in a trench is a difficult proposition at the best of times, but Stockhausen didn't know this and was certain he would die. The thousand-pound bombs whistled down and he bit his lip to stop himself from screaming. The bombs detonated around the flak positions, the most exposed of the German targets, hurling one into the air as it exploded next to the thin layer of sandbags. Nobody else was killed except for the three man crew. Then the planes raked the trenches with machine gun fire, failing to hit anyone before flying north.

Ritter appeared from a foxhole and ran over to Stockhausen. "Six casualties sir, and we only have a single 20mm gun left."

"Why didn't the light machine guns fire?" growled Stockhausen.

"I ordered them not to. We have limited ammunition for the Masdens and I thought we better save it for the next infantry attack."

Stockhausen nodded. He was sick of playing the part of an army commander and every attack just reinforced how unprepared he was for the task.

"First time I wished I was back at sea," he muttered.

Ritter nodded. "Sir, I wouldn't know the first thing about manoeuvring a U-boat into an attack position."

"Feel free to make quick decisions without running them through me, Ritter. I don't want the battalion destroyed because time was wasted checking with me."

"Thank you, sir," said the Hauptmann.

An hour later heavy shells started to explode in the valley. The British had brought up their twenty five-pounder Mark II guns, which lacked the later muzzle brake that eliminated the instability caused when firing twenty-pound armour piercing shells. This wasn't the case for the eight guns that now bombarded Stockhausen's battalion. Overhead a Royal Navy Supermarine Sea Otter spotted the fall of shots and directed the guns effectively onto the German trenches. This cooperation between the British army and navy was unusual but the requirements of the campaign had forged closer ties of cooperation. For the first time, Stockhausen's command started to take serious casualties.

The shells rained down for twenty minutes, with the mortars joining the attack. The air was thick with the smell of wet earth, smoke and cordite. Stockhausen hugged the wall of the command trench and tried not to scream. To him it felt as though he was once again in the belly of a U-boat as depth charges exploded in the surrounding water. Men called for help and others screamed as shrapnel tore through their bodies. The ground vibrated with each impact and the sound became a continual roar. It was different in some ways to being under attack in a submarine as Stockhausen didn't have the wait before a depth charge exploded. The British were firing at a rapid rate so each of the eight guns was shooting four times every minute. Then there were the mortar shells which dropped at an even higher frequency.

When the bombardment finished, Stockhausen waited for a moment before he lifted his head above the trench. As he did he noted British infantry only one hundred meters from their position. Leutnant Schaefer was already yelling for the men to start shooting. The two remaining anti-tank guns fired high explosive rounds into the enemy while a few of the machine guns also began to rake the enemy. On the eastern side of the valley the sailors were slow to respond and the British were among them before they knew what was happening. These men tried to surrender but in the heat of battle a number were gunned down before British officers got their soldiers under control. On the western side of the road Schaefer's quick action and the use of the anti-tank guns as direct fire weapons forced the enemy to go to ground.

Stockhausen managed to regain his senses for long enough to realise that without artillery support his command was going to be overrun. He turned and ran along the trench to the radio position but turned a corner to find a shell hole. Pieces of equipment and men lay scattered around and it took him a moment to recognise Ritter's body. The Hauptmann lay covered in earth, his eyes staring blankly at the sky. Most of an arm and one of his legs was missing yet his expression appeared calm. For a second Stockhausen wondered what the man had been thinking when he died. Then the chatter of machine guns and the clank of tank tracks brought him back to reality. Two Churchill tanks drove slowly up the road, then opened fire with their three-inch howitzers. A third sat a little further back and contented itself with spraying the German trenches with machine gun fire.

The 50mm guns hit the British tanks with a number of shells but all broke up on the thick armour or bounced off. The Churchills had 100mm of armour on the front of the hull and 90mm on the turrets, but the German weapons could only penetrate 80mm at the present range. The anti-tank guns were quickly destroyed and the resourceful Leutnant Schaefer wounded (he was later captured by the British and treated on a hospital ship. Schaefer survived the war and became a teacher in Munich). The battalion started to come apart and groups of sailors leapt from their trenches and started to run. Others threw up their hands to surrender.

Stockhausen ran. He was able to follow the curves of the trench for thirty meters before climbing out and sprinting a short distance to a gully that had been carved by melt water, away from the road. The firing seemed to die down behind him and soon the only sound was the clanking of the tanks' tracks and the odd burst of fire.

He found other men clustered in hollows at the top of the slope, their eyes wild and faces smeared with dirt.

"What will we do, sir?" whimpered a Matrose.

"Retreat. There's nothing else we can do here."

He led twenty men, many whom had lost their guns and other equipment, over the high plateau until they descended back down into the valley four kilometers from the battle. One of his men spotted a German armoured car creeping along the road and managed to signal its commander with a piece of glass from a broken pair of binoculars, flashing the sun until it caught the man's attention. Stockhausen took his exhausted men back down onto the road and found the Feldwebel looking at him curiously.

"We were to come forward and see how your battalion was fairing, sir but I'm guessing we are too late," said the young red-haired non-commissioned officer.

"The British overran us about an hour ago. The battalion has been destroyed and the enemy will come down this road at any moment. They're probably just cleaning up the stragglers."

The man nodded and then dropped down into the hull of the Sd.Kfz.222 before appearing again a moment later.

"Sorry sir, just radioing it in. I've been told to direct your survivors down the road to Budardalur."

"Is there any chance of vehicles picking us up? These men are exhausted," said Stockhausen.

"I'm sorry sir, there's nothing available."

"Then we'll be captured by the British before we've walked five kilometers."

"I doubt that, sir."

The sound of aircraft came from the southeast and Stockhausen saw the young Feldwebel smile. "Those are ours, sir."

Four Fw 190 A3s dipped low over the hills, followed by another two similar looking aircraft, but these were twin seaters.

"They are the new Fw 205s," said Stockhausen.

The planes dived down into the valley and he heard the chatter of machine guns and the slower thump of 20mm cannons. Then the Fw 205s dropped their two fifty-kilo bombs and single five hundred-kilo weapons and turned south. Stockhausen didn't see any of the German planes go down but noted a pillar of smoke rising beyond the intervening hills. He didn't know that fourteen British soldiers had been killed and the leading Churchill tank destroyed. More importantly, the enemy didn't start moving south again until nightfall.

V

Stockhausen made it back safely to Reykjavik with about one hundred survivors from his battalion. The men were formed into a single company but they were mainly used to dig trenches and work at improving the defences around the town. The German counterattack took place in a wide valley on the coast, ten kilometers north of Budardalur. The British lost heavily to the Panzer IIIs, IVs and the Marder IIs. The Convenanter tanks with their two-pounder guns were destroyed en masse but when the heavily armoured Churchills with the six-pounder guns arrived, the tables were turned on the attacking Germans. The enemy advance was halted temporarily but the Allies continued to move forward toward Stadur. Eventually, naval 88mm guns stopped the advance of the British here too, but nobody thought it would be for very long.

Stockhausen went to his office and threw himself onto the old couch and dropped off to sleep in seconds. He woke to the sound of sirens a little later, but decided he wasn't moving. Rolling over, he dozed until woken by a soft voice.

"Sir, the General is asking for you," said Matrose Mila Roth.

She passed him a hot drink and sat on the edge of his desk. Her normally immaculate red-gold hair was sticking out in strands and there was blood on her white apron.

"I thought you were working at the hospital?" Stockhausen asked.

"They sent me back to my room to get some rest, but on the way a Feldwebel from the General's headquarters intercepted me and asked if I knew where you were."

Stockhausen groaned and Mila smiled. "They said it was urgent," she added.

"The army always thinks that. I don't know why, as my command has been smashed."

He noted Mila's complexion whiten and cursed himself. Slowly he stood and stretched out his protesting muscles before sipping at the drink. It tasted surprisingly good for ersatz coffee. He gulped it down and attempted to straighten his clothes and smooth his hair.

"Do you feel any better now you've slept?"

"I think so, I just need to shake off the cobwebs." He finished flattening his clothes and stood tall. "Well, that will have to do."

"The general knows you have come from the front, sir. I'm sure he'll be understanding. Anyway, he's not navy."

Stockhausen grinned at the comment and then nodded. "Get some rest Mila. I think you are going to need it. I'll try and find you later."

v

Lieutenant General Karl von Oven had moved his headquarters to the basement of the library building. He stood looking at a map of eastern Iceland, his hands folded behind his back and his face creased with worry.

"You asked for me, sir?" said Stockhausen.

The general turned and his eyebrows went up a notch. "Yes, Stockhausen, your command did well to hold for as long as it did. I believe it no longer exists?"

"About one company eventually made it back to our line, sir. I believe they are working on the defences of Reykjavik now."

"Not anymore. Your Commander and Chief wasn't happy that the ad hoc battalions were created and then destroyed. He saw the death of the mechanics and technicians as a waste of well-trained men, and I suppose I can see his point. Still he's not here and doesn't understand how desperate the situation is."

Stockhausen decided it was best not to comment. If Wever was unhappy with his cooperation with the army in these matters, it could limit his chance of a future promotion. However, that would need to be a concern to be dealt with in the future.

"Your defence of the valley gave us time to launch our counterattack. Unfortunately both the strikes by units of the 22nd Air Landing Division, and the armoured attack at Budardalur failed to do anything more than halt the advance of the enemy. Now the 2nd Canadian Division has landed some of its troops, and the disparity between our forces and theirs is growing. The 22nd Air Landing Division has only managed to transport one regiment and half a dozen Marder IIs. Even with the Somuas, their armoured strike wasn't enough to break through the British positions on the Boreyri road. We have stopped the Allies for now but that may be as much because of their supply difficulties as anything else."

"Has the navy interfered with the landings, sir?"

"They tried but that's not what is slowing the enemy's build up of resources. I suspect it's the problem of trying to unload heavy equipment at small fishing ports. The British have to unload from their freighters into landing craft in the fjords and then ferry their equipment ashore. They have almost two divisions to supply, as well as the thirty or more aircraft at Isafjordur. We have noted transport aircraft on the airfield so munitions and fuel are being flown in, but it's an emergency strip so can only handle a small number of planes."

None of this concerned Stockhausen, though he appreciated the general taking the time to explain the situation to him. "What would you like me to do, sir?"

"We can't hold Iceland. The enemy can reinforce but we can't. They control the waters around the island. The Kriegsmarine lacks the strength to interfere with the landings, because air losses in the Mediterranean were so high, or that's what I've been told. I want you to start organising a list of personnel to be evacuated, starting immediately. Concentrate on the western side of the island. Every night transport planes land at Reykjavik and the eastern airfields. We need to move some of our people by road to the east and fly out others from here. There are a few U-boats we can use, but you'd know more about that. We need to keep a small number of mechanics here for now as there is still a small air contingent of Bf 110s, He 112s and Fw 205s still operating. However, pilots without a plane need to go."

"What about the wounded, sir?"

"Fly out those who will be able to fight again first. By that I don't mean the lightly wounded. Concentrate on those who could be back in the fight in three months to a year. I'll leave the details to you."

Stockhausen noted three officers hovering in his peripheral vision and realised the general had other matters to attend to. He saluted and left the room.

The first task he undertook when he arrived at his office was to locate Mila. He needed her and a few others to deliver messages and organise the necessary paperwork to ensure the efficient evacuation of the island. He was told she was sleeping and left her alone, making his own way by motorcycle to the hospital. There he found the doctor in charge and explained the orders. He told the man that written instructions would follow but the medical staff needed to have the first batch of wounded ready to fly out tonight.

Mila arrived with two other women in tow. All had been clerical assistants, but now were to spread the word and help him organise the removal of all surplus personnel back to Norway. A slightly wounded Matrose joined them. The young man had been hit in the thigh by shell fragment and was to be their motorcycle rider, delivering written orders to different commands.

A convoy of carts was organised to take mechanics and technical staff across to the eastern airfields, while the wounded were flown to Norway from the airstrip at Reykjavik.

Ju 290s flew in late in the day carrying ammunition and fuel, and left full of wounded a few hours later. On the far side of the island Me 323s flew out large numbers of people every night. These huge six engined machines needed refuelling en route as they only had a range of eight hundred kilometres and the effort of pouring fuel into the empty tanks while the planes were in the air was a major inconvenience. Ju 252s and Ju 290s could carry enough petrol to make the journey to Iceland and back without this problem. U-445 and U-604 were available to transport people back to Norway so they were loaded with mechanics from the dock area and others from the airstrip, before leaving the following evening. Each boat took thirty passengers, leaving behind most of their torpedoes and some provisions.

In three days Stockhausen evacuated two thousand people. He used Do 24s seaplanes to land at the eastern fjords to pick up more personnel and even managed to get some of the more seriously wounded soldiers out of the country. Three Ju 252s were hidden under camouflage nets to evacuate high ranking officers at the last minute. One aircraft disappeared on the return flight to Norway and two more were shot down by P-38s as they came into land at Reykjavik, forcing the arrival time of the transports to be moved back to dusk.

On the fourth day he ordered Mila and her two friends to leave the following night on a Ju 290. The Allies had broken through at Stadur with Canadian forces racing along the coast road toward Blonduos while the US 1st Ranger Battalion landed at the village of the same name to cut off the fleeing Germans. The US unit was badly placed as there were other roads east that bypassed their position. However, two companies of the 16th Infantry Regiment of the 22nd Air Landing Division backed by the two remaining Souma tanks launched an assault on the battalion and were driven back with heavy casualties. However, twelve US soldiers were killed making them the first American ground troops to die fighting the Germans.

There was very little to stop the Canadian advance eastward across the island and the Heer was also being forced back west. Budardalur had fallen and the British 4th Division had advanced roughly twenty kilometres further south but had again been stopped in an area of high hills and valleys. The problem for the German armed forces was that their eastern flank was wide open, with the southern road from Stadur only being held by a single battery of 88mm guns, two Panzer VIs and a scattered infantry battalion.

The situation in the air was almost as bad, with only a handful of Fw 190A3s, a couple of Fw 205s and half a dozen He 112s still operational in the west. The German occupation of Iceland could now be measured in days. The main issue slowing the

Canadian advance was now fuel, so the pursuit of the remains of the 22nd Landing Division's 16th Regiment was postponed with all supplies being diverted to the advance at the crossroads between Baulan and the bridges over the Nordura River. There were two more natural choke points before Reykjavik, around the Skorradalsvatn Lake, which ran east-west across the line of the advance, and the Hyalfjordur inlet, which did likewise. Both bodies of water were surrounded by steep hills and it was good defensive country. The problem for the Germans was they had very few troops with which to hold it.

A day later the small force of panzers and 88mm guns was destroyed after a stiff engagement with British armour. Again the lighter Covenanter tanks proved wanting, with fourteen being knocked out before Churchill tanks and artillery destroyed the heavy German anti-tank guns and drove the Panzer IVs off. The Heer had to retreat quickly from the hills to the west or they'd be cut off. As it was they were forced to abandon a number of artillery pieces and some of their wounded. Enough German troops escaped to make a stand in the hills surrounding the fjord. A delaying action was fought in the pass between the hills and the Skorradalsvatn Lake. Here the narrow road was surrounded by open hills which climbed to nine hundred metres. The Canadians stopped to catch their breath, while the British assaulted the village of Hofn on the coast. The area was a coastal plain of over a kilometre in width, overlooked by the eastern edge of the same hills that blocked the Canadians. The British were forced to slow as the Germans used the high ground to direct artillery fire down on to the advancing Allied forces.

It took British paratroopers, in cooperation with the US Ranger battalion, two days to clear the hills so the 4th division could push forward. The extra time allowed the Germans to harden their defensive positions around the Hyalfjordur inlet. The main problem both sides now faced was the shortage of supplies. For the Allies, the arrival of three landing ships, the Misoa, Tasajera and the brand new LST-1, alleviated the situation as two of these carried thirty trucks each, and the LST-1 brought ashore twenty M3 Grant tanks.

These soon made their presence felt at Hofn, and later, fighting the last German armour around Grundartangi. Unfortunately for the Germans, a sudden breakthrough by the Canadians on the eastern flank cut off a number of German battalions before they could reach the Hyalfjordur inlet, severely weakening their defences.

Stockhausen appreciated the extra time the tenacious German effort gave him to evacuate more people. Reykjavik was only thirty-five kilometres from the front line during the later stages of these battles, but the airstrip remained in operation. Raids by US Flying Fortress bombers diminished as the enemy seemed to use their air bases in Greenland to resupply forces in Iceland. A steady trickle of P-38s replaced any losses the Allies incurred, while the Germans struggled to bring any more fighter aircraft to Iceland. The effort at Stalingrad seemed to swallow resources, with the Luftwaffe having little in the way of planes to offer for the defence of Iceland. Meanwhile the Kriegsmarine licked its wounds after the battle of Jan Mayen and only managed to deliver supplies via the air bridge or with U-boats. Attempts were made with destroyers to get fuel and ammunition to eastern Iceland, but both attempts failed with two vessels being sunk. Now that the British controlled the Faroes, their aircraft hunted the German navy's surface ships in the southern half of the Norwegian Sea.

When the guns of the Prince Eugen started firing on the advancing allies outside Reykjavik, Stockhausen knew it was time to leave. The eight-inch weapons fired at Canadian forces around the village of Grundartangi, twenty-five kilometres from the ship. It was just another illustration of how close the enemy were. The collapse came the next day as ammunition almost ran out. Some battalions fought on with small arms but most of the heavy shells were gone. Stockhausen stayed until the British were reported at Grundarnverfi, only ten kilometres away. He flew out on a plane full of junior officers and pilots, just as the last of the light bled from the autumn sky. The Ju 252 flew away from the town where Stockhausen had spent the better part of a year and dipped low, to avoid any lurking US fighters. The pilot followed the southern coast before flying through the darkness, over the sea and back to

Norway.

Chapter Five: Winter 1942/43

"Has he forgiven you?" asked Admiral Canaris.

"Our leader is totally absorbed by the disaster unfolding at Stalingrad," said Grossadmiral Wever.

"I think he is very unhappy with the intelligence service. You did well to make it sound like our relationship was under strain."

"Well, I hope the Führer believes me. I'll portray our meeting up today as an argument, with me giving you a dressing down. Unfortunately we won't be able to see each other again for some time."

The two men sat in Wever's office in the small town of Sazznitz on the island of Rugen. In reality it was his second office, but he was spending more time here than in the past as he liked to be away from the politics of the capital.

"He wasn't happy that Iceland was lost, but the attack on the 6th Army and before that, the stalling of the advance in the east, meant that I only had to endure a week of his ranting before it all settled down."

"What does he expect of the navy now?"

"That we prevent convoys making their way to Russia and continue to attack British convoys."

"All of which is nearly impossible in the depths of winter," said Canaris.

"True, however the Führer has ordered all of the Kriegsmarine's Ju 290s move east to help with the airlift. It seems Kesselring's warning that the Luftwaffe couldn't supply the 6th Army is coming true."

"So he'll finally let Paulus break out," said Canaris.

"An attempt to reach the 6th Army is being organised I believe, but I don't know the details. If that fails, our Führer will have no choice but to let the Army escape, but who knows? If he doesn't and the 6th is destroyed, he won't be able to blame anyone else as he was warned they couldn't be supplied by air. I believe the

216

10th Panzer Division, three infantry divisions and an elite parachute division have gone east. They were to help the relief attempt but had to be used to prop the Italians. Luckily, nothing is going on in the Mediterranean right now, except for Rommel's little war."

"That won't last. The Allies will land somewhere in the south: Greece, Sardinia, Spain, or maybe North Africa."

"True. Any idea exactly where?"

"None, though my money is on Spain or North Africa."

"Yes, well the Führer won't be interested in guess work. He still thinks Norway might be next."

"Doubtful at this time of year. In the meantime, part of your reconnaissance force will be pulled into the mess."

"All of it is to go east."

"When?"

"It's already happening."

Canaris sighed and stared out the window. It was an impressive view from the 3rd floor window of the Hotel Lovel. In truth, the main town was five kilometers to the north but Wever liked to take walks on the long sandy beach to clear his head most mornings. He could drive across the causeway to Berlin when he had to, or he could fly.

"What about our plans to get the folio to the Allies, outlining Hitler's design for the Jews?" asked Canaris.

"The sticking point is Marseille's mother. We have a few people working on it but need the corpse of an old woman for our plan, and they are harder to get your hands on than you'd think. Also we need an air raid."

"You plan to fake his mother's death?"

"That's all we can come up with that will allow us to hide the involvement of other parties in her disappearance, and protect her if it comes out that he has deserted to the enemy."

"It's a good idea, you'll just need to wait for the right time. Then our ace can fly to the Allies?"

"That's the idea. In the meantime I'm trying to keep him alive. At the moment he is training pilots not far from here. He could fly to Sweden but I don't trust the authorities there not to hand him back. When the time's right, Marseille will have to return to the front. Then he can fly straight to an American or British base, when we give him the signal."

"You've got someone watching him?"

"A young woman. With his history it's the perfect fit."

"Unless she becomes involved."

"She has been told to keep her distance. Though her cover is that they are lovers, so easier said than done."

"We will just have to hope. On another front, I've finally had some interest from a few generals about removing Hitler. It seems our recent reverses have brought the reality of the war home to a few people. Rommel is still stuck in Egypt and Iceland is gone. Now the 6th Army is trapped and our army is about to face another winter in Russia."

"You were right my friend, as soon as the USA entered the war Germany was destined to lose."

"The strange thing is we could have won. The problem started when our leader believed he was military genius."

"Yes, but from what we now know, we probably don't deserve to win."

V

The storm came from the north, causing snow to swirl around the Ju 290. Kapitän Helmut Bruck watched as Luftwaffe men loaded cans of fuel and bags of flour into his aircraft. Nearby others did the same with Ju 252s and Ju 90s. Me 323s and even He 111s had been loaded with ammunition and petrol for the panzers trapped with the 6th Army. He had heard rumours that the attack by the Feldmarschall Erich von Manstein had stalled fifty kilometers from the closest point to the pocket. The Soviets were still attacking everywhere and the Italian 8th Army was under extreme pressure with its front threatening to collapse at any moment. In the meantime, his Staffel had been commanded to keep flying supplies to the surrounded German troops.

It was obvious that despite the Luftwaffe's best efforts, the transport aircraft, even supported by a number of bombers, couldn't deliver what was needed to keep two hundred and fifty thousand men alive. Still, they needed to keep trying.

"We're ready, sir," said Matrose Helmut Khole.

"Crew of only four again," said Bruck.

"Yes, sir," said the short man, a frown spreading across his face.

"Chin up, Khole. In this weather we are unlikely to face any fighters. We don't need the extra gunners but out troops could certainly do with two more hundred kilo bags of flour."

"I suppose so, sir."

Bruck smiled and slapped the rear gunner on the back. Then he clambered through the belly hatch and made his way forward to the pilot's seat. Oberfänrich zur See Hals Bruner was already waiting for him.

"Conditions are supposed to slowly improve skipper, as we fly east, but not by much," said his co-pilot.

Bruck nodded and then went through the pre-flight check. The four BMW 801D engines started one after the other and soon the large plane was taxiing down the snow covered runway. The airfield at Tatsinskaya was mostly used by Ju 252s and Ju 52s but the odd bomber took off from there as well. The Soviets were advancing from the northeast and Bruck wondered how long it would be before the base was overrun. He hoped it would be evacuated in time, because if it wasn't, the Luftwaffe would lose a lot of aircraft.

The flight to Pitomnik would take an hour. This was a little faster than the journey for the other transports as the Ju 290 was faster than the Ju 252. His plane was also better protected, which was just as well because Russian fighters often tried to intercept the

222

lumbering aircraft. The fighter escort from JG 52 did its best to fend off the Yaks and Mig 3s but many avoided the German Bf 109s and attacked the transports anyway. Bruck climbed to a thousand meters and joined up with three other aircraft from his Staffel. The four planes then flew east across the frozen landscape toward Stalingrad.

So far his command hadn't lost an aircraft and Bruck put this down to the superior poor weather flying skills of his men. His Staffel had suffered from the lack of maintenance facilities, particularly at Pitomnik. German aircraft made the flight into the Stalingrad enclave fully loaded, then landed on an ice hardened runway, often pock marked by artillery impacts, and then the same machines were expected to take off again with very little work being done on them. It was insane. So far he'd flown back three Ju 52 crews and a He 111 crew. This was always a source of annoyance for him as these men took the place of wounded soldiers who needed to be flown out of the pocket and moved to better medical facilities.

The cloudy conditions had cleared two days ago and Stalingrad was enjoying its second day of high visibility, even though it was bitterly cold at night. The foggy conditions on the 16th had closed down most of the airfields in the morning and it wasn't until the afternoon of that day when flights had recommenced. The temperature today was expected to reach -8 celsius with weather conditions expected to deteriorate in the near future. Bruck was determined to make two flights before the clouds returned. He flew at two thousand meters, watching the sky for Russian planes but only saw four Bf 109s flying above him. He was glad of their company and disappointed when they turned away a little later. They must be low on fuel, he thought.

As he descended toward the airfield at Pitomnik, Bruck spotted the wrecks of various aircraft around the runway. The flak positions protecting the base were also clearly visible, as were the large tents where at least a little maintenance was carried out. He touched down smoothly and came to a stop near a group of men clustered around a number of carts pulled by ponies. As soon as he stopped and shut down the engines, Luftwaffe personnel offloaded the bags of flour and jerry cans of fuel.

A major rushed up to him as he climbed out of the aircraft to supervise the loading of the wounded. The man's face was wrapped in a thick scarf and he wore a long army great coat lined with sheep skin around the collar.

"We are really glad you boys are putting in such a big effort today," said the officer as he cleaned his spectacles with the fingers of his gloves.

"Why's that?" asked Bruck.

"The order has come down that the army is to break out tomorrow and the panzers will need every drop of fuel they can get."

"The 6th is leaving Stalingrad?'

"Well, Manstein can't get any closer and despite your best efforts, not enough is being delivered to keep the army going. Story is that out leaders were warned it was impossible to supply so many men from the air and finally they have listened."

"What about the wounded?'

"Another reason it's important that a lot of transport planes arrive today. When we break out it will be impossible to take those who can't walk. Some will be loaded onto the horse drawn carts but the poor animals are on their last legs due to the lack of fodder and some have already been eaten. There's little in the way of motor transport still running, and the panzers will be carrying assault infantry, I'm guessing."

"Well, load them up. We will take off as soon as you're ready."

Fifteen men on stretchers were put aboard the Ju 290 as well as a single nurse to look after them on the hour flight. The young woman was wrapped in odd layers of clothing and her eyes were bloodshot and sunken. Bruck felt for her.

"We will soon have you back in Rostov," he told her, and she graced him with a tired smile.

They taxied into position to take off when Matrose Helmut Khole yelled a warning. The short gunner had positioned himself in the dorsal turret and started firing the 15mm cannon at an unseen target.

"Russian attack aircraft skipper, coming in fast," yelled Khole.

Ilyushin Il-2 Shturmovik planes flew low, spraying the runway with their cannons and dropping bombs. Most of the attacks were inaccurate as the heavy German flak forced the Russian aircraft to take evasive action. Bruck's Ju 290 sat alone at the end of the runway and stood out. A Shturmovik riddled the port wing with shells, and another hit the fuselage with a burst. Bruck heard the wounded scream as he gunned the engines. He saw warning lights flick on and was forced to abort his take off. Both engines were smoking and he shut them down before they caught fire. Using the starboard engines carefully he taxied back to the dispersal area and turned off the engines.

"The nurse was hit," said Bruner as he returned from the cargo hold. "Two of the wounded were killed.

"Is she dead?" asked Bruck.

"No, but she took a slug through the leg and another in the shoulder."

"We need to find a doctor quickly and patch her up, then she goes on the next plane out."

"I'll see to it," said Bruner.

"Meanwhile, I'll find out if this bird will ever fly again."

Bruck could have flown out on one of the other Ju 290s, or even on the Ju 252s that took off later in the day but he wouldn't take the place of one of the wounded soldiers, particularly knowing what was about to happen. He ordered Bruner off with the rest of his crew but later discovered Khole had disobeyed his orders.

"Couldn't leave you alone, sir," said the gunner. The little man was carrying a MG 15 with its seventy-five round magazine. Over his shoulder he carried a sack which bulged with a variety of items.

"What goodies have you got in there?" Bruck asked.

"Well, I got the gun from a wrecked Ju 52 and a few extra drums of ammo, and I brought a little food and a few blankets. I started carrying them as soon as I saw the situation we were flying into, sir."

"All I did was eat a big breakfast," said Bruck.

"You've got your Mauser, sir?"

"Yes, and a single spare clip. I've also got a cheese and onion sandwich and that's it."

"Better than nothing, sir. Oh, I also managed to find a winter combat suit on one of the wounded men killed on our plane. It's small so I'll need to wear it. For you I found a woollen greatcoat, which I got off another poor sod. They both have a bit of blood and a few holes in them I'm afraid."

"Unless we fly out tomorrow morning we will need them."

There were no more flights and Bruck found himself leading one hundred Luftwaffe personnel with Major Paul Bach. The small unit armed itself with whatever weapons it could find and connected to the 100th Jaeger Division. This unit, along with the attached 369th Croatian Reinforced Infantry Regiment marched to the north-eastern side of the pocket as the attack commenced with a final artillery barrage, before the German gunners destroyed their guns. The 16th and 14th Panzer Divisions led the way, though both formations could only muster about forty tanks each. Despite this, the Russians were caught by surprise and the 6th army immediately broke the Soviet ring. The 6th army then started its desperate trek west.

The 100th attacked over a stretch of open steppe, moving toward Ssokarewka while the 16th and 14th Panzers moved with the 29th Motorised along both sides of the Reka Karpovka River toward

Pruboy. The advance would then turn southeast in order to link up with Manstein's thrust. The 100th had been moved from the city of Stalingrad itself to hold the north-eastern flank of the pocket, while the 24th Panzer and 60th Motorized Divisions had the daunting task of being the rear guard. The Russians had been slow to respond at first but now their artillery was coming down everywhere, and large scale infantry attacks were being fended off from the north. If it wasn't for the fact that a few Soviet units had been pulled further west to try and keep the momentum of the attack toward Rostov going, the rear guard of the 6th army would have been in desperate trouble. German reserves that were to guard against possible allied landings in the west had been shifted to the Stalingrad front in order to try and stabilise the situation, and to some extent they had been successful. The Allies weren't going to attack for at least six weeks so the German troops could fight the Soviets instead. The Herman Goering SS Panzer Grenadier Division and the 10th Panzers had combined with the 501st Heavy Panzer Battalion with its Tigers and Panzer IIIs. These forces counterattacked to save the Italian 8th

Army near the headwaters of the Don River. The 334th Infantry Division and the 2nd Parachute Division helped try and plug the line further south.

Shells rained down around Bruck and Khole as they hugged the snow. The air was full of smoke and earth as the Russians dropped shells down on their position. Both men had found a slight depression in the ground, and they now endeavoured to burrow as deeply as possible into their little crevasse. Bruck thought he'd soil himself; such was the terror he was experiencing. It was too late for second thoughts but he was regretting his decision to give his place on one of the departing transport planes to the wounded. Raising his head slightly he could see a line of infantry lying along the same depression, all of them barely moving. Somewhere a man was screaming and there was a continual shriek of the shells.

When the barrage stopped Bruck stood up, but one of the infantry Feldwebels yelled at him to stay down. Suddenly more shells fell and Bruck was glad he'd taken the non-commissioned officer's advice. It seemed the Russians would send a final quick barrage down on their enemy, to catch any German who emerged from cover. Bruck shook his head, understanding that he knew little about how to say alive on the ground.

"Right sir, we're moving," said Khole as he picked up his heavy bag and the machine gun. Bruck carried a Kar98k bolt action rifle and a few clips of ammunition he'd taken from a badly wounded man, but he was still trying to remember how to use it. He hoped he didn't have to fire it in anger any time soon.

In front of him a battalion of the 227th Regiment of the 100th Jaeger Division jogged in open order over the shell-churned ground, toward a distant line of trees. The unit was now south of the river as the march of the 6th Army pivoted toward the advancing forces of Manstein to the southeast. They'd been told there was a shallow creek ahead where they could rest. To the east panzers from the 14th Panzer Division had advanced sixteen kilometers toward the village of Buzinovka. The village was slightly short of the halfway point the retreating army had to cover. The 100th had covered about two thirds of the panzers' advance. The 76th Infantry Division was attacking to the west toward the Don River but it had been savaged by artillery and had only moved eight kilometers.

Bruck was surprised they had made it this far in the last two days. He'd sat back and followed the initial breakthrough, but after that the Soviet response had been brutal. Now the path forward was much more difficult. He'd long since devoured his sandwich and managed to eat a couple of sardines and another slice of bread since then. Already he was incredibly hungry and wondered how the infantry managed to move forward at all without sustenance. Behind them a line of carts pulled by men followed. Many of the pack animals had been moved east in September due to the lack of fodder. It wasn't believed they were needed as the 6th Army was locked in a battle of attrition in the suburbs of Stalingrad, and had barely advanced more than one hundred meters in a day. Now those horses were sorely missed and men were forced to take their place.

Soldiers dragged a 75mm 18 light infantry gun on makeshift skis, while others pushed a sled carrying ammunition and food.

234

About three hundred men moved forward in an evenly spaced formation, wearing a variety of uniforms from the full winter jumpsuits to greatcoats. Some even wore captured Russian uniforms. The felt boots of the enemy were particularly prized.

"Movement," hissed Khole.

Bruck spotted something among the snow covered trees and then there was a sudden chatter of a machine gun. All along the line of foliage small lights started winking. A burly soldier threw him to the ground as two other men were chopped down in front of them.

Dirt and snow flew up in spurts around them and men screamed in pain. Bullets ripped into flesh and Bruck was working the bolt of his rifle and firing back. He didn't really aim at anything; he just worked the bolt and pulled the trigger until the clip was empty. Next to him the soldier who had pushed him down was firing his Haenel machine carbine (MKb 42). He used short controlled bursts and Bruck thought he could see where the man's bullets were hitting. Then Khole opened up with the MG 15. The heavy gun roared and the traces flew straight at one of the enemy positions. Immediately one of those small lights went out. What Bruck couldn't see was the impact of the bullets on the Russian crew of a DShK 12.7mm machine gun. The weapon's shield was hit twice with one of the slugs ricocheting into the head of the loader. Two more deflected off the metal, then another went through the gap near the sights and hit the gunner in the throat. Khole then switched to another target and repeated the process. Bruck couldn't believe the man's accuracy. Every time he fired; another Soviet position ceased to exist.

"Your man can really shoot, sir," said the soldier.

"Reload for me please, skipper," said Khole.

Bruck dug into the bag and found another seventy-five round magazine. He removed the old one, almost burning his hands in the process, while fumbling to fit the new one into place. In the meantime the soldier lying with them kept firing.

"That's it, I'm out," said the man, as he pushed the gun away.

Khole started firing again while the infantry crept forward. The 75mm close support gun roared and more of the enemy disappeared in an explosion of flame and dirt. Then the men of the 227th Regiment surged over the Russian lines and the fighting was hand to hand. Bruck only glimpsed swinging rifle butts and flashing bayonets but when he reached the Soviet trenches he saw the damage they had caused to human bodies. What little food there was in his stomach came up and splashed over his boots. He wiped at his mouth and watched as the burly Soldat picked through the enemy weapons. Khole grabbed a TT-33 semi-automatic pistol while the German soldier found a STV-40 with a sniper's scope. He dug around for spare magazines and even stuffed a few grenades in his belt.

"Sir, I suggest you grab a gun," said Khole.

"Take the Papasha, sir. They're tough and easy to use," said the soldier. The man was busy wrapping a captured scarf around his face while Khole pulled some boots off a corpse. Bruck looked at a submachine gun with a large round magazine. He found more ammunition and helped himself to a grenade.

"And sir, lose the field cap. Russian snipers love to shoot officers, so it's best not to make your presence obvious," said the man.

"Thanks. What's your name, soldier?" asked Bruck.

"Muller, sir. I was with the 3rd Motorized sir, but I lost my unit in a bombardment. I think they are somewhere to the northwest pushing for the Don. Don't know if I'd be able to get back to them in this mess so I might stick with you if that's okay. I don't want one of the Military Police to think I'm a deserter."

"We'll vouch for you Muller, and keep the Chain Dogs off your back," said Bruck.

The three men joined with the rest of the regiment as it moved away to the southwest. Bruck thought the strength of the unit couldn't be more than that of an over manned battalion. The

100th Jaeger Division had obviously taken heavy casualties, but at least they were still moving in the right direction.

"Found this, sir," said Khole.

He held up three carrots and a few pieces of black bread. Muller's mouth started to chew involuntarily at the thought of the food and Bruck restrained himself from not snatching the morsels out of the man's hand.

"There's also a canteen of vodka, some matches and tobacco. Oh, and I also found a couple of beets, but I thought we might want to save them for tomorrow," Khole continued.

"That's a good idea," said Bruck, though part of him wanted to eat the lot now. As it was, they devoured the food quickly before any of the other men noticed their luck. They walked forward with the unit for another four kilometers, following the watercourse before camping among trees as the light disappeared. The foliage gave the soldiers cover and small groups of men managed to get a few fires going, though they were careful not to let any light show.

The men ate what little food they had found on the dead Russians, but this was only enough to give each soldier a mouthful. After a day walking in the cold, carrying or pushing heavy equipment, it wasn't enough. Men slept in relays, lying near fires or warmed by the body heat of a friend. Later, positions would swap until most of the men got a few hours' sleep. Bruck was completely exhausted. He was colder than he'd ever been in his life and his stomach growled like a wounded tiger.

The following morning there was a warning yell from one of the officers. Men ran to the southern side of the creek bed and crouched down in the ice and snow. A line of white clad Russians walked toward them with rifles slung over their shoulders, chatting to each other as though they didn't have a care in the world.

"They don't know we are here," said Muller.

"They soon will," said Khole as he leaned over his Mg 15.

The officer in charge waited until the enemy were only two hundred meters away when he gave the order to fire. The Russians were cut down like ripe wheat. They immediately fell to the snow and started shooting back but they had little cover. Then someone gave the order to charge and the Germans were up and running forward.

"That's unusual," said Muller. "Usually we'd wait until they were destroyed."

"Do we have time for that?" asked Khole.

"I suppose not," said the big soldier.

Everyone jumped to their feet and surged toward to enemy. The remaining Soviets fired at the running men, but many of them had already been killed or wounded. The Germans were on their enemy before they knew it, shooting them at close range. Khole was firing his machine gun from the hip, killing Russians who were running for their lives. Every burst seemed to knock three of four men to the ground, until finally there wasn't anyone left to shoot at.

"That's it for this beast. Most of the ammo gone," said the little gunner.

"Try the DP-27; it's a good gun, or so I've heard," said Muller.

Khole looked suspiciously at the Soviet light machine gun with its flat round magazine on the top. It lay near two dead Russians, one of whom carried a bag containing more ammunition.

"They've got food!" yelled a soldier from nearby.

This set off a mad scramble to search the corpses and soon everybody was stuffing their mouths with pieces of bread covered with fat. Others found carrots and beets, as well as vodka. A few were even lucky enough to discover a few biscuits. To Bruck it felt like a feast, though it was probably no more than a few mouthfuls. It certainly raised the spirits of the men as they continued southwest for another eight kilometers until they reached an even smaller creek. The Reka Donskaya was little more than a gully with a few patches of frozen ice at the bottom. One hundred and fifty meters in front of them was a thin line of snow covered trees. The waterway meandered southeast and northwest, in some places almost reaching the neat line of pines. They didn't know it at the time but the 100th Jaeger was twenty-eight kilometers from German lines, while the 16th and 14th Panzer Divisions were only six kilometers from the small village from Krepinskiy. If they could take the town, then the 6th Army was slightly over halfway to the German lines.

The area seemed to be flat, but in reality was cut with many gullies of varying depths and all of them provided excellent defensive positions. The problem for the 6th Army at this point, wasn't what was in front of it, though that was still formidable, it was what was snapping at its heels that was the issue. The advance of the Germans created a moving pocket of troops shaped like an egg, with the elongated end moving toward Manstein's army, and the fat end dragging almost all the way back to the old defensive positions of the original lodgement. Now however, the forces that had surrounded the 6th Army were free to attack the Germans in open country. There were no trenches to hide in and no fortified positions to fire from. A lot of Russians had been held back to make sure their enemy didn't escape and though the initial break out had taken them by surprise, they were now snapping at the German rear guard with renewed determination.

The 24th Panzer and 60th Motorized Divisions only had thirty tanks between them. Anti-tank guns held back the first Soviet attacks but they had to be abandoned due to lack of transportation and fuel. Soon the remaining Panzer IIIs and StuG IIIs would either run dry or be overwhelmed by the perusing T-34s. The infantry at the side of the pocket was also struggling from a barrage of constant artillery and infantry attacks. It was only the constant Luftwaffe air support which allowed the Germans to shake themselves free of the enemies' embrace and keep moving.

The 100th were lucky they were on the leading edge of the advance. They had been spared the worst of the attacks from the Russians who had been stationed around the surrounded 6th Army's original positions. To the south Manstein prepared to make another lunge toward the pocket of German troops. He'd just received fourteen Tiger tanks and twenty Panzer IIIs as well as a brigade of parachutists. With this force he wanted to try and force a path through the Russians.

V

Soviet 45mm guns fired from dug in positions among the pines, and the men of the 27th Regiment followed a series of low ravines toward the trees, trying to stay low as heavy machine guns fired over their heads. Khole, Bruck and Muller watched from a position near the junction of two small creek beds. Below them the gully was filled with pools of frozen water and pockets of dirty snow. Squads of men crept along the watercourse, trying to get closer to the trees. Then the German 75mm guns started firing back at the Russian positions. Soon a duel began with the support weapons attempting to knock each other out. There were more of the Russian weapons but they weren't designed for the task, and eventually all of the 45mm guns were destroyed. The German weapons, however, were almost out of ammunition so the firing pins were removed and they were abandoned.

The enemy retreated in good order and the 27th moved probably another kilometer before coming to a halt in another series of shallow ravines. To their northwest the 5th regiment and the 100th Reconnaissance Battalion found themselves in a similar position. That's when the division had a stroke of luck. Six Drache helicopters, each carrying one six hundred kilos of cargo, landed from out of a cold grey sky. Cold meats and a lot of pre-baked biscuits were handed out and some of the wounded were flown west. The following morning the helicopters returned with more food, though their loads now also consisted of ammunition. Again, more of the sick and injured were flown away.

Bruck saw the morale of the men lift and when he heard there were eighty helicopters doing this along the entire line, he began to hope. There was even a story of two Me 323s landing near a column of panzers. Both were loaded with 50mm shells and cans of fuel. Later it was discovered that six of the giant aircraft had taken off, looking for the leading troops of the 6th Army. One was shot down, one landed near the rear guard, and two turned back.

None of the planes could become airborne again and the pilots had to join the retreating soldiers.

To the south they could hear gun fire. Bruck didn't know it, but the spear head of the 14th Panzer Division was only sixteen kilometers from joining with the Tigers and parachute troops who were grinding their way northeast. The 100th was still a few kilometers further back and it was now fracturing into groups of six hundred to a thousand men. Behind them some of the infantry divisions were starting to disintegrate under the Russian onslaught. The 24th Panzer still fought a desperate rear-guard action but the 60th Motorised Division had almost been wiped out. If the pocket didn't reach safety soon it would start to implode as the flanks and rear gave way.

A cold wind whipped ice granules into Bruck's exposed cheeks. He tried to cover his whole face with a thick scarf but it just wouldn't stay where he wanted it to. At least he wasn't feeling as hungry as the previous day. His group of six hundred men trudged southwest, past the small village of Krepinskiy, over wind swept steppes and along gullies carved by the melted water of spring. They made it through to an area of shallow channels after crossing another small frozen river. Some of the depressions were less than half the height of a man and proved little in the way of shelter. Bruck marvelled at the monotony of the landscape and wondered why the Führer wanted this country. It was unlike anything he'd ever seen in Germany. It seemed to go on forever to horizons that were impossibly distant. In some way it frightened him. It was certainly nothing like his home in Silesia.

The clank of tank tracks was a nasty shock to the men of the 27th Regiment. They turned as one to stare northwest and saw white shapes speeding across the flat landscape toward them. Soviet tanks charged at them firing cannons as they churned the snow. The T-70 light tanks then started using their machine guns on the German troops. Bruck dropped into the gully and pressed his face into the snow. The enemy armour charged right up to the hidden Germans and fell down into the gully, before attempting to climb out the other side. Men and tanks went in every direction;

some of the soldiers fell under the tracks where they were crushed, while others died as the Russian tanks fired their machine guns.

A Feldwebel managed to clamber onto one of the vehicles as it tried to climb out of the gully, and opened the top hatch. He tossed a grenade inside before jumping off. Bruck heard a muffled bang and the tank stopped moving, its nose buried into the wall of the trench. The Russians then discovered that the gully was too steep to navigate their way out of and they couldn't escape. Some managed to drive along the waterway but others became stuck. German troops quickly climbed onto the tanks and forced the hatches open. The two man crews were dragged out and shot, while others were destroyed by satchel charges or grenades. In the end, four T-70s were captured and another eight destroyed.

"We were lucky they weren't carrying troops," said Muller.

"Can we get them moving?" asked Bruck.

"I heard a couple of the men say that they can probably mange them. First we'll have to collapse the walls of the gully," said Khole.

Eventually the wall of the shallow waterways were dug away and the four light tanks drove up on to the surrounding steppe. Wounded men lay on the engine grills, enjoying the warmth, while others clung to any hand grip they could find. The officers ordered the drivers to move slowly and stay with the regiment, which they did, grinding along in a low gear. Fortunately the tanks were half full of fuel and had a good load of ammunition. The remaining men walked behind the armoured vehicles as they drove toward the distant sound of guns.

They reached the lines of Guderian's army early the following day. Only two of the T-70s were still running by then and they were almost shot at by Tiger tanks, however one of the German helicopters warned the panzer troops that the approaching men were from the 6th Army. Bruck had never been so relieved in his life. He wrote a note about Muller and his bravery, and gave it to the man before being whisked away with Khole on a large cart pulled by a team of horses. Later in the day both men were moved, with a number of other soldiers, by truck to Rostov. Bruck leaned against the canvas and sighed. He'd escaped.

Only half of the 6th Army made it to safety with the rear guard being totally destroyed and a number of the infantry divisions being cut off and sliced up by Russian cavalry and armour. The 16th and 14th Panzer Divisions were reformed, though they had lost most of their equipment. The 100th Jaeger managed to escape with roughly half its numbers, as did five of the eleven infantry divisions. The 94th and 44th Divisions escaped with three quarters of their strength, while the other units varied from a third to only a few hundred soldiers. Only twelve men from the 305th Infantry Division made it to German lines, not counting its wounded who were evacuated before the breakout attempt.

None of the divisions were battle ready and all were moved to Poland and Germany for reequipping and reforming. Hitler wanted them to become his strategic reserve but they weren't even close to being ready when the next hammer blow fell. In the meantime, the German line in the east stabilised at roughly the same position it had been before the summer offensive had begun. Manstein managed to hold on to Rostov and a small part of the Kuban Peninsula but otherwise the Germans were back where they started, minus a lot of panzers and guns. Then there was the casualty list, though as the ever positive Kesselring said at the time, 'It could have been worse.'

Chapter Six: Spring 1943

They had all known the Allies would land somewhere and when they came ashore in Algeria and Morocco, some in the German High Command were almost relieved. The problem for Hitler was that after the losses and commitments in the east there was precious little in the way of units to spare. The 114th Jaeger Division was pulled from occupation duties in Yugoslavia and the 264th Infantry Division had to hurriedly finish its training in Rouen and move to North Africa. The first unit to be flown in however, was the ubiquitous 22nd Air Landing Division with its new contingent of Marder III tank destroyers. The unit landed unopposed and rushed to block the advance of British commandos and the US 34th Division. A number of fresh Italian divisions, some of high quality, also landed in Tunisia.

In the meantime, the Luftwaffe and naval air contingents of the Kriegsmarine also flew south, to oppose the allied attack. Rommel had been fighting the 8th Army in front of Tobruk and had recently been forced to retreat further west. Now Wever looked to his airmen to attack the allied armada sitting off the beaches at Algiers.

V

The Me 155 wasn't as easy to fly as the He 112 but Kapitänleutnant Hans-Joachim Marseille was getting used to it. The plane was certainly a lot faster than his old mount and climbed quickly, yet it didn't turn as sharply and wasn't as light on the controls. Still, the range was just as good, and the four 13mm machine guns and single 20mm cannon packed a punch. He now flew with fourteen other fighters as they escorted an equal number of Ju 188 bombers southwest to attack the British. The new torpedo planes were an improvement over the older He 111s. They'd have to be good though, to escape from the improved fighters the Allies were using.

It was a long flight from Sardinia to Algiers and the chance of running into enemy aircraft only really existed in the final stretch. Marseille thought back to his final meeting with Charlotte and his mother, who often laughed with the young woman about the fact they had the same Christian name. Marseille recalled the three of them sitting in the kitchen eating potatoes and beans and talking about the defeats in the east. Charlotte talked openly about the war now being lost, and though his Mother tried to remain optimistic, though the older woman admitted she couldn't really see a situation where the Allies would sue for peace.

"The USA is such a powerful country and Russia is vast," said Charlotte.

"The Führer said we had to attack the Soviets because they were a threat to our way of life," said his mother.

"I could never see why. I mean, Stalin is the same as Hitler in many ways," said Marseille.

"We attacked first in Poland, with Russia, so we are the aggressor. I thought at first that the Führer was trying to restore Germany's borders and even accepted the attack on Poland, but when we went into Russia I was lost. At first we are their allies and then our army suddenly marches into their country," said Charlotte.

"Most Germans don't see it that way. They believe what they are told. It's only when you listen to the BBC and other radio stations you get a different perspective. I suppose they lie too and the truth is somewhere in the middle," said Charlotte.

His mother's face paled. "You can be shot for listening to the BBC."

"Mother, they play the best music and it's the only way we can find out when our forces have lost a battle," said Marseille.

They spoke to his mother frequently about what was happening to the Jews, and Nazi plans to destroy the Slavs and to even extinguish the clergy. The old lady was beginning to understand the policies of Hitler and his cronies.

"I don't know how we voted them into power," she muttered one afternoon.

"We didn't. The highest number of people who chose Hitler was forty four percent. It was when the Catholic Centre Party voted with the Nazis to pass the Enabling Act that Hitler received his autocratic powers," said Charlotte.

"How do we allow such monsters to rule us?" asked his mother.

"People were pleased when Hitler rebuilt the economy. Lots of unemployed Germans were back in work and our national pride was surging. Everyone was willing to blame the Jews for our problem and then there was the myth of the stab in the back," said Charlotte.

"You see Mother, the army *asked* for the armistice in the Great War; nobody stabbed them in the back," said Marseille. He had only recently discovered the truth about his nation's defeat in World War One from Charlotte, though when she explained it to him he wasn't surprised. "But everyone believes that the leadership at the time betrayed the armed forces."

"So what do we do about it?" his mother had asked.

Charlotte glanced at him at this point but they had said nothing. The young woman had later pulled him aside and said she was going to explain everything to his mother in the next few weeks. Unfortunately Marseille had been transferred to the Mediterranean before they could share the plan to get the old lady to safety. He left it to Charlotte to tell his mother that he was going to fly to the Allies with papers proving to the world what his government was doing to the Jews and other groups who were considered 'undesirables'. The idea had been for him to fly to Sweden from the air bases on Rugen where he was training new pilots, but Grossadmiral Wever thought the neutral country might hand him back to the Nazis. Now he was on Sardinia, Marseille needed a different strategy. He could still fly to the Allies with the incriminating folio, but he wouldn't be able to reassure his mother. That task would have to be undertaken by his lover.

Marseille was also concerned about the young woman's safety. He had fallen for Charlotte completely and had almost stopped drinking to prove his dedication to her as she didn't like it when he was inebriated. The night Charlotte had finally pulled him into her arms was a week after the death of her brother at Stalingrad. The first time she kissed him, Marseille held her but refused to take advantage of the situation. It took all of his restraint not to take her to bed but when she dragged him into his room a few days later he didn't resist.

"When I fly to the Allies they'll come after you," he said one night as Charlotte lay in his arms.

"I know. We have plans for that too. Within the space of a couple of weeks I'll be dead and then the same fate will befall your mother. But of course both of us will be safe, with different identities."

"What about your corpse?"

"That's what we are yet to work out, but best if I don't tell you any more than that."

Marseille didn't know what to think, however he was relieved that the German resistance had a plan to keep the two women he loved most in the world safe.

"So when I've heard that you are both gone, that's my signal to leave?"

"Yes. It's nice and simple, but make sure you grieve or people might be suspicious. You might even have to attend a funeral or two. Don't go to the Allies straight away, maybe wait a few weeks. If you just jump in a plane and fly away, the Gestapo might get suspicious and start looking into your mother's death, and mine."

Marseille nodded and kissed Charlotte's hair. He remembered the feeling of his heart racing when he considered the dangers of what they were trying to do. Anything could go wrong and they could all end up hanging by a rope.

v

"Skipper, target's coming up in twenty minutes," said his wingman Leutnant zur See Emil Clade.

Marseille snapped back to the present. He checked his gauges, taking careful note of how much fuel remained. The distance to Algiers was almost five hundred and fifty kilometers; well within the range of the Me 155 when it carried drop tanks. He scanned the skies looking for enemy aircraft and saw none. At that moment the USS Ranger only had a combat air patrol of six Wildcat fighters, the rest of its planes were attacking targets in and around the harbour of Algiers. However, American flown Spitfires were already ashore and some patrolled just off the coast near the allied transport ships.

Five minutes later a large carrier and a group of warships came into view. There was a smaller flat top off to one side of the group, steaming near a battleship. The Ju 188s started a shallow dive toward their targets and soon the sky filled with black puffs of smoke.

"Skipper, Wildcats nine o'clock high," said Clade.

Marseille had already seen them and ordered his Staffel to turn toward them.

"Don't let them get through to the bombers," he ordered.

The Wildcats had the advantage in height and the men who flew them were well trained. These same pilots had shot down a few French fighters the previous day so weren't completely new to air combat however they had never faced the veterans of the Kriegsmarine. At least half of Marseille's Staffel had flown missions over Iceland or Malta. Some were returning to combat after being wounded and others had just finished stints as instructors. The six Wildcats were swept aside in a few minutes of hectic combat with Marseille and his wingman, both making a kill. None of the Me 155s were lost.

Below, the torpedo bombers skimmed the waves, flying through a hurricane of flak as they tried to approach their targets. HMS Duke of York threw up the greatest amount of fire and attracted the attention of at least half of the Ju 188s. The large battleship maneuverd nimbly for her size and her gunners were credited with shooting down three of the torpedo bombers. At the last moment, just when it looked as though the battleship might make it through the attack unscathed, one of the missiles struck. The hit was right where her outer port propeller shaft exited the hull. Turning at maximum revolutions the shaft twisted and ruptured the hull, allowing three thousand tons of water to rush into the ship. The speed of the battleship dropped to fifteen knots and the Duke of York was forced to leave the North African coast and return to Britain. A transport ship was hit and sunk as well, taking fifty tanks and a large number of trucks to the bottom of the sea. Marseille flew with his usual expertise but his heart wasn't into combat anymore. He had shot down one hundred and sixty eight planes, twenty of them in Russia, but now he didn't really want to fight. The enemy were men who were just trying to halt the aggression and murder perpetrated by his nation. Marseille didn't believe in the German cause. In the past he'd thought the grievances of his country needed addressing but now he understood Hitler's intentions, he wanted out. Yet when he saw the Spitfires descend on the fleeing Ju 188s he acted out of instinct.

"Follow me down Clade," he yelled into the radio.

The Spitfire Vs weren't the newest mark, and were flown by Americans from the 308th Squadron who had trained in the planes in southern England for two months to become familiar with them. They were still dangerous fighters and needed to be treated with respect. The last aircraft in the formation came into range as Marseille eased out of his dive. The Me 155 closed the distance but he hesitated to press the firing button; instead he eased his sights a little to the left, then fired his first burst. Cannon shells and machine gun bullets chewed through the Spitfire's wing and the plane fell away, smoke pouring from the engine. Marseille watched with satisfaction as the American bailed out close to the allied fleet. His wingman fired a long burst at another Spitfire as the formation of fighters scattered, breaking in all directions. The enemy aircraft shuddered from hits to the tail and wing before catching fire. Another pilot jumped from his stricken plane, though Marseille suspected this man would have received a number of burns before he made it out of the cockpit.

The Ju 188s headed for Sardinia but now only numbered eight as the bombers had suffered heavy losses. Marseille didn't know how the attack pilots managed to keep going when every assault on an enemy warship lowered their chance of making it through the war alive. Attacking merchants was even a risky proposition these days as many carried at least one anti-aircraft gun, possibly more. He climbed back to four thousand meters and noted that all of his pilots reported in. He couldn't see all of them, but that wasn't unusual as combat often scattered a Staffel. The range of the FuG 7 radio was about fifty kilometers in good conditions and none of his pilots were further away than that.

This was Marseille's first taste of combat since returning to the front and he hadn't enjoyed it. Everything about the experience confirmed in his mind that his decision to take the folio on the murder of the Jews to the Allies was correct. The sooner the news of his mother's death arrived, the better. When he knew she was

265

safe he would climb into the nearest fighter and fly to an American airfield.

V

Berlin was always beautiful in the springtime. Fregattenkapitän Hans-Gerrit von Stockhausen admired the green shoots pushing up through the ground in the Tiergarten. He couldn't believe he was here in the capital after having survived the invasion of Iceland and his consequent role in its defence. Now he had a staff job organising supplies and training schedules. With the losses the U-boat arm of the Kriegsmarine was sustaining in the Atlantic at the moment, he was extremely happy to be back in Germany, despite the air raids. These were light at the moment and did little damage.

Stockhausen was due to return to Danzig in a few days to supervise the selection of crew for another U-boat. In the Atlantic, losses were escalating. Twelve boats had been destroyed in March and another fifteen in April. By all accounts the Allies had lost many tankers and freighters during this time as wolf packs formed and savaged convoys. The number of U-boats at sea was finally large enough to inflict substantial losses on the enemy's merchant fleet, though the damage to the Kriegsmarine in terms of the men who never returned was high. Still, Stockhausen thought for the first time the navy had a real chance of forcing the Allies to the negotiating table. Ju 290s flew long range patrols, finding the convoys and reporting their location. A new version of the reconnaissance machine also hunted enemy aircraft, with gunships attacking Flying Fortresses, Liberators and Catalina Flying Boats. The heavy cannons of these German aircraft outmatched the machine guns of the allied planes, but the American aircraft usually used their greater speed to escape, except in the case of the flying boat, which was a sitting duck.

A soft breeze tickled Stockhausen's cheek and he thought about stopping at a small café for lunch. He'd accumulated a few extra ration tickets and wondered if there might be a little bacon or ham on offer. There wouldn't be any coffee and he'd have to drink that acorn muck or perhaps the chicory substitute. He bought a paper and wondered why he was so lucky. Sitting at a small table at the window Stockhausen was delighted to discover the café did have bacon, and though it was expensive he ordered as much as his ration tickets allowed him. The papers reported on the damage done to the allied fleets off Algiers and how the enemy would soon be thrown out of North Africa. Stockhausen noted that Rommel's army was now back in Tripoli and the rest of the German army was fighting in Tunisia. At least the situation seemed to be stabilising in the east. 'Der Angriff' wrote of the defeat of the Soviet thrust west, but didn't mention that the Germans had been thrown back from the Volga and now fought outside Rotov. All the major cities: Kursk, Kharkov, and Orel seemed to still be in German hands with the line following the Donets River until it reached the Oskil River. He had no way of knowing the losses the German Army had incurred just to end up almost back where it had started from, or the complete destruction of most of the Italian, Romanian and Hungarian armies that had been involved.

He finished his meal and enjoyed the sunshine for a moment before paying and walking out on to the street. After walking a short distance he crossed the Spree River, then followed Paulstrasse until he hit the railway line. In the distance, on the other side of the road, he spotted three women walking together. One of them had a familiar shock of red hair.

"Mila!" he called and stepped out on to the road. The truck came around the corner from Flemingstrasse and was speeding up when it hit him. The impact wasn't hard but he went under the wheels, one of which crushed his neck. Fregattenkapitän Hans-Gerrit von Stockhausen died not knowing what had struck him. Mila and her friends rushed to the scene with a number of other people. She recognised her old commander and sadness overwhelmed her. This man had faced death a number of times and survived only to be killed by a truck in Berlin. Later, when she thought about it, Mila decided there was no clear reason why one person lived and another died. Everything happened by chance and sometimes a person's luck ran out.

Later, Mila was transferred to Rugen Island where she worked as a clerical assistant until the end of the war. After that she moved to Canada where she married and had two children. Her luck never ran short.

v

"We have lost the battle for the Atlantic, at least for now. I have failed the Führer," said Admiral Karl Doenitz.

"Your forces have been overwhelmed by superior forces and new technology," said Grossadmiral Wever.

The tall, sharp-faced man rubbed at his chin and stood. Wever thought he looked exhausted but he felt little sympathy for him. Doenitz was a Nazi who worshipped his Führer. Also, Doenitz had never seemed to understand the importance of technological developments, until now.

"They always are one step ahead of us. The number of times our refuelling submarines were sunk has been remarkable," said Doentiz. "Five have been destroyed by enemy aircraft!"

Wever said nothing but he had a growing suspicion of how that was occurring, and decided he needed to have another meeting with Admiral Canaris as soon as possible.

"We have lost forty-one boats and the month isn't even over," said Doenitz. "That's a quarter of my operational boats!"

"And we haven't sunk many merchants?" asked Wever.

"Thirty-eight in the Atlantic and a few more elsewhere, but we can't afford these losses. If it continues like this, then our U-boat arm will be decimated by summer."

"Withdraw them for now. We will look for other vulnerabilities, maybe in the South Atlantic or off the coast of West Africa."

"Most of the type VIIs don't have the range to go that far and we have lost so many of the refuelling submarines that I can't fill their tanks," said Doenitz.

"Send the type IXs and bring the smaller boats home. Increase training and accelerate the development of the snorkels.

271

Also we need those decoy devices rolled out to all U-boats as soon as possible. You have been resistant to some of these developments and now is the time to put those feelings aside," said Wever.

"That is unfair, sir."

"Is it? I've read the reports you sent saying development of new technologies must not be at the expensive of production."

"I believed that was a reasonable position to take at the time. There was no way of knowing the allied technology would advance so quickly."

"We don't even know how far they have come. Obviously they have more escorts than before, and something else has changed. Maybe they are reading our mail, but that wouldn't affect the outcome of the wolf pack attacks on convoys. It's time the Kriegsmarine put all its efforts into regaining our edge. I just hope it isn't too late."

Chapter Seven: Summer 1943

"Enigma is compromised, but I suspect you already knew that," said Grossadmiral Wever.

Admiral Canaris stiffened slightly in his chair, however he didn't speak.

Wever sighed. "I know you believe Germany has no right to win this war and perhaps you are correct, but I will not be party to the death of a single sailor."

"The Generals needed defeats before they would listen to me," said Canaris.

"Not at the expense of my men!" yelled Wever.

"For most of last year I tried to find allies to help us be rid of the monster who rules our country, but nobody was interested. Some even said the policies in the east were necessary. Many of the top generals are complicit in the policies to kill the Jews and to let the Slavs die of starvation."

"I know, and it was only natural that people tried to justify to themselves what was happening, however this policy hit us harder than the army. I won't have my sailors dying in order to convince a few generals to join us."

Canaris sighed. "I didn't like keeping my suspicions quiet. Others ran investigations but they never had all the evidence. The fact the Allies are reading some of our mail didn't lead to Stalingrad, that was our leader's doing."

"Yes, and it brought a number of high ranking people over to us. They can see there is no way we can win. Now, I want you to announce you have discovered Enigma is compromised. You will get the credit and it will impress our leader. He will think more highly of you and that might be useful."

"You know we will have to kill Hitler," said Canaris.

"I was hoping to arrest him but I can see that you are right. It would be too dangerous to let him live."

"The problem is, the man has the Devil watching over him. There have been a number of attempts on his life; the bomb in Munich in 1939 came close."

"Most of them have been random attacks haven't they?" asked Wever.

"Nearly all. There was an attempt recently to blow up his plane but the bomb didn't detonate."

"Why wasn't I told! I would have had the Navy ready to act in support."

"I didn't know until after the failure. It was an army plot."

"These actions need to be coordinated or we will end up with Himmler in charge."

"They both need to be killed at the same time. The problem is that our leader rarely visits the front and his security is extremely tight," said Canaris.

"I still see him, though I'd prefer not to be the man to do the deed. I need to be around to make sure the navy supports the new regime. What's the plan now?"

"You and a number of the Generals would form a committee to run Germany. Then we would approach the Allies for terms. I don't know if the Russians would listen, and Roosevelt and Churchill have agreed with this unconditional surrender position."

"Again, I thank you for your trust. The unconditional surrender proclamation must be for propaganda purposes. Why would they lock in the death of thousands of their men if we are willing to give up?"

"Stalin wouldn't care, but America and Britain might waver. What would we give up?"

"Everything, if it kept the Russians out of Berlin. We must, however, avoid another stab in the back scenario."

"We were never stabbed in the back in the Great War! That's a myth."

"I know that, and so do you, but *everybody* has to understand that is the case."

"We will need to round up and put on trial the men who have perpetrated war crimes."

"Agreed."

"Luckily your friend Heydrich isn't alive, he'd have been at the top of the list," said Canaris.

"He was never my friend. And, yes, those assassins did us a favour. This all needs to occur before the Allies land in France. They'll try at some stage."

"First they will need to finish us in North Africa," said Canaris.

"That's only a matter of time. Now Rommel and Arnim are locked up in Tunisia, all the enemy needs to do is squeeze them backwards into the sea. It will be a disaster on the scale of Stalingrad, probably worse, as fewer men will be able to escape."

"Another seven divisions destroyed, two of them panzer formations."

"The generals can see it coming and are trying to evacuate essential personnel by air."

"I believe Rommel stung the Americans a few times, but now he's back in Germany, ill."

"He did, but it made little difference in the end."

"You know his name has been mentioned as a possible disaffected general."

"If he joined us it would add credibility to our cause!" exclaimed Wever.

"He has been fighting with the Führer about withdrawing men from Tunisia. Hitler doesn't want anyone to leave; last man, last bullet. Our leader says that's what the 6th Army should have done."

Wever shook his head. "After France I thought the man was a genius. I hated his policies toward the conquered but thought when the war ended everything would settle down. I couldn't have been more wrong."

"Now, what of our young fighter pilot?" asked Canaris.

"We have a plan to fake the deaths of his mother and contact, then he'll fly the papers to the Allies."

"The Führer won't be pleased."

"I'm sure Marseille will make it look convincing. He knows what's at stake."

"I hope you're right. If he doesn't, the Führer will be very unhappy with the navy."

"I'll ride it out if that's the case. The main thing is we need a coordinated plan for what happens next and I'll have to stay close to our leader."

V

The sea was calm, for the Artic. Admiral Ciliax stood on the bridge of the Graf Zeppelin, watching as the rest of the fleet steamed north to destroy the British convoy. Grossadmiral Wever had ordered that not a single ship was to make it to Murmansk. The new carrier, the Jade steamed off to port with thirty planes. In front of the Graf Zeppelin, the mighty Bismarck cut the ocean, while the Scharnhorst brought up the rear. The repaired Hipper sailed on one flank and the Moltke on the other. The fleet was surrounded by eight destroyers who prowled back and forth searching for enemy submarines.

The Bannak air base in Norway had been reinforced, with the addition of fourteen Ju 188s to add to the twenty-four Ju 88s, and twelve new Me 155s. Another force of older He 111s and Bf 110s were based at Bardufoss, a little further to the south.

Ciliax knew that the Allies probably believed the fleet wasn't going to attack convoy JW54A. False Enigma messages had been sent from the northern command about engine problem on the Bismarck and that the Scharnhorst was about to return to Germany after hitting a hidden reef. These signals might affect the composition of the allied covering force, though it was hoped it might allow the two German carriers to get close enough to the convoy to hit it hard. Ciliax didn't want the allied merchant ships to turn back before he was in range.

There was a question as to why the enemy would risk a convoy in the middle of summer with the long periods of daylight, but it was surmised they were under pressure from the Russians to do so. There was also the belief that the Allies might want to bring the Kriegsmarine to battle, to defeat it with their growing material strength. The enemy would probably attempt to stay out of range of the German naval aircraft unless they thought the German fleet was not going to move. Records after the war now show that was exactly what they allies did believe, and it tempted them closer to the coast of Norway than would have usually been the case.

Late in the afternoon Ciliax received reports of the enemy convoy further north than he had anticipated. It seemed the Allies had chosen a route closer to the Spitbergen Islands than they had used in the previous convoy. The pack ice had retreated, which increased the distance Kriegsmarine bombers would have to travel to attack the British ships. It also added at least a day to the usual fourteen day trip to Russia. The weather still held and there would be no darkness in which the British could hide. Their best chance would be for one of the summer storms to appear at any time, or fog, which might occur if the still conditions remained for a little longer.

The first strike hit the enemy convoy at five pm and sunk the destroyers Whitehall and Hussar, as well as the merchants Junecrest, James Smith, Ocean Vanity, and Fort Yukon, all of which were freighters. Ciliax wasn't happy with the number of ships sunk, and was even more annoyed that there was only one damaged vessel, the Ocean Vanity. When a reconnaissance Do 24 reported the convoy had turned around, he decided to follow and strike one final time. That's when the Bismarck's radar reported two air contacts. Both these planes were Grumman Avengers from the USS Ranger and they reported the position of the German fleet before the CAP shot them down. Ciliax realised there was at least one enemy carrier within range and that he needed to find it.

He was lucky a Ju 290 was returning early from its patrol over the ocean to the south west of the Spitbergen Islands due to engine trouble. The allied covering fleet of three carriers and two battleships was spotted about sixty kilometers to the west of the main convoy, with another group of three cruisers in between the two groups. The Ju 290 was hit by two Seafires and damaged, just reaching the rocky island one hundred and thirty kilometers to the northeast, before crash landing. Ciliax knew it was too late to run, and radioed the information to shore commands. He hoped the land based bombers might be able to frighten the enemy away, but thought any intervention from Norway would probably come too late. Three carriers were more than his fleet could handle, but he was determined to become involved in a strike of his own, so he turned his carriers into the slight breeze and started launching his aircraft. In the meantime, he ordered another Do 24 which happened to be patrolling north of Bear Island, to locate the enemy fleet and give a more current position of the allied ships.

Allied aircraft found his ships first. Coming from the west, planes from the USS Ranger, the HMS Victorious and the USS Princeton attacked the German fleet, running the gauntlet of Me 155s and flak. The CAP from the Graf Zeppelin and the Jade was only fourteen fighters, and though these outclassed the Wildcats that escorted the allied strike, the German aircraft were overwhelmed by the sheer number of enemy machines. One hundred and twenty five aircraft attacked in clear weather and though nineteen were lost, the German fleet was devastated. The Jade was hit by four torpedos and sank within ten minutes taking most of her crew down with her. The Graf Zeppelin was struck by four one thousand kilo bombs and ripped apart. Explosions tore through her interior and at least a quarter of her crew were killed. Destroyers took off the rest and scuttled the hulk later in the day. Admiral Ciliax was killed when dive bombers strafed the bridge, the heavy machine gun bullets punching through the metal shutters that were already damaged by bomb blasts.

The Mighty Bismarck was hit by three bombs and three torpedoes, and sank an hour later whilst the Hipper struggled east at ten knots after being struck by a torpedo and a bomb. The Scharnhorst continued with her reputation as a lucky ship. A torpedo hit on her bow failed to detonate, though a thousand-pound bomb did knock out the Anton turret and killed thirty-two crewmen. The gunners on the battle cruiser then shot down at least three Grumman Avengers as they flew low over the water. None of them managed to drop their torpedos before they either blew up or crashed into the waves.

The German surface fleet was wrecked in this one massive strike. Only the Moltke remained undamaged. Later, the Scharnhorst would be repaired but would never again attempt to take on the allied fleet, settling to attack convoys instead.

Fifty German planes flew to find the allied ships and did so after receiving final coordinates from a Do 24 (the float plane was shot down in the act of radioing the enemy's position). They were met by thirty Wildcat and Seafire fighters. There weren't enough

German planes to break through. The Stukas were swept from the sky with only the Fw 205 torpedo bombers managing to launch any effective attacks. However, the flak was ferocious and most of the attack aircraft were damaged or dropped their ordinance at too great a range. The surviving German planes then turned north and attempted to reach Spitbergen Island. Most off the pilots made it, with the crews bailing out over the long valley at Sveagruva. A U-boat picked up sixteen pilots and eight other crew from this location four days later. They had sheltered in a nearby fisherman's hut, living on emergency rations until rescued.

The battle, however, wasn't over. Bombers flew from their Norwegian bases to attack the allied fleet. The He 111s and Bf 110s completely missed their target, scouring the ocean until lack of fuel forced them to return to their airfield. The Ju 188s and Ju 88s had more luck. They were joined en route by four Ju 290s, all of which carried experimental precision guided munitions. The raid met the full force of the allied CAP and many Ju 88s and Ju 188s were damaged or shot down. The crews bravely pressed on and a single torpedo managed to hit the battleship HMS Anson on the bow, blowing a five meter hole in the ship and forcing it to slow until a patch could be put in place.

High above, not spotted by the Allies due to the attack by torpedo planes and low level bombers, the four Ju 290s released their bombs. This was the first use of the Fritz X, a one thousand three hundred kilo, armour piercing glide bomb. Two were guided straight at the USS Princeton, one narrowly missed and caused little damage. The other struck between the elevators, punching through the wooden flight deck and hangars before exploding. Structural damage was minimal but a fire started which quickly ran out of control. When bombs in the magazine started to detonate because of the heat, the ship was doomed. Only one hundred and twenty eight men were killed, with most being rescued, but the carrier blew up a little after eleven pm, with the sun sitting low in the sky.

The other two Fritz X bombs both struck USS Iowa, one punching through the armour just in front of the forward turret, detonating within and probably killing the gun crew. A second bomb struck the starboard side near the bow. This hit was perilously close to the first and probably allowed the blast to reach the forward magazines. A huge explosion resulted, blowing the turret overboard. This caused immediate catastrophic flooding to the front of the ship and it capsized before breaking in two. It all happened so quickly that only one hundred and twenty crew were rescued. The Allies didn't know until after the war that the Ju 290s had delivered the fatal blow to the American battleship.

Though the convoy was partially destroyed and the enemy had lost a battleship and a carrier, the Germany Navy was severely defeated. Wever and his admirals had thought the land based aircraft would swing the battle in their favour, but the allied carriers had discovered the Kriegsmarine's ships first and launched their strike with ruthless speed. Wever also misjudged the strength of the enemy and the depth of their resources. Not only was his surface fleet ruined, the number of planes he had left to strike at allied convoys was drastically reduced. The only morsel he could take to the Führer was that convoys to Russia stopped until late autumn.

V

The bombing of Hamburg was the Luftwaffe's Stalingrad. The attack started on July 24th but the real damage happened on the night of the 27th. Eight hundred bombers of the Royal Air Force attacked on a night of unusually dry conditions. The resulting firestorm reached temperatures of eight hundred degrees celsius and created cyclonic winds that snatched people from the streets like leaves. Asphalt streets caught fire and people suffocated in their thousands as they hid in bunkers and cellars. Forty-two thousand people died during the course of the raids but the attack also gave Charlotte the chance to disappear, and Admiral Canaris the body he needed to take the place of Hans-Joachim Marseille's mother. Three days later there was a house fire in Berlin and the fighter ace received the tragic news of her death. He immediately received leave and went to the capital where he attended his mother's funeral. Marseille wondered how Charlotte had convinced

289

the old lady to disappear. He was sure the letter he had left would have helped and his lover was a persuasive woman. Maybe his Mutti now understood how corrupt and morally repugnant the leadership of Germany was.

After the funeral Marseille stayed at a friend's house near the Zoologischer Bahnhof. At times, as he lay in bed, he could hear the trains rumbling by. In the morning he found a note slipped under his door saying it was a pleasant day to visit the zoo. Marseille thought this was probably one of his contacts from Grossadmiral Wever but decided to proceed cautiously anyway. He dressed, ate, and walked the short distance, buying a ticket and wandering around the various exhibits. The zoo had only been slightly damaged by bombs in 1941 and most of the animals were still in good condition. He walked past the elephants and the lions, stopping to admire the elephant seal.

"He is a very large specimen, don't you think?"

Marseille turned and found himself looking at a middle aged man in a plain suit. The individual wore glasses and regarded him with intelligent eyes.

"Do I know you?" asked Marseille.

"My name is not important. I have a message for you and want you to listen carefully. Your mother is safe, as promised. She isn't in Germany but that is all I will say. Charlotte of course, didn't die in Hamburg and is out of harm's way with a new identity. Are you ready to uphold your part of the deal?"

"Can you keep them safe?"

"There are no guarantees. Hopefully, if circumstances change, their location will no longer matter. For now though, well, it's the best that can be done. The biggest factor in their favour is that nobody is looking for them."

"Well, I hope my disappearance will be blamed on enemy action, when the time comes; however, there's no way of knowing what the enemy will do once they have me."

"You can make it look like you were shot down?"

"It's possible. I just have to lose my wingman in battle. A little cloud cover will help, so circumstances need to be right."

"Then I'll report you are ready."

Marseille nodded. "I hope you and your friends can save Germany. This madness needs to end," he said.

"We will do our best."

Marseille never found out that he was speaking with General Hans Speidel, Field Marshal Rommel's new Chief of Staff.

V

It was amazing he was still alive after all the combat he'd seen. Finally the navy had seen fit to grant him a training position, though he didn't know how long he'd keep it. Fregattenkapitän Bernhard Jope was at least now able to visit Emma more frequently. His fiancée was regularly sent to help at one of the many concentration sub-camps in the area and she preferred this to working at Ravensbruck itself. Jope was seeing her tomorrow and hoped she would be in better condition than the last time he'd visited. Emma often seemed to be distant, as though part of her had shut down. He tried to talk to her but often only received single word responses. This time she would be catching the train to Sassnits and he would drive to town to pick her up. Emma had two weeks leave and he planned to make it a special occasion for her.

V

They drove back to the small village of Breege near the northern tip of the island. The thirty kilometer trip took them over fields untouched by war, along the coast past lagoons and next to beaches of white sand. They only saw the odd sea plane flying overhead, otherwise the scene was peaceful. Emma said very little, content to stare out the window at the sea for long stretches of time.

"How far away is Sweden?" she asked as they approached the outskirts of the village.

"About eighty kilometers. Most of the training flights head west, or northwest toward Denmark, but sometimes we fly east, all the way to Danzig."

"The city we took back off the Poles?"

"Yes, the very same."

Emma turned away from him. "We shot some women from there recently, Jews and Poles. The Hauptsturmführer ordered a selection; women too weak to work, or ill. We usually ship them off to be gassed but this time there weren't enough to bother putting on a train, so we shot them."

"You killed them?"

"Oh, I didn't pull the trigger. They don't give the women guns; well, a few have received the right to carry a side arm, but not many. No, I help select the victims. Then I stand by and watch as they are shot. I don't have to, however if you walk away some of the guards think you aren't really dedicated to the task. I often wonder what it would be like to pull the trigger, but in a way, I don't think there's much difference."

It was all said in such a matter-of-fact way that Jope wasn't sure if he had heard correctly.

"Why are they killed?" he asked.

"To make space for more prisoners."

"No, I mean what was their crime?"

Emma laughed. The sound was bitter and she turned and met his eye. "Not being German."

"Well, they are enemies of Germany, so I suppose that's reason enough."

"That's what I tell myself, over and over. When the blood flows in the gutters I remind myself they had it coming. I wonder what will happen if we lose?"

The change in direction was sudden and Jope scrambled to reorientate himself. "We will win," he said.

"But we have been pushed back in Russia and have just evacuated North Africa. There are rumours a huge sea battle was recently fought and lost, and lately two of the guards lost husbands and boyfriends who served on U-boats. It doesn't sound like it's going well. Didn't British bombers also burn Hamburg to the ground?"

"There have been setbacks but I retain my faith in our Führer. He has led us to great victories."

"Hmmm, they seem to have dried up of late. I suppose you are right though. If we lose, they'll hang me for what I've done."

"We will win and the work you do is keeping our country safe, you need to believe this."

Emma sighed. "I try to. I just wish I didn't have to wade through so much blood to keep my country safe."

After a meal of Baltic herring with white wine sauce, Jope took Emma to bed. She was distant and disinterested in sex, and he found the experience unsatisfying. Later she curled up against him and slept. He dozed but awoke to a whimpering noise. Next to him Emma shook slightly and a gentle keening sound leaked from between her lips. Jope woke her and she started to cry.

"I hoped that next to you it wouldn't happen. Then there would be a chance I would be forgiven," wailed Emma.

"There is nothing to forgive," said Jope.

"Have you read the Bible? It's quite clear what's in store for me. I'm going to burn for what I've done. You can't send a child's mother to her death and not see your own in those innocent eyes. Some of the guards say the children are little rats, born from vermin, but I can't see it anymore, I just can't."

He had no words to calm the horror on her face. Emma had watched more people die than he ever had. She was responsible for the execution of hundreds of women and it was weighing her down. Jope tried to tell her that they weren't really people, but they looked just like Germans, so he could see why it would be difficult to watch them die. It confused him at times. He knew individuals who were his father's friends from the Great War; Jews who had bled with and fought next to the old man. Yet the Führer said they had conspired against Germany for centuries. He shook his head and held Emma tightly as she sobbed. Eventually they both fell asleep.

In the morning she wasn't there. Jope hoped to catch her downstairs so they could eat breakfast and go for a walk. He felt a little groggy as he walked into the dining room and realised he hadn't had enough sleep. Emma was nowhere to be seen. He noticed the owner of the small hotel clearing away some plates, and he approached the old man.

"Excuse me, have you seen my fiancée?" Jope asked.

"Ahh yes, the lady, Emma. She gave me an envelope to give to you and left about an hour ago," said the owner.

He retrieved the sealed envelope from under the front counter and gave it to Jope who tore it open.

It read, 'My Love, I always wanted to see Sweden. Forgive me.'

"Which way did she go?" Jope barked.

The old man's bespectacled face went pale. "The young lady was walking toward the beach. Is everything alright?" said the owner.

Jope was running. He burst through the front door and sprinted for the beach. It was only five hundred meters but he was exhausted by the time he reached the water's edge. A soft breeze blew from the south, barely ruffling the top of the sea. In the distance he could see a couple walking but there was no sign of Emma. He turned and ran north for a few seconds until he found a man leaning on a crutch, throwing a stick to his dog.

"Have you seen a young woman walking by herself?" Jope panted.

The man looked at him in alarm but shook his head. He turned and ran back the other direction for a few hundred meters when he saw a jumper and thin coat lying on the beach. Picking it up, he noticed they were Emma's. A set of footsteps led to the water and he waded out until his feet couldn't touch the bottom. Then he screamed her name.

The police station was austere and cold. Jope had changed his clothes but it hadn't taken the chill from him body. Emma had managed to swim probably two kilometers before exhaustion had robbed her of the strength to move, then the tide and local current swept her body further east. A local naval launch found her just before nightfall and brought her ashore. Jope identified the corpse and slumped in a chair in the outer office. The local officers briefly interviewed him, then drove him back to the hotel where they spoke to the owner. Both of the older men looked at him with sad eyes and he wanted to scream at them. Instead, he looked at them and bit his lip.

"It was too much for her, what they asked her to do, far too much," he said.

Both of the men looked away and shuffled their feet. Yes, you don't want to know what happens at the camps, he thought to himself. None of you do. That way you can pretend it wasn't you; it was the

300

Nazis who took such drastic action against our enemies. Cowards.

He strode to his room and slammed the door and that's when the doubts came. It was only then he started to understand the torment that Emma must have felt.

Chapter Eight: Autumn 1943

"So we are back at the Dnieper River," said Grossadmiral Wever.

"Retired there in good order, according to my sources," said Admiral Canaris.

It was the first time the two men had seen each other in over two months and they both had a lot to catch up on.

"The summer offensive was a complete failure. It took the army so long to start the attack toward Tula and Kaluga that the enemy was waiting for them."

"Manstein broke through; it was the diversionary attacks by the Soviets to take Belgorod and Kharkov that bled the strength away from our thrust. That and the Russian offensive to open a land route to Leningrad."

"Everywhere they grow stronger, while we become weaker."

"And the fact the Artic convoys have been stopped, turns out to be worthless. The Allies are just sending the Russians war material via Persia."

"All those ships lost, for very little return," said Wever.

"But the Führer doesn't see it that way?"

"We managed to convince him it was a strategic victory, though he wasn't very happy about the loss of capital ships. The sinking of enemy battleships and a carrier mollified him somewhat."

"I thought one of the battleships didn't sink," said Canaris.

"Our Führer doesn't know that yet, and I'm going to put off telling him for as long as possible."

"That seems wise."

"Now that the Allies have landed on Sicily I have been ordered to transfer all of our naval air reserve south."

"Just at the time the British will start sending convoys via the Artic again."

"We probably have a month before they will try, however that's not what worries me. It's the overwhelming strength of the allied air forces. The Luftwaffe lost five hundred day fighters in the last three months and one thousand five hundred aircraft of all types, compare with the loss to our naval air contingent of two hundred and forty-three aircraft. We are making enough aircraft now to replace those destroyed but it's the pilots that are the problem. There just aren't enough of them. Training time has been cut again, as has the fuel allocation to the flight schools. I'm keeping the most experienced units in the Artic where blind flying and navigating over vast distances is important but..."

"That means those men facing the full strength of the Americans and the British over Sicily are under trained."

"Exactly."

"The writing is on wall."

"Yes, we have truly lost the war. Hamburg, Stalingrad, Tula and the destruction of our fleet at the Battle of Spitzbergen all underline this fact."

"If we replace Hitler and try and sue for peace, Germany will have little to bargain with," said Canaris.

"Space and casualties, that's all we will have left. We still hold much of Europe."

"Less every day."

"Indeed, and the Soviets won't care about the price they need to pay in blood for defeating us. The Allies might."

"Roosevelt and Churchill hate us."

"They hate Hitler and his cronies."

"Well, we have to show that we can be trusted. At the same time, we bleed them."

"The Russians must be held. It may be necessary to give ground in the west, perhaps even open a clear path for the Americans all the way to Berlin," said Wever.

"I hope it doesn't come to that," said Canaris.

"If it becomes the only option, then we take it. We don't want Stalin west of the Oder."

"On that, I think all Germans will agree."

"In the meantime, this coup needs to be well organised. When Hitler dies so must Himmler, Goebbels and Bormann."

"With your assistance and the recent defeats, more Generals are coming on board."

"We have to be ready by the end of the year. If the war stretches into 1944, Germany will be lucky to survive."

V

The bomber grew in his sights. Kapitänleutnant Hans-Joachim Marseille aimed at the wings of the B-17, hoping to cripple the aircraft rather than kill the crew. He knew that with the closing speed of the two aircraft he only had a couple of seconds in which to fire. He waited until the bomber filled his sights, then depressed the button. Bullets and cannon shells ripped through the wing and the inner port engine. A slight touch on the rudder sent more projectiles into the outer engine. Marseille eased back on the stick and flashed across the top of the formation with his Schwarm. His target was drifting out of box of enemy bombers with two smoking engines, while another spiralled toward the ground. He led his group upward while a group of Italian Fiat G 55s streaked toward the enemy. Another plane fell in flames while two more suffered damage.

Marseille had been back with his Staffel for a week now, but the opportunity to fly to the Allies had yet to present itself. So far he had been defending Rome against attack by heavy and medium bombers. He didn't know that this raid would be the last as President Roosevelt would declare the city off limits for US bombers, however the port town of Naples would still be attacked and the American aircraft would be escorted by P-38Hs. Marseille didn't think the US heavy fighters were particularly difficult opponents, however they were still a distraction.

He needed a mission that would take him close to Malta or the allied landing grounds on Sicily. From the air base near Naples his Staffel was in striking distance of the allied fleet. Yes, it was a flight of four hundred and fifty kilometers, but that was well within the range of the Me 155. All that was needed was an escort for a force of German bombers, as they tried to hit enemy ships. The problem was the naval air attack contingent of the Kriegsmarine had been decimated during recent attempts. The Germans had few attack aircraft to send at the Allies, and so the Me 155 Staffels found themselves defending cities and factories from enemy bombers.

His fighter came down lightly on the concrete runway and Marseille taxied it into one of the earthen barriers. He walked back to the briefing room past Italian fighters sitting in hangars while being repaired by mechanics. Germany's allies now had some very good planes and he wished they'd made them operational earlier in the war. These were Macchi 205 and had been used to fly missions protecting the mainland. Marseille heard they had fought a large battle against American B-25s and P-38 fighters the previous day. He'd flown all of the three late war fighters and thought the Reggaine Re.2005 the best, though in reality there was little difference between them.

After reporting his one hundred and eightieth kill, he walked to the command building but was met on the way by a Matrose from the wireless room.

"Sir, orders for tomorrow," said the young man.

Marseille took the piece of paper and suppressed a grin. They were to escort a group of Ju 188s on a special mission. Some Fiat G 55s were to go with them and the orders were very specific about staying with the bombers and making sure they made it to their targets. Marseille didn't care about the mission itself; he was more interested in the opportunity it gave him to fly to an allied air strip.

The briefcase containing details of the Final Solution to the Jewish Question, along with photographs and maps, were placed in his cockpit in the morning. Marseille planted the case whilst he pretended to check the maintenance work from the previous night. He put a grenade and a small bottle of Schnapps under the seat then took off. The grenade was to destroy the aircraft and the bottle was for a quick drink before going into captivity. The truth was he didn't partake of alcohol much anymore, but this would be a special occasion. The Staffel formed up around him and he led the fighters south over the ocean before flying over Sicily itself. Just off the coast of the island they met the Ju 188s. Marseille thought he could see a strange device hanging beneath each of the twelve machines but he had no idea what they were. As they flew, the cloud thickened, but not enough to be a hazard. Marseille was glad of the extra cover as it would allow him to slip away from his Staffel more easily.

It only took half an hour to fly over the hilly interior of Sicily and reach the invasion beaches, where the 3rd US infantry Division was coming ashore. He noted a number of transport vessels and cruisers in the distance and waited for the Ju 188s to make their attack runs. However, when they bombers were still five kilometers from their targets they all released the strange devices that hung under the bellies of the aircraft. A flare burst into life on the back of the unusual bombs and Marseille watched them fall toward the distant ships. Suddenly he noted that some of the bombs changed direction. That was when he understood these were the new guided munitions which were rumoured to have been used against enemy ships off the coast of Norway.

Flak exploded nearby. The bombers were well inside the range of the allied ships. They had held their fire until now in order not to waist ammunition. Now that the Ju 188s had dropped some sort of weapon they all started firing. The problem for the bombers was they had to fly straight and slow down as the bombardier guided the Fritz X onto its target. Still, they were more accurate than normal bombs and lowered the chance of being shot down quite markedly. One Ju 188 was hit and another damaged, yet six of the missiles hit their targets. A Fritz X hit the number 3 turret of the USS Savanah, passing through three decks to explode in the lower ammunition handling room. The device blew a hole in the keel and tore a seam along the hull. Secondary explosions then wracked the ship but eventually the crew sealed the damaged sections and made a slow journey back to Tunisia. The light cruiser HMS Uganda was also hit, but didn't survive as the guided bomber penetrated the forward magazine and the ship blew up with a huge roar. A destroyer was struck near the stern. The USS Pringle drifted helplessly, while other destroyers took off her crew before she sunk two hours later. A freighter was also destroyed and a sloop heavily damaged by a near miss.

Marseille saw none of this, as Spitfires from the recently occupied island of Pantelleria dived out of the clouds straight at the Ju 188s. Fiat G 55s met the attacking British fighters but an American P-38 Lightning also tried to intercept the German bombers. Marseille led his Staffel in a tight turn straight at the enemy formation. The two groups flashed through each other, neither being able to line up a shot. The sky was suddenly full of twisting and turning aircraft and Marseille used the opportunity to hall his stick into his chest and climb vertically for about five hundred meters. This maneuver lost his wingman and allowed him to turn away from the fighting in order to fly south to an allied air base.

He saw the two Spitfires out of the corner of his eye at the last second and hauled the Me 155 around in a tight turn, narrowly avoiding a burst of cannon fire. These planes were Mark VIII types with normal wing tips and arguably the best Spitfire ever made. Marseille's turn brought him into position to make a snap deflection shot on the second machine. The quick burst slammed into the engine causing a stream of black smoke to pour from under the aircraft .The plane immediately went into a dive, then the canopy snapped back and the pilot tumbled free, the parachute opening a second later.

Marseille had no time to feel pleased that his opponent had escaped as the second Spitfire had rolled over and was now trying to get on his tail. Flight Lieutenant George Beurling had already made thirty kills over the Mediterranean, mainly over Malta and then, after he'd escaped the fall of the island, over Tunisia. Marseille half rolled and then dived to gain a little speed before performing an Immelmann turn to face his opponent head on. Beurling chose not to exchange fire but dived, then tried to turn behind Marseille. Anticipating the move Marseille climbed and dived, forcing his opponent to follow him. The scissor maneuver caused Beurling to overshoot. As soon as the British pilot realised his mistake he threw his aircraft into a tight turn. The deflection shot was difficult but Marseille managed to hit the tail of the Spitfire with at least three cannon shells and a number of bullets.

The Spitfire struggled to maintain lateral control and Marseille closed in and placed a short burst into his opponent's engine. Flames erupted, flowing back toward the cockpit. The British pilot hesitated before jumping and received burns to his face and hands before leaping free. Marseille watched the parachute open before radioing to his Staffel that he was hit. Immediately his wingman called for his location so Marseille answered with a scream and shut his radio down. He then flew into a bank of cloud further inland before turning back out to sea ten minutes later.

Cruising at four hundred and fifty kilometers per hour the flight to his old base at Pantelleria only took fifteen minutes. Four Spitfires met him off the coast but he dropped his wheels and waggled his wings as a sign that he was going to surrender. The British fighters followed him down as he lined up with the tarmac, and Marseille understood that any suspicious move would see his aircraft shot out of the sky. As he came in to land he saw a pair of jeeps loaded with armed men and noted all the anti-aircraft guns were manned. He smiled as he landed and taxied to a stop at the end of the runway. As the jeeps raced down the concrete he climbed out of his cockpit and dropped the modified grenade on the seat. One of the armourers had told him months ago that it was a variety with a twenty second fuse. He pulled the cord and had jumped down off the wing and walked away from the fighter. Marseille carried his briefcase in one hand and his hip flask in the other. He took a swig and felt the liquid burn as it ran down the back of his throat.

Two men in British uniforms ran toward him carrying rifles and some strange submachine gun with the magazine protruding from the side. He took another long swig before placing the flask and the briefcase on the ground.

"Keep them up, Fritz," said one of the men.

His partner moved toward the fighter and Marseille decided it wouldn't be a good idea if he started his captivity by blowing up a British soldier.

"Ah, I wouldn't go over there just yet," he said in slightly accented English.

The man stopped and eyed him suspiciously. Then an explosion tore open the cockpit of the Me 155 and Marseille winced.

"Now we should probably move away in case the fuel tanks go up," Marseille said.

The second jeep arrived as the two soldiers hustled Marseille away from the plane.

"You are welcome to the spirits," he said to one of the soldiers.

The young man bent to retrieve the hip flask, then picked it up and took a sniff.

"Whisky?" he said

"Better, its Schnapps," said Marseille.

The other man was older than the one holding the flask and his face wrinkled. "He's not your new mate, Stompy," the man growled. "Come on Jerry, you better come with us."

The men from the second jeep walked over and Marseille could see one of them was a pilot and probably an officer. He saluted the man.

"My name is Kapitänleutnant Hans-Joachim Marseille and I surrender myself to you. Oh, and your superiors might be interested in what's in the briefcase," he said.

"Not the Marseille, the naval ace?" asked the young officer.

"You have heard of me?"

"Sir, it is a pleasure to meet one of our most respected foes. Your ability and chivalry are well known on this side of the lines. There are many people who will want to talk to you."

"I expect so," said Marseille.

V

The Ju 290 flew out over the Bay of Biscay with three other machines. Kapitän Helmut Bruck knew that this was the best defence against the marauding twin engined British machines. The newer Mosquito fighters were the greatest threat. With their high speeds, long range and heavy armament, they were deadly to the Ju 290s. The only protection the four engined reconnaissance plane had was fighter escort or mutual support. As most of the Kriegsmarine fighters had been sent to Italy, and the Luftwaffe was busy defending the Homeland, then flying in groups was the only answer.

Today the Ju 290s carried Henschel Hs 293 anti-shipping guided missiles. These weapons weren't armour piercing but were perfect for destroying enemy destroyers and frigates. A convoy had been spotted by U-706. The boat had subsequently disappeared and had probably been sunk. Bruck felt for the men in the submarine arm as their life expectancy these days seemed rather short. Now it was the submarines that often as not called the Ju 290s to a target. The new guided ordinance had been in use for some time and certainly increased the chance of hits, while making it easier to survive an attack. The problem was making it to the target in the first place.

At least since the codes had changed, the enemy convoys didn't seem to disappear before the German bombers arrived. The flight was uninterrupted and soon Bruck noted smoke on the horizon. The plan was to sink as many of the escorts as possible, allowing the U-boats to attack unimpeded. Unfortunately this rarely happened as the enemy just called up more escorts, of which there seemed to be an unending supply, or enemy aircraft found the submarines and drove them away or sank them.

Bruck shook his head and wondered at the point of it all. Now the USA had ramped up its production, the amount of enemy planes and ships increased exponentially. He'd seen so many of his friends die or fail to return from missions and he felt it was just a matter of time before he'd join them. Bruck shook his head. He was a professional and there was a job to do.

When they were about ten kilometers from the convoy, the flight split into two groups. Bruck wasn't expecting single engined fighters, as an escort carrier hadn't been spotted. He grunted and thought of his Staffel's last attack when British Hellcat fighters had shot down two Ju 290s in a matter of minutes. Bruck and another plane only escaped because of the thick cloud cover in the area. Today the enemy didn't have one of the small carriers attached to the convoy, though Bruck pondered it was wouldn't be long before nearly everyone did.

"Not much cloud today team, but watch the crosswind. It may make the rockets a little harder to guide," radioed Bruck.

Flak exploded nearby, causing flashes of red, followed by a black puff of smoke.

The range was extreme for the enemy guns as the Hs 293 had a range of almost six kilometers at the altitude they were flying. The range of the four point seven-inch guns was fifteen kilometers, but beyond four it became very difficult to hit a moving aircraft. The rate of fire of about ten rounds a minute did increase the chances of a hit, and Bruck understood that his plane was still vulnerable.

He waited until his bombardier released the missile and then turned parallel to the target. The bombardier guided the weapon downward and then over the wave tops until it smashed into the side of a British I-class destroyer. The Isis was struck near the bow and lost most of that section of the ship. She filled with water and sank quickly taking most of her crew down with her. Bruck turned the big aircraft away, satisfied he had chipped away at the enemy's strength. The rest of his flight weren't as lucky and the only other hit was on a merchant vessel, which was badly damaged.

As they flew east the weather started to cloud over. That was probably why the four Ju 290s didn't see the Mosquitos until they were on top of them. One of large German aircraft caught fire as 20mm shells raked it from end to end. A second Ju 290 lost a wing as the four cannons in the nose of the British aircraft cut through the structure near the fuselage. Bruck immediately ordered the two remaining aircraft to dive, only levelling out at one hundred meters above the waves. He put out frantic calls for help as the four enemy planes circled before diving in to attack from behind. Recently promoted Ober-matt Helmut Khole immediately opened fire from his position in the tail. The gunner hadn't lost any of his skill and his shells punched through the port engine of the leading machine, causing it burst into flames. The British pilot pulled up sharply and shut down the engine which made the extinguished the fire. The other Mosquitos turned away and flew in a circle before following the Ju 290s from a distance. One of the enemy machines then turned and flew home with the wounded fighter, while the other two approached the two German bombers head on.

The Ju 290 on his left caught a full two second burst through the cockpit and forward gunner's position. The plane dropped like a stone and smashed into the ocean, disappearing in an explosion of water. Bruck jinked his plane sideways as soon as he saw the first shells leave the cannons of the other Mosquito. A line of spray indicated where the fighter's bullets had hit the water. Then the plane flashed by and started to climb. Khole took aim, but it moved out of his field of fire and none of his shells hit. The two planes turned back and Bruck felt sweat trickling down his spine. The British fighters wouldn't miss his aircraft again. Two Fw 190 A-5s dropped through the clouds and caught the enemy by surprise. Both of the Mosquitos were hit. One caught fire and cartwheeled across the sea as it struck the ocean at a shallow angle, while the other escaped into the clouds with smoke pouring from the starboard engine. The two Luftwaffe fighters then pulled up next to the Ju 290 and waggled their wings before flying off to the north east. Bruck laughed and tried to stop his hands from shaking. He'd been sure they were going to die.

"Our famous luck still holds, skipper," radioed Khole from the rear of the plane.

Yes, but for how much longer, thought Bruck.

Chapter Nine: Winter 1943/44

"The uniform demonstration is tomorrow. This time it is definitely going ahead, so we need to be ready," said Admiral Canaris.

"You've made sure the bomb is one of the best?" asked Grossadmiral Wever.

"This is a special explosive we stole from the British and I believe it's quite stable until the right detonator is used to make it explode."

"We can't afford anything to go wrong. As soon as we receive news Hitler is dead, the plan needs to swing into action."

"There are two young officers who are part of the plan tomorrow. One will trigger the bomb and the other will immediately notify us of its success."

"What of the backup plan?"

"There is an older officer who can also relay news of the attack, though he won't be in close proximity to the blast."

"Good. I've taken care from my end. Rommel is in Berlin on my invitation and will only become involved once success has been proven to him. Field Marshal Erwin von Witzleben will take control of the army and General Beck will mobilize the replacement army. I've also created a number of battalion sized units commanded by officers loyal to me. They are on their way to key locations around Germany to facilitate the takeover. Every group has a list of people who must be arrested."

"Claus von Stauffenberg will stay in Berlin and attempt to persuade commanders of frontline units to support us. He know who must be shot."

"We will have to arrest Reichsmarschall Kesselring. He has not responded to any of the tentative suggestions that something needs to be done about Hitler. He still thinks the new weapons, like his jets, can save the day. I don't know who he thinks is going to fly them. We have lost so many pilots of late, it's become distressing," said Wever

"As an aside, the navy will have some soon won't it?"

"I've made it a priority to have at least one Staffel of Arado Ar 234s in service by June 1st. Other projects are also being fast-tracked, like the four engined Heinkel He 343. Anyway, they might not even be needed if we can pull this off."

"I have to thank you for joining us. Without your resources and support any attempt to kill Hitler and take over the country would probably have failed."

"My conscience wouldn't let me do otherwise. When the fate of the Jews and the future plans for our country became clear I was disgusted, and I also understand that we can't win this war and our country will be destroyed if I stand by."

"The Allies are already doing a good job of that from the air. Did you hear that a long range American fighter was shot down near Berlin yesterday? If our enemy can escort their bombers all the way to the targets then we will probably lose the air war."

"Jets, or no jets, eh," said Wever.

"The Me 262? It won't be operational until June."

"In the meantime the Allies have taken the bottom half of Italy and the Russians now have Kiev and are across the Dnieper River. The SS counterattacks have failed to dislodge them."

"One of the operations came close."

"Yes, but in the end the Soviets held and now the SS formations are exhausted."

"Not necessarily a bad thing. A weakened SS is good for our plans."

"The Crimea has been cut off, and US and British bombers are pounding Berlin."

"But the Allies haven't landed in France yet," said Canaris.

"Now, on another front, have you seen the proposed peace deal that Stauffenberg and his crew want to offer the Allies? It is pure fantasy. Germany at its 1914 boundaries, keeping Austria within the Reich, and no handing over of war criminals to the Allies. It's insane. They will never go for it."

"I know, but let Stauffenberg try. We need to start formulating our own conditions."

"The Russians will be the problem. Stalin wants to occupy Berlin and destroy the country."

"We can't let that happen."

"So we will bend all our demands to that effort. If the Allies are just going to destroy our country anyway, then we'll fight on," said Wever.

"Agreed," sighed Admiral Canaris.

V

The area for the demonstration of the army's new winter uniforms was one of the bunkers at the Wolf's Lair in East Prussia.

The room was cold despite the electric heater sitting in a corner glowing merrily. Hauptmann Ewald-Heinrich von Kleist was only twenty-two years old, but already he'd seen death and destruction. He had fought in Russia and been wounded there the previous year. Von Kleist had always hated the Nazis and the sacrifice that he planned today would take that loathing to it natural conclusion. He loathed the man who now walked into the cold bunker with his entourage. Martin Bormann was there as was Field Marshal Wilhem Keitel. Von Kleist detested both men and was glad that both would soon be dead. Three SS guards were deployed to the back of the room and he decided it was time to strike. Hitler walked toward the row of dummies wearing the uniforms and then turned to look at von Kleist.

"Don't I know you?" asked the Führer.

Von Kleist pulled the cord attached to the bottom of his briefcase and strode forward. He recited the Lord's Prayer in his mind and tried to remember how long the fuse was. Ten seconds or five?

Three paces from Adolf Hitler the bomb detonated. The briefcase was packed with small pieces of steel as well as the two kilo charge of explosives. The time it took for the detonator to explode was twelve seconds and there had been a moment when Kleist stood in front of the German leader with his face white and his hand shaking. At that point the Führer's eyes grew wide and he turned his head to say something. The blast cut him short and everyone in the room died as small pieces of metal flew about the room. It is probable that the blast alone would have killed everyone in that small room, as there was nothing to deflect the force of the explosion.

Outside the bunker Colonel Wessel von Loringhoven was surprised by the force of the blast, but rushed into the room to make sure everybody was dead. It took a moment for him to see through the smoke and when he did he almost gagged. Body parts were thrown around the room and the walls were covered in blood. It was obvious that nobody could have survived the blast. He relayed the information to Major Axel von dem Bussche, who then walked into the main conference room where he pulled out his Walter PPK service pistol and started shooting people. Generaloberest Alfred Jodl was the first to go down, followed by Otto Dietrich, then Bussche ordered everyone else to surrender. A few officers rushed at him, and he shot them as well before drawing a second weapon; this time a Luger P08 to deter any other possible attackers and the rest of the officers were held captive. This move was designed to create confusion while General Erich Fellgiebell rang Admiral Canaris and also General Fromm to pass on the news that Hitler was dead. Then with the help of others involved in the plot, all communications from the Wolf's Lair were shut down, with telephone lines being cut and radios smashed. A gun battle broke out with the SS guards and eventually the surviving insurgents retreated into the nearby forest, where many of them fought to their death. Bussche died trying to shoot his way out of the command bunker, but he and many of his hostages were killed by grenades. The battle raged for over an hour, completely disrupting any chance of the General Staff interfering in the coup.

Then Operation Thor swung into action. Phone calls were sent to all plotters stating that the SS had killed Adolf Hitler and an interim military government would take control and prevent this stab in the back from derailing the war effort. A six man squad made their way to the Reich Ministry of Public Enlightenment and Propaganda, while a company secured the Reich Chancellery across the road. These six officers burst into Josef Goebbels' officer and shot him dead as he rose from behind his desk. Hans Fritzsche and Hasso von Wedel were then found and killed, as these two important men were deemed too dangerous to keep alive. The home of Radio Berlin, the Haus des Randfunks was occupied by a company of naval infantry and the announcer told to broadcast the story about the SS assassination of Adolf Hitler and the Army and Navy's determination to not allow this stab betrayal to undermine the German war efforts. Heinrich Himmler was blamed for the death of the German leader and a string of arrests then took place.

All did not go to plan as the SS school at Bad Tolz tried to send officer cadets to nearby Munich to take control of the city and these men clashed with soldiers from the 174th Reserve Division. Twenty SS men and eight from the army were killed in a firefight, before the former company withdrew to their training facility. Around Berlin SS troops mainly drifted toward Niederkirchnerstrasse and the SS Reich Main Security Office. Both Heinrich Himmler and Ernst Kaltenbrunner were in residence when the coup started, and attempts to arrest both men resulted in gun battles between Kriegsmarine troops and SS guards. Gestapo men blazed away with submachine guns and pistols, while others fired down into the streets with MG 42 machine guns.

The naval company were forced to retreat, leaving dead on the roads. Other SS men fought their way to the area, some ending up in battles with soldiers from the army who had set up roadblocks. Units of the SS however, made it through to the SS Reich Main Security Office, swelling the numbers defending the area.

For the coup leaders everything was going as well as could be expected. Many Generals agreed to follow their lead, for now, while

Rommel went on radio and swore to defend Germany and protect the country against the SS. The two panzer schools had been brought over to the coup forces at least two months earlier and the heavy equipment they provided proved essential. The division Panzer Lehr advanced from Verdun into western Germany. It sent three columns of infantry, armour and heavy guns to Frankfurt, Stuttgart and Cologne.

The panzer school at Zossen was supposed to send its forces straight to Berlin. Instead, it was forced to deal with SS guards who blocked its way. These men were under the command of Standartenführer Anton Kaindl. Indeed the SS guards at many of the camps became a major issue over the following days, as they either fled or joined a growing insurrection against the new government.

A day after the coup, most of the army had agreed to support the new regime. The strongest SS units were at the front, but Oberst-Gruppenführer Sepp Dietrich surprised the coup organisers by agreeing to cooperate with them, as long as they didn't persecute his men. Most of the SS divisions were in Russia except for two new formations which were in France. The leadership agreed not to break up the formations, with the exception of the 12th SS Division forming in Belgium. In Germany itself the SS mobilised using security personnel and SS guards. It was fortunate these units had little opportunity to get their hands on heavy equipment, and those that did, didn't have the training to use it correctly.

The naval forces had deployed effectively and quickly throughout Germany, placing Admiral Doenitz and Reichsmarschal Kesselring under house arrest. 88mm guns were moved by truck or half-track to locations where fighting was occurring with the SS, providing the fire power to force these units to surrender. However, in the middle of Berlin, Reichsführer Heinrich Himmler still held out. The area around the Reich Main Security Office was quickly fortified and reinforced with flak weapons taken from local Luftwaffe units. Of course, at the front, the war continued as though nothing had happened. Leningrad was free from its siege and Russian forces had reached the border of Estonia, but elsewhere the lines hardly moved. This wasn't the case in the air, with raids occurring on Berlin the night after the coup, followed up by another the following evening. During the day however, the skies were clear.

V

Himmler had betrayed Germany, but worse he had betrayed Emma's memory. His fiancée had been driven to take her own life by what the leader of the SS had forced her to do, and now this man had killed their country's leader. Fregattenkapitän Bernhard Jope was enraged by the news he was listening to. Field Marshal Erwin Rommel was speaking on the radio about how everyone in Germany must rise up to defend the country from those who would destroy it. This man was one of the most revered Generals of the war. His broadcasts had made it quite clear that Himmler was the one behind the attack which had killed the Führer. Rommel was obviously ready to support a regime that stood against Hitler's killer.

The base commander stood before them, his face grey. The briefing room was filled with men of all ranks, and the older officer signalled that the radio be turned off.

"You've all heard the news and it's shocking. I'm not really sure what's going on but I've just received disturbing orders," said the older man. "Our security forces, or at least a far part of them are being sent to Ravensbruck and the surrounding camps to disarm the SS."

The room filled with muttering and Jope leaned forward to hear as the commanding officer called for quiet. "Alright, there's more," the man yelled.

The room hushed and their commanding officer looked down at a piece of paper he held in his hand.

"We've been asked to bomb SS positions in Berlin, namely the Reich Main Security Office."

A gasp went up from the assembled group and Jope felt a vein in his temple throb.

"It is believed that Reichsführer Heinrich Himmler is in the building and trying to take over the country. Luckily the Heer has prevented him from doing so, if you believe that's what has happened, but he is fighting on."

"You don't believe that the Reichsführer killed the Führer, sir?" called a pilot.

"I don't know what to think; however, I'm loyal to Grossadmiral Wever and follow his orders. He wants us to bomb this target, so we shall. I'll take one of the Ju 88s and a crew of volunteers. I recognise it is difficult to ask you men to attack other Germans; so despite my orders, which I will obey, I will not ask you to do likewise. This trip is strictly for volunteers."

Jope didn't hesitate. "I'll go, sir," he said.

The commander nodded. Eventually four other pilots agreed, though not every aircraft had a crew. No one wanted to go with Jope and he didn't blame them. Many of the men couldn't kill other

Germans, while others remained unsure of what was really going on.

After looking at street maps of Berlin, and a briefing about the weather and expected opposition, Jope found himself alone. He had agreed to pilot his aircraft by himself and now tried to understand how Germany had just been turned on its head. He wasn't worried about flying the plane alone, knowing that the navigation to Berlin would be easy and he could drop the bombs himself. The range was just over two hundred kilometers from Rugen Island and he had flown to the Tempelhof Airfield more than once to pick up important parts. He wondered why the Luftwaffe weren't performing this mission but then decided that perhaps they were going to sit tight until the change of leadership had settled down and the traitor Himmler and the plotters were all destroyed.

He would do this for Emma. She had been destroyed and now betrayed by the very organisation she had trusted. He remembered the cold attitude of her commanding officer Chef Oberaufseherin, Anna Klein. The woman had given him her condolences and then stated she never thought Emma was suited

to the role of guarding the scum who would bring Germany down.

He remembered the fury he felt at the time. The Chef

Oberaufseherin must have noted it too, as her eyes grew wide as

she stepped away from him. Now that anger would be released on

those who let Emma down.

The Ju 88 flew through low cloud and the occasional shower

of rain until reaching the forests around Templin, about seventy

kilometers north of the capital. There were raids by the US 8th Army

Air Force but these were all further west near Munster, Hannover

and Brunswick. The area around the capital was clear of enemy

planes. Over the city it seemed calm until Jope turned his aircraft

toward central Berlin. Then the odd burst of ground fire rose up

from different locations, especially near the air base. It seemed the

Luftwaffe was sending a signal for the Kriegsmarine to keep its

planes away. 20mm and 37mm automatic weapons sprayed shells

into the sky and the occasional 88mm shell exploded near the Ju

88s.

The commander of the four attack planes led the flight in a route that took them away from the airfield and over the zoo and central gardens. Then all of the Ju 88s dropped lower and started a shallow dive toward Niederkirchnerstrasse. Jope knew the target would be difficult to hit as he didn't want to accidently bomb a civilian building. There was however a park to the south of the target, and this was the direction that Jope and his companions had been told to attack from. As he followed the other planes in, flak erupted from guns on the roof and from the park behind the building. His leader's aircraft was immediately hit in the wings and cockpit. It fell sideways, flames licking along the fuselage and from the engine, before it ploughed into the ground just short of the target. The resulting explosion blew trees and park benches into the air. The second Ju 88 panicked when it saw the aircraft's fate and pulled out too soon, its bombs falling on the Foreign Office which now occupied the old President's Palace. The minister, Joachim von Ribbentrop, was in the cellar at the time the weapons detonated and the building collapsed as six five hundred kilo devices blasted the palace into rubble.

As the third aircraft attacked, it sprayed the roof of the building with 20mm shells, killing one of the flak crews. The pilot pushed his attack until the last moment and then had to pull out of his steep dive quickly. In doing so he pulled the bomb release too late, the weapons landing on the New Reich's Chancellery Building. A number of SS troops fired from the windows of the building until the bombs blew a section of the front wall across the street.

Jope witnessed the failure of his comrades to destroy the Reich Main Security Office, and felt his heart pounding. Something told him this was the moment he could strike a blow for Emma and perhaps make a statement for Germany. He lined up his plane on the five story building and made a careful approach. Every gun in the area aimed at his Ju 88 and he felt the aircraft shudder as 20mm shells ripped into the fuselage. A 37 mm projectile smashed into the starboard engine, almost pulling the controls from his hands. He glanced out of the cockpit window and saw a ribbon of fire spread along the wing. I'm sorry Emma, I hope my message of revenge reaches you. He aimed the plane at the lower floors of the building and rode the burning aircraft all the way into the structure. When the Ju 88 exploded most of the building erupted in flames, before collapsing in on itself.

Heinrich Himmler was on his way down to the basement via the stairs as electricity had been cut to the area and the lifts were out. He had just reached the ground floor when the Ju 88 impacted the rear of the structure. Ruptured fuel tanks spewed petrol through the lower areas of the building before catching alight. The leader of the SS and his entourage were covered in the liquid and quickly became living torches when the fuel ignited, then the building crashed down on top of them.

V

Field Marshal Erwin Rommel walked through the ruins of the government area of Berlin with Grossadmiral Wever. They were accompanied by an escort of men from a detachment of the Panzer Lehr Division which had sent a mixed force to the capital. SS men

344

sat with their hands tied behind their backs while naval ratings stood by pointing rifles in their direction.

"So it is over, Field Marshal?" asked Wever.

"There is still some fighting in the south near Dachau and Munich, but mainly it's done. The cooperation of the navy and your organisational skills helped us coordinate most of our efforts. We owe you our gratitude, Grossadmiral."

"My conscience gave me no choice."

"Be that as it may, you took a huge risk and it succeeded."

"We all took a risk."

"But you were involved a lot longer than I was. I thought the stories of Nazi atrocities were exaggerated. I've been trying to find out what happened to my wife's uncle, a Polish priest, for years and now I discover he was killed days after I visited him in 1939. Its only now that I can access the records and I know that the SS were keeping this from my family." Rommel sighed. "I've been a naïve fool."

"To start with I thought our Führer was exactly what our country needed, and I supported his plans. I read his book and thought Germany did need living space; however, I didn't realise that we would murder and starve the Slavs until the east was empty."

"Our nation has behaved without honour, and now I hear there are death camps across the Reich and occupied territories?"

"It is true and it's a horror we must soon confront."

"First things first. We need to make sure we form a new government and the people are reassured. It is a pity we will have to keep the story of the SS killing the Führer going. I don't like lying."

"We must for now, but the day will come when we can share what we did with the country and explain our actions."

"As for the government, it is confirmed that Beck will be president?"

"Yes, and I will be chancellor while Goerdeler will be vice chancellor. We were wondering if you wanted to lead the army?"

"God no, my place is at the front. I need to be with my troops. I suggest von Rundstedt runs the whole show with von Manstein in control of things in the east and give Guderian the west, though make Speidel his Chief of Staff. "

"Why? I thought you would want to keep Speidel close to you. He is also being considered as our Foreign Minister."

"He is one of the smartest military minds in the army, and I also don't trust Guderian. That man needs watching. Has Kesselring come around?"

"Now that it's all over, he says he will cooperate. I think his focus, however, is on the developing air battles over the capital. At first he was furious, but now I think he sees what we have done as a necessary evil," said Wever.

"I suppose we need him, for now."

"Kesselring is not irreplaceable but I would like to keep disruption to a minimum."

"We will still have to clean house. The roots of the Nazi Party have spread throughout our country," said Rommel.

In the distance they heard a volley of rifle fire as a group of SS officials were executed.

"We have already started."

"There should be a proper process," objected Rommel.

"Time is of the essence. Our government must take control quickly."

"As long as we don't end up being the same as what we have replaced."

Wever shook his head. "I won't let that happen."

Chapter Ten: Spring 1944

Rommel held the handkerchief to his nose. The stench

emanating from the barracks was so overpowering that it made his

eyes water. He wished he was back in France preparing his army for

the coming invasion, but Grossadmiral Wever had thought it

important Rommel see what Hitler and his cronies had perpetrated

in Germany's name before he returned to the 7th Army.

Grossadmiral Wever stood beside the gate of Buchenwald

Concentration Camp. Inside, a number of army personnel wearing

masks rushed in and out of buildings with buckets of disinfectant.

Prisoners stood around in small groups, their skeletal arms visible

through the thin material of their striped uniforms.

"This is just a taste of what we have found, Herr Field

Marshal," said Grossadmiral Wever. "An SS Standartenführer who

used to serve here as a guard crucified priests in an upside down

position, and liked to hang prisoners in the forest by the wrists. The

guards called the local woods the singing forest because of the screaming. I thought this was an exaggeration but the commandant, one Herman Pister ignored the behaviour. It's all written down in the camp records."

Rommel's face flushed and his fists clenched. "Where is this monster now?"

"The torturer was eventually found to be even too depraved even for the SS and was sent to a frontline formation where he was killed. However, that's not the point. He is one of the few the SS found to be extreme. There are countless other cases of beatings and mass executions, and you know of the gas chambers."

"I do now."

"We had all heard the rumours, and many people knew them to be true. All of Germany is guilty for letting this happen. Now we have to care for these poor souls."

"Why did you want me to see this?"

"So you understand our county's crimes are not exaggerated. This will all be documented and those closest to the corruption charged and punished. We may need to let the Allies take part, or at least watch us bring justice to these monsters. I may need your support on this if the other generals object."

"You have it."

"No matter where it leads."

"I'm not giving you carte blanche, but overall, anything that leads to this," Rommel waved his hands at the barracks, "will bring me to your side."

"I can't ask for more."

Wever left the camp and flew back to Berlin where Fredrick von Schulenburg would meet him. The new Foreign Minister had just returned from Sweden where he had seen the representatives of all the major allied powers. The small group met in the study of Chancellor Beck at his home. Naval men protected the property, while the army brought armoured cars and parked them at either end of the street. The room was large for a study, but seemed crowded to Wever as he sat there with the three men. Schulenburg and Canaris were there along with Beck and himself.

"How did it go?" asked Beck.

The Foreign Minister shook his head. "They laughed at me."

Beck's eyes widened. "What do you mean?"

"The Allies said they want our total and unconditional surrender. They will not talk to us about the boundaries of a future Germany. The Soviets want our country broken into pieces and the Americans want us completely disarmed."

"And the British?" asked Canaris. "Did you get their representative alone?"

"They were more receptive. Now that Hitler and his cronies are gone, Churchill's representative seemed willing to listen. Your idea of letting them advance into Greece and Bulgaria; perhaps even Romania, got their attention," said Schulenburg.

"I'm not surprised. Churchill has always been a canny politician and he was willing to attack the Soviets in 1940. He distrusts Stalin as much as he did Hitler," said Canaris.

"That, and British manpower losses have been high," added Beck. "Churchill probably has an eye to the future."

"One thing is for certain; no one will accept our 1939 borders. The provinces of Alsace and Lorraine will have to be returned to France, and Austria will need to become independent again. Forget holding anything in Poland. The Americans indicated they want the borders of that country to move west, though I think they are complying with a Russian request there."

"This isn't good. Does anyone have an idea of how to convince them to compromise?" asked Beck. "Obviously our initial claims are unrealistic."

As Canaris and I told you, thought Wever. The head of the intelligence services reached into his pocket and withdrew a folded piece of paper.

"This is something Grossadmiral Wever and I have been working on. It is rough but we have to start somewhere," said Canaris.

The men gathered around the small map. Wever knew that on the back were a number of handwritten dot points.

"As you can see, we anticipated the American demand. Wever and I think that the border needs to run along the Vistula River until it turns toward Warsaw here at Bydgoszcz. Then the border follows the Notec and Warta rivers until they flow into the Oder at Kustrin."

"According to this we will lose some of Silesia, as the border follows the river almost until it reaches Czechoslovakia," said Beck.

"We need to make sacrifices to keep the Allies happy. On the back you can see we have invited all of the Allies to view the criminal trials of those involved in the murder of the Jews. We will even offer the Soviets the opportunity to extradite the most notorious of our Generals and occupying authorities," said Wever.

"That won't make the army happy," said Beck.

"I doubt it will ever happen," said Canaris. "The Soviets won't agree to a peace deal. They will want to destroy Germany."

"We are giving the Allies a lot here," said Schulenburg.

"It may be the only way to maintain an independent Germany," said Canaris.

"There is one more proposal which should help. We will offer the British and Americans the opportunity to send occupying forces into Poland," said Wever.

Beck whistled. "That will make Stalin furious."

"The British entered the war to defend Poland. This is their chance to fulfil their pledge to that nation. That's the way we will sell it anyway," said Canaris.

"I'll show this to the others, though I don't know if they'll like it," said Beck.

"Remind them of what is happening in the air. Our cities are getting pounded every day and the Luftwaffe is losing the battle," said Wever.

"Besides, we drip feed this to the Allies. I wouldn't offer it all at once. Also, we need to work on the British. They realise the danger the Soviet Union presents. The American President seems to naively trust Stalin," said Canaris.

"I'll tell them," said Beck. "What do we do in the meantime?"

"Bleed them, and give ground slowly. Strike back when we can, and show them that if they want our unconditional surrender, it will cost them," said Wever.

v

The office looked out over the Baltic. Clouds blew down from the north sweeping the ocean with tendrils of grey. It looked like a spring storm was going to hit the island, thought Wever. He turned to face Admiral Kurt Fricke. It was strange not seeing Ciliax in front of him but of course his old friend had gone down with his ship.

"So the Scharnhorst will take years to repair?" Wever asked

"We were lucky to make it back to the fjord. Four heavy cruisers proved too much for us to handle. The Moltke made a mess of the Artic convoy, sinking twelve ships, but was shattered when those destroyers put two torpedoes into her," said Fricke.

"Well, it looks like one of the American heavy cruisers sank and two of the others will be out of action for at least six months. The air strikes seemed to go well."

"Another six freighters were sunk, as well as a sloop."

"But we lost eight planes."

"Our air contingent is the only way we will be able to stop the convoys now. And every time we attack one with an escort carrier we lose more planes. The Hellcats the Allies are now using as naval fighters are almost a match for the Me 155, and the British are using a plane called the Corsair. It is probably a little better than our aircraft."

"I'll reinforce Norway with another Staffel. There's a small reserve here at Rugen so I will draw on that. Connected to the crippling of the Scharnhorst is my next issue, and you won't like it," said Wever.

"The transfer of some of our personnel to the army?"

"Yes. The losses in manpower on the eastern front have been crippling. There is no point leaving a crew of one thousand six hundred men on a damaged ship. I keep sending U-boats to sea and they just disappear under the weight of the enemy escorts. I'm wondering if it's a waste of resources."

"The navy has performed beyond expectations. We can continue to do so," said Fricke. "Less U-boats are getting sunk in transit, thanks to the new radars and radar detection units."

"Yes, but as soon as they attack a convoy they are destroyed! I've promised the army two hundred thousand men and

I'll find them. The Luftwaffe is doing the same. These troops will go to units in the west that have been pulled from Russia and have a core of veterans."

"If you are right about the timetable of the Allies and they do land in France this summer, then our men will only have two or three months to be integrated into their new units," said Fricke.

"That can't be helped. The situation is desperate and I'll do whatever I can to keep Germany from being ruined."

V

Rommel looked at the map in front of him. He had driven with his escort across Germany and France the previous evening and now stood next to Oberst Han-Ulrich Back, commander of the 16th Panzer Division.

"I think you are correct sir, to keep our formation close to the beaches. The weight of allied air power I experienced in Italy showed me how hard it is to move a motorised formation when you don't have air superiority," said Back.

"Your formation and the 21st Panzer will stay here behind the possible landing sites in Normandy. The 14th Panzer and Panzer Lehr will stay near the sites near Calais. I'm also allocating the 29th Panzer Grenadier Division to this area, though they will be closer to Cherbourg," said Rommel.

"They have panzers now, sir?"

"We have given the unit forty of the new Hetzer tank destroyers. Your unit will also receive ten."

"That's good news sir, but we will still be below strength."

"Beck, everyone is under strength, and you are at ninety percent, I checked."

"Yes sir, but we only have twenty Panthers, the rest of my armour is made up of Panzer IVs or assault guns."

Rommel shook his head. "Make do, be inventive. The 21st Panzer has many strange and wonderful vehicles thanks to Major Becker. He has mounted 75mm guns on a variety of captured

French equipment and has made the 21st the most mobile unit in the west."

"I've heard sir, but I don't have an engineer of his skill."

"Hmmm, true. I'll send him to you and to the 14th to see what he can do for you. In the meantime, train hard and put as many fortifications as you can in place. Camouflage everything extremely carefully, because our other problem will be naval bombardment."

"We will need to move and attack at night?"

"Where possible; so get to know the area. Sometimes it won't be an option but if you can move under cover of darkness do so."

The Oberst nodded and promised to try. Rommel left with an escort of an armoured car and a truck load of infantry driving back toward Paris. He wished that Speidel was there waiting for him. His chief of staff had proved to be an intelligent and decisive officer, but now he was in Berlin. He'd spoken to the man on the phone the previous evening about the situation in the East and the attempts to interest the Allies in a peace agreement. There had been little attention given to the attempt at a cease-fire as yet, and the Russians were spreading their attacks along the front line. The Battle at Narva seemed to be grinding on as was the fighting around the bridgeheads over the Dneiper River in the Ukraine. A Soviet airborne drop had been destroyed but an assault by the 3rd Tank Guards Army forced a crossing further north of the giant bend in the river and held, despite terrible losses. Yet in spite of the Soviet efforts, the line held. Rommel supposed the withdrawal of the 17th Army from the Crimea had certainly bolstered the number of German troops available for the battle. The same situation had occurred in the north of Russia where an infantry division, two mountain divisions and the SS Division Nord had been moved out of Finland and into the front around Smolensk (though the 169th Infantry was moved into reserve in Germany).

In the air the situation was deteriorating. The offensive by the US 8th Army Air Force had devastated the ranks of the Luftwaffe fighter force, with the loss of experienced pilots being particularly troubling. The switch to free fighter sweeps ahead of the main bombing raids by the US had been very effective, with the heavily armed Fw 190s being caught and shot down before they could reach the B17s. To make matters even worse the Allies had just started attacking oil facilities throughout Germany, Hungary and Romania. This was a disaster for the oil poor Reich.

Rommel went over his reserves in his mind. Many of the panzer divisions had been kept in Russia but he needed some striking power if he was to bleed the Allies. Most of the units he had were survivors from North Africa and Stalingrad. It was true these formations had fought in Italy and some, such as the 100th Jaeger Division, were still there. Rommel needed panzers and though he understood the policy to keep the SS in the front line in Russia where they couldn't do any harm to the new regime, he would have loved to have had the 1st SS Panzer Division in reserve. He had the 9th Panzer Division reforming after battles in Russia near Paris, however that was it. The 11th Panzer Division was in southern

France, but it was still a shell with only forty tanks and ten assault guns. The new 116th Panzer Division was technically available to him as it trained in Holland. Rommel understood that it was part of the Reich General Reserve and could just as easily be sent east. The 1st Panzer Division was in transit from the east, but it too was only at fifty percent of full strength and the 7th Panzer was also reforming after taking heavy losses in the battle around Kiev; though this unit was in Denmark.

This is what he had. It would have to do. At least the transfer of troops from the Luftwaffe and navy had fleshed out most of his units with decent, if half trained, infantry. The veterans they would fight next to would show them how to survive, hopefully.

In the meantime he would drive to the Luftwaffe base and have a look at the photos the new jets were bringing back from England. He was extremely pleased that the experimental aircraft had been allocated, at his request, to gathering information on the Allies' intentions. If he could narrow down the possible landing sites then it would make the placement of his forces a lot easier. The

Arado Ar 234 was fast enough to reach England and avoid interception. Gone was the ridiculous rear firing 20 mm cannons, to be replaced by two forward firing 13mm machine guns in blisters either side of the main cockpit. The machines Rommel had procured however, were unarmed, but they would prove more deadly than any aircraft of the war.

Chapter Eleven: Summer 1944

"So the English approached us for details on how their forces could land in Greece?" asked Grossadmiral Wever.

"Yes, and also what route they could take to move into Bulgaria. They were interested in possible timetables for such an advance. All hypothetical of course," said Admiral Canaris, a smirk pulling at the corner of his mouth.

"They are interested then, though we probably won't see any movement on this until after the invasion of France."

"The Americans are committed to the attack and still won't budge. Roosevelt wants an unconditional surrender and sees our nation as a militaristic threat to the future of a peaceful Europe."

"And what does he think the Soviets are?"

"Our contacts believe Roosevelt has a close relationship with Stalin. He wants the Soviets to sign up to a new version of the League of Nations, one in which the USA will actually participate."

"The fact we are cleaning house and the Russians massacred over ten thousand Poles doesn't matter to the Allies."

"My dear Wever; Hitler, no Germany, killed *millions* of people. Over four million Jews are dead, and then there are the prisoners of war, Russians and the other groups that the Nazis decided were enemies of the state."

"Stalin has killed as many in Russia."

"We think Churchill understands this, but the Americans don't."

"Then our nation will fight on."

"They leave us no other choice."

"Meanwhile, we now think we have a definite landing site worked out. Normandy, I believe, is where the Allies will come ashore?"

"The reconnaissance by jets is conclusive, though many of our agents are still telling us otherwise. I think these men have been turned and I don't trust their information. The jets have been taking photos of large areas of southern England and our experts have been pouring over them. It's taken time, and we have had to take all the radio traffic and intercepts out of the analysis. It impossible to know what is real and what isn't, but we are fairly sure that the Allies going to cross the Channel soon. The weather is poor at the moment so we should have time to get the 503rd Heavy Panzer Battalion across the Seine and the Panzer Lehr Division is already moving to Caen. The appalling weather is hiding the realignment from the enemy, though the destruction of all the bridges over the Seine are slowing the transfer of troops."

"If we can defeat the invasion, the Allies will be forced to the negotiating table."

"A big if. Then there is the Russian Juggernaut to stop as well," said Canaris.

"It's fairly quiet in the east isn't it?"

"The Soviets have launched attacks on Finland and our allies look as though they are getting ready to surrender, or at least make peace with the Russians. We delivered over ten thousand panzerfausts and a thousand panzerschrecks to them and they have an air force of over five hundred aircraft. Still, despite their strength in the air the Finns can't hold out long. This will release more Russians to attack us elsewhere."

"Where?" asked Wever.

"We think, in the south. The line along the Dnieper River still holds, though there are a number of bridgeheads on the western bank from which the army hasn't been able to dislodge the Soviets."

"We have reserves in the area?"

"A number of regular panzer divisions are present. The SS division are all on the central front, except for the 9th and 10th SS which are chasing partisans around Zhytomyr. We have not given the SS divisions replacements or panzers, so they all remain at about fifty percent of their strength. Rumour is though they have scrounged together over two hundred Soviet panzers and reconditioned them. They have welded command cupolas into some, put in radios, and in some case taken off the turret and placed one of our anti-tank guns in its place."

"But they aren't getting any more men are they?"

"To be honest, some of the SS guards from the camps have gone to them, as have a number of SS administrative personnel from Germany. We thought it was better they were at the front, where many will become casualties."

"Ruthless, but necessary," said Wever. "Alright, that's the front. What about the house cleaning?"

"It goes on. The trials of the worst defenders begin soon. The immediate executions of the most dangerous Nazis of our regime have ended, now we are arresting middle ranking officials and camp commandants."

"These trials need to be very public. We should invite the Allies to them."

"They already have a lot of the evidence. It seems sending Marseille to the English wasn't necessary," said Canaris.

"It was insurance in case the coup failed."

"Well it has created a sense of outrage and may have backfired."

"Do you regret sending him?"

"No, it was the right course of action. If we had been caught, or Himmler had taken control of Germany, then the world wouldn't have found out about the Nazi crimes until after the war is over."

"And now we are trying to save as many lives as possible."

"Yes, our coup has probably saved a million people, maybe more," said Canaris. "Of course if the war had lasted past spring next year, it would have been more like two million."

"Now it's the lives of our own people we are trying to save."

"At least the Allies have stopped bombing the capital."

"Yes, except now they have hit our oil facilities," said Wever.

"Even that has stopped. The allied air force is directing all its power into attacking communications in France."

"Yes, the invasion must be only a few weeks away. As soon as the weather clears, the British and Americans will attack."

That evening, as the storm in France eased, the Allies stormed ashore on the beaches of Normandy.

V

Kapitän Helmut Bruck eased the large bomber through the cloud cover, trying to get a view of the coast. The English Channel was full of ships, though they could only be glimpsed through the dark, due to the flares dropped by fast moving Ju 188s and Arado jet bombers. Below, a ship burned, struck by a Fritz X dropped by an earlier attack. Bruck knew that the Luftwaffe and Kriegsmarine Air Force were making an all-out attempt to disrupt allied shipping coming from Britain tonight. Wever and the High Command decided that the Allies had to be stopped.

Already there had been a victory with the destruction of the Omaha beachhead, as the Germans now knew it was called. The US forces had been mauled coming ashore and a battle group from the 16th Panzer Division based around a panzer battalion from the second regiment, and the panzer reconnaissance battalion crashed into the 1st US Infantry Division before they could become established, rolling up the Americans and forcing the survivors back into positions held by the 29th Infantry Division. The US navy had to evacuate the battered units and over six thousand prisoners were taken.

At Utah beach the Americans came ashore unmolested but were swiftly counterattacked by the other battle group from the 16th Panzer. This time the panzerjaeger battalion hit the troops from the 4th Infantry Division at Chef du Pont, forcing the allied troops back from the village. The scattered paratrooper drops from the 101st and 82nd US Airborne Divisions slowed other units from the panzer division until the tanks from the 70th US Armoured Regiment were ashore. In the end it hadn't mattered as the US forces proved too strong and forced the Germans back to the Carentan Chanel in the west and Valognes in the east. The British and Canadian lodgement was larger, taking in portions on the east bank of the Orne River to just past the town of Bayeux. The gap between the American position and the British one was still over thirty kilometers in width, and it was through this area that Bruck and his Staffel had flown.

The Americans and the British 50th Division had tried to close the gap, with the 2nd US Armoured Division landing on Gold Beach to assist in the operation. Despite the pounding the 16th Panzer and 362nd Infantry Division were receiving from offshore naval bombardments, and the strong attacks of the enemy, they were holding firm for now.

"We are looking for transport ships; these modified Fritz X devices won't penetrate the armour of anything heavier than a light cruiser," said Bruck over his radio.

Below he could see the thin line of the coast and the odd ship dimly reflected in the flare dropped by other planes.

"Skipper, there is another aircraft going down out to sea. Can't tell if it's one of theirs or ours," said his rear gunner Ober-matt Helmut Khole.

Bruck didn't reply. He knew the two Fw 190 day fighters that had accompanied them had peeled off the attack of an American night fighter earlier. A P-61 Black Widow was shot down, but the German machines couldn't find their way back to Bruck's plane in the darkness. Ju 88s fighters and even the Arados took on the enemy that evening over the beaches, after dropping flares. German torpedo planes of all types snuck in to make low level attacks while medium and heavy bombers attempted to bomb the beachheads. Bruck was looking for something large to hit with his two glide bombs.

"I see something burning near the beach," he said quietly.

"Looks like a ship," said his co-pilot. "Somebody has been effective tonight then."

"That's a breakwater nearby. We must be near the artificial pier the enemy have set up," said Bruck.

They were flying above the Arromanches Mulberry Harbour. There were two of these, the other having been moved to the Utah beachhead after the Omaha landing collapsed. The Allies were attempting to increase the amount of material landing in France, though a lot of equipment was still delivered straight onto the beaches.

"Skipper, I see a ship at the end of one of these piers," said Khole as they flew past the installation.

"Alright, let's have a crack at it. If we sink something at the end of one of the wharfs that must inconvenience the British a little," said Bruck.

He turned the Ju 290 around and flew back the way they had come, losing a little altitude as he did.

"I see it," he said.

The ship was the Mount Hood, a fourteen thousand ton freighter. She was carrying seven thousand tons of ammunition, of which only a thousand had been unloaded when Bruck released his two glide bombs. Flak exploded around his plane as his bombardier guided both weapons toward the target. Usually he would have dropped one at a time, as it was very difficult to guide both devices at once. In the end it didn't matter. The flak and glare of the burning ship didn't put the bombardier off and he managed to strike the Mount Hood with the first weapon, the second hitting the pier and failing to detonate.

The freighter exploded, obliterating the vessel and killing all of her crew, but this was the least of the destruction. All of the nearby piers were ripped apart and hurled into the air while ships capsized or were destroyed as they were caught in the blast. A staggering twenty-three landing craft sank immediately. The shock wave blew sailors off ships over five kilometers from the scene of the explosion. The force of the detonation left a trench in the mud below the ship over a thousand meters long, and over twenty meters deep. Two thousand men were killed with a similar number wounded, and the allied supply schedule was severely disrupted. When an enormous summer storm blew in three days later and wrecked the American artificial harbour, the situation became critical for a few days. Then supplies started to land directly onto the beach; but with both piers destroyed, this slowed the allied efforts to provide their troops the food and ammunition needed to attack the Germans.

"What was that?" yelled Bruck as the Ju 290 was caught by the blast wave.

"Skipper, that ship has disappeared," said Khole. "It must have been carrying ammunition."

Bruck laughed and headed inland. As he was turning the big aircraft to fly to its air base near Paris, his gunner yelled a warning.

"Break left, break left," screamed Khole.

Bruck's quick reaction saved his crew from a fiery death. As it was, the attacking Mosquito riddled the port wing with 20mm cannon shells. He heard the thump of the rear gunner's cannon and then a curse.

"I think I winged him, skipper, but I can see fire coming from our engine," said Khole.

"Shutting it down," said Bruck.

He looked out of the window a moment later and saw the fire still burning.

"Shit, we will have to bail out," he said. "We are almost over our own lines."

"Skipper, that wind is from the south. It will blow us back toward the allied positions," said Khole.

Bruck glanced at the wing and watched as the flames grew. "We have no time. All crew bail out now. That's an order."

In the time they'd been flying, Bruck thought the plane would have already covered about ten kilometers. He called out over the radio, checking to see if everybody was gone and then wedged the controls in position. Flames now ran between the inner port engine and the fuselage, and he worried that either the fuel tank would explode or the wing would buckle and then tear loose. Bruck made his way to the hatch after turning the plane gently back toward the coast. He hoped the aircraft would drop on allied troops rather than his own. As he reached the opening he glanced down at the darkened countryside and wondered what he was about to drop into.

There was a ripping sound and the plane started to twist. Bruck grabbed at the edge of the hatch but his grip was almost torn free as the Ju 290 lost its wing and started its plunge to the ground. Bruck fought against the forces that were trying to drag him back inside the aircraft with all of his strength. The hatch was right in front of him and he just needed a final effort to hurl himself free. Something else gave way within the structure of the plane and he was rocked forward. Seizing his chance he pulled himself through the door and into the night. Cold air whistled past him as he scrambled to find the release cord for the parachute. Above him fire expanded into a ball as the tanks on the Ju 290 tore apart, adding what was left of the plane's fuel to the conflagration.

But Bruck was clear. His hand found the ripcord and pulled. The parachute snapped open above him and suddenly he was floating. The only noises came from the wind, the material of the parachute, and from distant gun fire. He was almost on the ground when a huge detonation occurred somewhere to his north, back toward to invasion fleet. Bruck wondered what it was but had no time to think on the matter as the earth rushed up to meet him. He had drifted with the wind and was coming down among the small enclosed field of Normandy known as the Bocage. The town of Bayeux was a few kilometers away and Bruck was landing near the front lines of the 352nd German Infantry Division and the recently arrived US 2nd Armoured Division.

He landed at the edge of field, hitting the ground heavily with his parachute snagging on the ancient trees overhanging a small lane. Bruck slammed hard into the dirt, the wind being knocked from him before managing to grab a handful of grass to stop himself being dragged any further. The breeze kept trying to fill the parachute and he fought to collapse it. Eventually he managed to free himself and staggered over the field. The trees loomed up in front of him and he was trying to think of what to do next when a voice yelled at him in German.

"Halt and identify yourself," called the unseen man.

"Kapitän Helmut Bruck, naval pilot," he yelled.

"Password!"

"I don't know. I just jumped out of a Ju 290! We weren't told what the password was for the front line as we didn't expect to be here."

A second voice called out. "Come forward slowly."

Bruck raised his hands and walked carefully to the thick hedge when a pair of soldiers appeared and pulled him into cover. He looked at three men wearing German helmets and carrying a variety of weapons, some them American. Then he remembered this was the unit that had held the US Army on the beach until the panzers arrived and threw them back into the sea.

The oldest of the three soldiers gestured at the hedgerow on the other side of the field.

"The Americans must be asleep. They are just over there," said the Feldwebel.

"I've got movement, sir," said a young soldat carrying an M1 carbine.

The man was peering across the open ground and pointed at a glowing red dot.

"The idiot is smoking. Must be new to the front, a recruit perhaps. Strange though, this unit we are facing is supposed to have fought in Sicily and North Africa."

"Shall I shoot him, sir?" asked the soldat.

"Next time you see it glow, yeh, then we better move," said the Feldwebel.

Bruck saw the glow, then the young man fired three quick shots with the semi-automatic rifle. As the last round left his weapon, the field on the other side erupted with gun fire. The young soldat was hit in the head and throat and the other man fell moaning with a bullet in the shoulder. Bruck and the Feldwebel hit the ground next to each other.

"It was a trap," said the older man. He pulled the wounded man with him through the foliage and Bruck crawled after them. Soon mortar shells started to land and Bruck was forced to lie in a shallow ditch, while shrapnel tore through the trees and bushes around him. What a night, he thought. From blowing up a ship to this. The Feldwebel managed to get the wounded man to his feet, and guided him to a series of trenches and fox holes dug next to a hedgerow. Bruck pulled himself into the shelter as small arms fire caused the ground around him to erupt in explosions. He dived into the hole, and when he looked up, saw a grinning Ober-matt Helmut Khole.

"We should both put in for infantry assault medals, skipper," said the diminutive gunner. The man was loading an American M19 thirty calibre Browning machine gun.

"Do I dare ask where you got that from Khole?" said Bruck.

"The soldier I took it from was wounded a moment ago. I think I've worked out the basics sir, but I'll need you to load."

Across from them the enemy fire continued to grow, and in some places the Americans crept forward and threw grenades. Khole lifted the machine gun up and placed it in a tripod before squeezing the trigger. Bruck held the belt of bullets and felt them shake as they ran through his hands. Next to him he saw Khole's mouth work as he counted to four, and then stopped firing, before repeating the process a few seconds later. The gun spat at the enemy, and Bruck noted the accuracy of the little gunner's shooting. Nobody came close to their fox hole and eventually the Americans melted back into the night. Bruck was about to get up and go looking for an officer when he heard the whistling sound. Throwing himself into the bottom of the hole again he covered his ears as shells exploded around them. The Americans had decided that as a parting gift they would saturate the area where they believed the Germans were dug in, with M101 howitzer shells. The barrage lasted for only five minutes, but for Bruck it felt like it went all night.

Then it stopped and the air was filled with the stink of burning trees and cordite. Somewhere nearby a man screamed, otherwise it was quiet. Soon there was the sound of movement and the noise coming from the wounded soldier dropped to a low moan after someone gave him a shot of morphine.

"Everyone alright in there?" said a voice.

"As well as could be expected," answered Bruck.

A figure slid into the fox hole and looked at Bruck. The man was wearing a pea dot camouflage smock and his helmet had a brown band in which tufts of grass had been tucked.

"Oberleutnant Hans Ritter at your service, gentlemen. May I compliment you on your use of the American machine gun. That was some fine shooting. I was wondering if you would lend your gunner to us for a while."

The man was grinning and looked to be no older than twenty years of age.

"This is Ober-matt Helmut Khole and I'm Kapitän Helmut Bruck of the naval air force. We were shot down over the coast after dropping..." There was a massive detonation to the north that interrupted him. "What was that Oberleutnant?"

"A new weapon I believe, sir. Some sort of rocket. We call it the Maybug, though I don't really know why. Basically it's a big unguided bomb that flies by itself until it runs out of fuel and then, bang. We were told our forces were going to start using them on the enemy tonight. The Ami and Tommies are so crowded inside their lodgement that they'll probably hit something."

Bruck nodded thoughtfully. If the rockets were landing here, then they were probably also hitting the embarkation ports in England, such as Portsmouth. It would be stupid to waste the new weapons on London.

"Good, then we are hitting back. We blew up an ammunition ship which was unloading onto an artificial pier a while ago. That must have hurt the enemy," he said.

"Ahh, that's what that rumble was. I told the boys it didn't sound like a rocket. Well I'm glad I'll be able to tell the whingers that the air boys are doing what they can."

"Speaking of which, we really should get back to our unit."

"Of course, I'll allocate a couple of men to guide you to battalion headquarters and they should be able to arrange some transport for you," said the young officer.

It took Bruck and Khole two days to make it as far as Paris, such were the dangers of trying to move in a car or truck in daylight hours. The weather had been clear and Bruck was staggered by the number of allied aircraft he saw. He realised what the German 7th

Army was up against and wondered how the Luftwaffe and the

Kriegsmarine Air Force could possibly prevail.

V

Grossadmiral Wever massaged his temples as he sat behind

his desk.

"So, you are telling me just as we contain the Allies inside

their lodgement the Russians launch an offensive the like of which

we have never seen?" he asked.

"That's about the size of it. They fooled us completely. We

thought they'd drive on Romania and clear the western Ukraine,

but inside they are heading for Warsaw and the Baltic Coast," said

Admiral Canaris.

"Are we holding?"

"No, but we had a stroke of luck. Remember when we

decided to leave the SS divisions in the front line but give them little

in the way of replacements and equipment?"

"Yes."

"Well, the army put all of the burnt out SS units behind the central front."

"But they were shells weren't they?"

"Some are, but others are still above sixty percent strength. Take the 10th SS Panzer for example. It still had seventy panzers and twelve assault guns when the Russians attacked. The 101st Heavy Panzer Battalion still had twenty-two operational Tigers and the 9th SS had forty Panthers and fourteen other panzers. Of course the 2nd SS started with only thirty tanks and a few thousand men, not much more than a powerful battle group really, but some formations have combined, such as the 1st and 3rd SS into a powerful unit of one hundred panzers."

"Where did they get all of those vehicles? I thought we hadn't sent them anything."

"Well, a little bit of equipment still trickled to them through their own depots but they have also been very good at repairing older panzers and fixing up captured Russian ones. The 5th SS has over twenty reworked T-34s and ten heavier Soviet tanks."

"So, completely by accident, we have a number of understrength panzer divisions and battle groups in place to oppose the Soviets?"

"Yes, and with the Finns still holding out, the Russians can't reinforce their main thrust any time soon."

"Yet the central front has been pierced?"

"In a number of places," answered Canaris. "Our forces are trying to retreat slowly but the Russians are more mobile than us. They are well equipped with American trucks and half-tracks while our infantry are on foot."

"Can we stop them?"

"Manstein thinks so, though he is screaming for reinforcements. So far only the 4th Panzer Division has been released to him. The prediction is we will lose Minsk."

"We need more troops."

"There is a proposal we shorten the lines. Withdraw from Estonia and half of Latvia, perhaps holding on to Riga."

"And abandon the Estonians to the Soviets?"

"It's necessary to save Germany."

"Isn't there an entire division of men from that country who have been fighting for us?"

"We will evacuate the families of these men to Germany or Denmark. It is one division against the repositioning of an army."

"It will free up Soviet troops as well," said Wever.

"This is true, but we are stretched too thin. The priority has to be the east now."

"The Allies haven't gone away. They have failed to join the American and British Lodgements but the Amis have pushed the 29th Panzer Grenadier and other units into Cherbourg and will take most of the Cotentin Peninsula."

"We will hold them and bleed them for a while longer; for now we must stop the Soviets. Perhaps then the Russians and the Americans will meet us in some meaningful negotiations."

Chapter Twelve: Autumn 1944

Thirty Me 262 jets flew toward the bomber formation at speeds of up to five hundred miles an hour. They had flown straight past the American Mustang fighters and were now approaching the B-17s from behind. General Adolf Galland wasn't supposed to be in the air. He had been banned from flying years ago, but with the new leadership still sorting itself out he decided to take a chance. Besides, he needed to know what combat conditions were like when flying the new jets.

Fuel shortages were starting to keep conventional fighters on the ground but jets could use kerosene or different types of fuel, however the preferred variety was diesel. This certainly helped with training and shortages, as gasoline was now difficult to obtain. Today only two hundred conventional fighters, mainly Fw 190 D9s and Bf 109 K4s had taken off to attack the enemy.

He eased the throttle gently forward and increased the aircraft's speed to an amazing five hundred and forty miles an hour, as the jets closed the distance on the bombers. He did this carefully and slowly as increasing the fuel supply to the turbine too quickly could cause it to flame out.

The rear gunners of the B-17s were firing at his plane now, though he knew he was still out of range. Galland was shocked at how fast the enemy bombers seemed to grow in his gun sights. He was below the B-17s at the moment and started to climb, as the distance between the two formations was only a couple of kilometers. His airspeed dropped and he lined up on one of the American machines. At six hundred meters he fired but noted the low velocity shells from the four 30mm cannons were falling under his target. He only had a split second to adjust and lifted the nose of the jet slightly. Galland watched as his fire tore into the bomber, blowing huge holes in the B-17's wing and engine. At the last second he pulled up, his jet narrowly missing his target and screaming through the American formation. Galland yelled as he narrowly avoided colliding with at least two bombers, then he was through and climbing toward the clouds.

"He is going down, sir," said one of the other pilots.

Galland turned his aircraft slightly so he could see the enemy formation. At least five bombers were burning, twisting and spinning as they dropped. In the distance another group of jets approached.

"Fighters coming down," a voice warned.

Galland glanced around and noted the Mustangs trying to build up enough air speed to attack the jets that were approaching the B-17s. He realised he and his wingman were in a perfect position to intercept the enemy fighters.

"Follow me Anton Two," he ordered.

The Me 262 bled off little speed as it turned, and Galland liked this aspect of the plane. As long as he didn't get drawn into a low speed turning dog fight, the jet would perform well.

As it was, the P-51 pilots were so intent on catching the Me 262s that were lining up on the bombers that they didn't see the two planes approaching them from behind. Galland closed the distance on the trailing American fighter to one hundred meters before opening fire. Only two of his 30mm shells hit the target but that was enough. One blew most of the tail off the enemy aircraft while the other punched a hole the size of a car's tyre in the starboard wing. The P-51 was travelling at high speed and the damage caused the structural integrity of the airframe to break apart. The Mustang tore itself to pieces in mid-air giving the pilot no chance to bail out. His wingman also destroyed a fighter, and the enemy formation turned rapidly as it sought to escape the cannons of the two jets. Below him Galland noted that the second group of Me 262s had just torn half a dozen bombers out of the sky. That day the American 8th Army Air Force lost seventy-two B-17s to flak and fighters. Four days later, in an attack on Ulm, the heavy bombers lost another eighty-one planes. Operations over the more distant targets in Germany were suspended for just over six weeks.

The attacks by the RAF on Germany tapered off as well, after the disastrous raid on Berlin in October. The British sent over eight hundred planes to attack the capital on a night of strong winds and clear skies. The wind scattered the bomber stream, allowing German fighters many easy targets. A number of naval fighter Staffels took to the air for the first time to operate in a night fighter role, much as the Luftwaffe had done in 1943. The main advantage here was that the naval pilots had been trained to fly by instruments in all types of weather and these fast single engined machines were able to avoid British night fighters. Sixty Me 155s took to the air above Berlin and shot down twenty-two Lancasters for the loss of six planes. The twin engined Luftwaffe fighters and flak accounted for all of the other British losses.

Naval Arado 234s with rocket assisted take offs attacked shipping off the Normandy coast and though losses were high, the new bomber had an early success sinking the heavy cruiser, the USS Quincy. No further night raids experienced the same success as the June 14th foray, but S-boats and destroyers attacked in a series of evening engagements throughout summer, until the German force was decimated. At least fourteen destroyers were lost on each side with the Allies also losing a light cruiser, but it wasn't enough to make a difference to the enemies' supply route. Divers and mini submarines were now the only method of penetrating the British forces protecting the freighters, and these dangerous missions were only pin pricks. U-boat attacks sunk fourteen enemy vessels whilst losing twenty submarines. This was unsustainable, and the submarines were withdrawn from the offensive. The new Type XXI Elektro U-boats would be ready by February 1945 and the smaller Type XXIII boats were just starting to move toward the English Channel.

V

Grossadmiral Wever rubbed the grit from his eyes and walked slowly into the briefing room. He stopped briefly and looked at the two huge maps on either wall. The only other man in the area was Field Marshal Rommel. He stood with his hands behind his back looking at the large scale map of the Russian front. Wever moved over to the Field Marshal, and after shaking the man's hand, looked at situation.

"So these are up to date?" Wever asked.

"As of this morning, yes," said Rommel.

"Minsk has fallen and Riga holds I see."

"The Soviets have almost reached the old Polish frontier. The line runs from Riga to Vilnius and from there to Grodno. After that it's almost a straight line to the Carpathian Mountains. Then the line follows the Dniester to the Black Sea. We had to evacuate Odesa by sea."

"We are also back on the Romanian border and have lost the Ukraine."

"It looks grim, but we withdrew in good order. Those SS divisions saved the day on the central front in the end. Their continual counterattacks allowed the infantry to escape to a new line, though it cost them dearly."

"I've heard that a number of the old formations have been joined together."

"The 1st, 2nd and 3rd SS are now one division and we are sending most of the old concentration camp guards to them, except for those we have imprisoned. The 10th and the 9th SS are also being amalgamated and the 17th SS is now part of the 5th, along with some of the foreign formations, like the French and the Walloons. It has also been decided to reequip these new SS divisions but they're not going to get the best equipment anymore. Those formations have proved to be too valuable to just break apart. They're reforming in Poland and will soon return to the front."

"The regular divisions had to give way in the south as well?" asked Wever.

"Once the river line on the Dnieper was breached it was a running battle back across the Steppes. We bled the Russians though and gave ground slowly. Now the High Command is discussing how we hold Romania."

"I suppose we still need their oil."

"We are already experiencing fuel shortages and that will only get worse if we lose those oil fields."

"It leaves precious little for Normandy. As it is the Allies have finally managed to link their lodgement."

Rommel snorted. "Only after blowing a hole in our line with hundreds of their heavy bombers. The 77th Infantry Division was smashed by the attack and so were elements of the Panzer Lehr. The problem for the enemy was they managed to drop bombs on their own troops as well. Then the Allies struggled to move their armour over the moonscape they had created."

"But their front is now continuous?"

Rommel sighed. "Yes, and it's just a matter of time until they break out. Still, we bleed them too. Eventually we will have to withdraw to the line of the Seine."

"And Rome is gone."

"The Allies now hold Italy except for the northern portion. The Gothic line runs just north of Florence and follows the mountains. I believe the rivers in the Po Valley are the next fall-back position and then the Alps."

"We have no chance of stopping them?"

"None! The war was lost either when we failed to take Moscow, or when the Sixth Army was mauled at Stalingrad, depending on who you speak to."

"So we try to slow them down."

"And convince them to negotiate. Is there any word on that front?"

"Fredrick von Schulenburg, our Foreign Minister has returned from Sweden with some good news. The British are talking with us, hypothetically, about how we would evacuate Greece, Albania, Yugoslavia and Bulgaria."

"We aren't in Bulgaria."

Wever waved the Field Marshal comment away. "It seems that the British have been in contact with our small ally and the Bulgarians are willing to surrender to them. It's just a matter of the British getting some of their forces into the area."

"That wouldn't make the Russians happy. I bet Stalin would love to take all of Eastern Europe."

"Churchill is aware of this, though the American President seems unconcerned."

"What about the Russians? I gather they aren't interested in peace?"

"Despite their enormous losses, Stalin drives them on. The man would stand on a pile of corpses if it helped him take most of Europe. The good news is that he is furious the British have been speaking with us and is putting pressure on Roosevelt. The Americans are also receiving pressure from the British. It seems that the English may need to amalgamate some of their divisions soon, their losses have been that high and they have manpower shortages. It has been reported some American senators have been asking why their government isn't putting more resources into the war against Japan. Canaris says there are signs that the pressure is getting to the US administration."

"It could all be wishful thinking," said Rommel. "In the meantime, the Normandy front has only received two extra panzer divisions, the 9th and the 2nd."

"I believe the army sent a number of Tiger formations your way?"

"The 503rd, 509th and 510th, all with Tiger Is and the Panzerjaeger Abteilung 654 with forty-eight new Jagdpanthers has just arrived. Still, it's the extra infantry divisions from Finland and Norway that have made the difference so far. They made up for the lack of armour, especially when supported by units such as the Panzerjaeger Abteilung 560."

"You also have a number of those independent assault gun battalions."

"Without them we wouldn't have held. They are perfect to ambush enemy armour within the bocage."

"But we can't hold them forever, especially with the majority of units and replacements having to go east," said Wever.

"No, though the fall back line on the Seine is slowly being built," said Rommel.

"Well, we have swept the Luftwaffe and Kriegsmarine for extra men and managed to scrape together another three hundred thousand. Then there are also the troops coming from the replacement army."

"It won't be enough. In the end they will grind their way into Germany, that's if they don't destroy us from the air first," said Rommel.

V

His hands shook as he held the controls of the Ju 290. Kapitän Helmut Bruck tried to steady them, then glanced out his side window at the ocean below. He didn't want to be here but knew it was unfair to expect the new crews and their pilots to undertake missions without him. He now wore the Knights Cross with Oak Leaves, but would rather have received a month's leave. The three other aircraft he now led were supposed to hunt for convoys west of Ireland but Bruck's mind wasn't really engaged. After the loss of half of his crew over Normandy he felt that he was living on borrowed time.

The sight of all those allied ships had rocked him. It seemed it didn't matter how many enemy vessels they sunk, the Americans could just make more. Bruck knew enough about the war to understand that his country was being squeezed from three sides. The death of the German leader during the previous winter had slowed the rate of territory loss but hadn't stopped it. The Allies were grinding their way out of Normandy and the Soviets had almost retaken all their old territory, including what they had stolen from the Poles. He couldn't see a future that didn't include the defeat of his country and his death. Sighing he glanced at the instrument panel and noted one of the engines was running a little hot. He wondered if he could use this as a reason to turn for home and immediately felt a spike of shame.

Since the night attack on Normandy and the explosion of the ammunition ship, the Allies had also lost their second artificial pier to a storm on June 19th. This must have slowed the allied build up, however plenty of materials seemed to still make their way across the beaches to keep the armies supplied. He hadn't attacked again but other naval Staffels had attempted to hit allied shipping at night. The results had been poor and the losses heavy. The British and Americans increased the number of night fighters over the English Channel and now Luftwaffe and Kriegsmarine units were reduced to dropping mines and then running from the area as quickly as possible.

His Staffel had taken heavy casualties and could now only put six aircraft into the air. Today they carried a modified version of the Fritz X flying bomb that wasn't equipped with an armour piercing head. The new bombs, such as the one he had used at Normandy, had been reconfigured so that the attempts of the Allies to jam the radio signals between the weapon and the operator were less effective. This had increased the effectiveness of the weapon, though again, Bruck understood it would only be a matter of time before the Allies found another way to jam them.

"Skipper, I see smoke in the distance, off to the northeast," reported the pilot of Bruno Two.

It took a while for Bruck to locate the tell-tale sign of an enemy ship but when he did, it became obvious it was only a small group of vessels, and one very large ship.

"It's big, whatever it is," said his co-pilot.

Bruck stared for a moment, then realised this was one of the fast ocean liners the enemy used to transport troops from America. These vessels were too fast for a U-boat to catch and hard for the air contingent of the Kriegsmarine to find. Usually though they travelled with a large escort, but the US and Royal Navy were feeling more secure since recapturing Iceland.

"It looks like we've got very lucky," said Bruck over the radio. "All aircraft line up with me. I want to swamp their defences by releasing all of our weapons at the same time."

As they approached the target, flak started to explode around them. A light cruiser and three destroyers accompanied the RMS Aquitania. He felt the sweat gather on the back of his neck as he considered which shell would hit his aircraft and blow it out of the sky. One of the Ju 290s was damaged but continued its attack run with the other aircraft. He felt his aircraft buck and jump as the explosions came closer, and he fought down the urge to scream. Then the bombardier announced that the weapon was on its way. Bruck watch the flare on the tail of the bomb as it was guided toward the target. The other devices were also streaking toward the distant ship. Suddenly there was an explosion near the front of his plane and holes appeared in the cockpit. He heard a scream and then watched as the Fritz X his bombardier had been controlling fell away and exploded in the sea.

The other three bombs either hit the Aquitania or exploded near her. Two smashed into the ship's stern, punching through ten decks to explode just underneath the vessel. A thirty meter hole was blown in the bottom of the Aquitania and two of her four propeller shafts destroyed. A second Fritz X hit just behind the last of the four enormous funnels and exploded in one of the boiler rooms. The force of the explosion ripped through the double hull and created another huge hole in the bottom of the ship. With more damage caused by the near miss, the ship started to settle quickly. It is thought that without all the watertight compartments the vessel would have gone down even faster. The loss of power to the ash expellers and the extinguishing of most of the furnaces due to the inrush of sea water, doomed the vessel. Of the seven thousand men on board the ship from the US 99th Division, more than half drowned. This didn't include the loss of most of the signals, military police, combat engineers and even the divisional band. Later US historians likened the destruction of the Aquitania to a minor military defeat in battle. In Maryland and Virginia the loss of so many soldiers at one time came as a shock as the division was formed from men mainly living in those states.

Bruck knew the ship was sinking but didn't know the extent of the casualties his Staffel had just inflicted on the Americans until much later. At that point he was more concerned about the damage to his plane and the condition of his bombardier. As it was, the man died soon after his plane was hit. The aircraft itself was remarkably unscathed, except for being a little breezy. Wind whistled through the cockpit, chilling his cheeks, but in a strange way it calmed him. The four aircraft flew back toward their base near La Rochelle, however the Ju 290 with the damaged engine dropped behind. After Bruck landed he waited for the plane on the runway for two hours but it never appeared. Later, after the war, it was discovered that two Mosquitoes flown by Australians in No. 456 squadron, shot down the damaged plane over the Bay of Biscay and all of the crew were killed.

He stood there waiting until it started to rain and then trudged back to his office. His gunner Khole was waiting there for him and the man had a grin on his face.

"Sir, we are going to Germany, they want to give us both another medal," said the short man.

Bruck smiled. "The best aspect of getting those pieces of tin is we get a few days off flying."

"Oh I'm sure we can string it out for a week or more sir, if we are inventive."

"Khole, I like your thinking."

v

During this period of time, secret talks between the British and Germans were convened in Sweden. Churchill was very interested in landing forces in Greece and then rushing troops forward into Bulgaria and Albania. Feelers were also extended to Yugoslavia, which had fallen into civil war in the autumn of 1942. Tito's forces now controlled large areas of the country and Germany only occupied small areas of the region, almost abandoning the rural zone and concentrating on keeping the mines and railways open. The communist leader had indicated he was unwilling to have troops from any of the Allies in his country, and that included those from the Soviet Union.

Of course these secret discussions didn't remain that way for very long and soon Stalin was screaming about the perfidy of the British and Americans. At this point he withdrew any pretence at free elections in Poland; despite Churchill promising that the talks with the Germans were only to investigate certain possibilities, and that the British didn't plan on entering Bulgaria. Stories of the mass rape of Polish women and the execution of members of the Home Army in areas taken by Russia and then retaken by Germany in counterattacks were broadcast to the world at this time. Stalin denied everything but the evidence was overwhelming. Churchill pushed for an investigation of the allegations and hardened his position against the Soviet Union.

President Roosevelt felt the growing pressure. He tried to calm Stalin's paranoia but also pushed for stronger reassurances on democratic elections for those area taken by the Russian army. These requests were met with shrill accusations and calls for the Allies to do more in their efforts to defeat Germany. Churchill's relationship with Stalin had gone through many ups and downs but this time it didn't bounce back. In the meantime, Finland made peace with the Russians, giving up land along its border, and the Soviets immediately redirected the soldiers engaged in that campaign to an attack on the Latvian capital of Riga. The offensive turned into an expensive battle of attrition for the Russians, taking two weeks to capture half of the city on the eastern side of the Daugava River. Vilnius, the capital of Lithuania fell quickly and soon the Germans were forced to completely abandon the Baltic States. The Russians were at the East Prussian border by late October and well inside the old 1939 Polish border as well.

German counterattacks and an extended supply line forced the Soviet advance to stop at this point and resupply. In the south the Russian attacks into Romania had been held at the Danube and the Carpathian Mountains, with part of the line stretching along the Siret River. Romania had tried to surrender to the Soviets but Germany quickly occupied the country and disarmed the army, taking all of its aircraft and panzers, and using them to reinforce their own units in the area. In this way German divisions in Romania took possession of over two hundred Panzer IVs, twenty Panthers, and one hundred tank destroyers and assault guns of different types. The most important aspect of the German defensive effort was that they kept their access to the oil fields around Ploiesti. Crete was completely evacuated with the twenty thousand men from the island going into the line on the Danube. The British immediately moved onto Crete, further inflaming Stalin's belief that Churchill was up to no good. At the time though there had actually been no arrangement between the Germans and the British.

During this period, the first British units were forced to amalgamate due to ongoing manpower shortages and the heavy losses incurred in the Normandy campaign. This is also often believed to be another reason why Churchill was looking for a way out of the war himself. He had an eye on what would happen to the British Empire once the shooting in Europe stopped, and his trust of the Russian intentions was also now paper thin.

V

"So Paris is now the front line?" said Grossadmiral Wever.

Admiral Canaris nodded wearily. "The 7th Army made it to the Seine but it did lose a lot of equipment in its retreat. The line follows the river further east to Sens. From there it runs through the hill country of the Morvan to the Swiss border near Bern."

"Do Rommel and the other generals think they can hold there?"

"For a while, though only if they receive reinforcements."

"The policy is that everything goes to the Russian front."

"Then the Allies will be in Germany soon."

"Maybe that's the only way out of this mess."

Admiral Canaris raised a single grey eyebrow.

"I'll see if I can shift some of the production of panzers back to the west but I can't make any promises. Speer has worked miracles and maybe some of the new panzerjaegers and assault guns can be sent that way."

"It may be enough. We need time. The cracks in the Allies are starting to appear now and we just need the breathing space for them to widen."

"I don't know if our enemies will give us that time."

Chapter Thirteen: Winter

1944/45

"Is it true? Is Roosevelt dead?" asked Grossadmiral Wever.

Foreign minister Fredrick von Schulenburg nodded while Admiral Canaris grinned.

"It's all over the American radio broadcasts," said the white haired man.

"I knew he wasn't a well man. I wonder what tipped him over the edge?" said Wever.

"Maybe it was the strain of dealing with his fractious allies, who knows?" said Schulenburg. "But it certainly removes a stumbling block to the peace process. The new man, Harry Truman is an unknown quantity."

"We need to reach out to him quickly," said Wever

"He has gone on the record in the past as being anti-communist and was critical of the Soviet pact with Germany in 1939. He also spoke out against Russian aggression in Finland," said Canaris.

"This is all promising but we still don't have any substantive offers from the Allies. Until we do then we are in great danger as a country," said Wever.

"Well the British have now said that they are happy with our time table to withdraw from Greece, Albania and then they will enter Bulgaria," said Schulenburg.

"The Bulgarians are alright with this arrangement?" asked Wever.

"The government isn't thrilled with the idea but they know the other option is eventual occupation by the Soviet Union. They are ready to choose the lesser of two evils," said Schulenburg. "We have repossessed the armour we sold them and sent it to the

Romanian front. It's only about one hundred panzers and the same amount of Bf 109s, but it all helps."

Suddenly Canaris sat a little straighter. "We should offer to withdraw from Poland now."

Wever frowned. "That would put the Russians on our doorstep. They have already reached East Prussia."

"Yes, but that province is probably lost to us no matter what we do. We have been toying with the idea of giving the area to the Poles anyway," said Canaris. "It may be necessary to draw the new German border along the Oder."

"I thought we were going to try to keep Danzig," said Schulenburg.

"That may be very difficult. The Russians are going to try and push their borders and influence as far east as possible," said Canaris. "As for the soviets rolling across Poland that may not happen, especially if we reach out to the Home Army. We know that a large number of Poles have joined their underground forces.

There are anywhere between six hundred and three hundred thousand ready to take up arms against us according to intelligence reports. We also know this army is loyal to the government in Britain. Why not offer them their independence and arm them? There are also a lot of Poles fighting for the Allies, whole divisions exist. Then there are destroyers and submarines crewed by Poles. The RAF has squadrons of bombers and fighters flown by Polish pilots. What if we let them go home, even offer to refuel their planes in Germany on the way?" said Canaris.

"It wouldn't stop the Russians," said Wever.

"They have whole divisions that are also Polish. Would brother fight brother? The Allies started this war to defend Poland. They would be hard pressed to ignore their plight, especially if the Russians start killing them. It would certainly put the new president in a difficult position. If he sees that Stalin is actually invading rather than liberating the very country over which the war started then maybe it would break the alliance."

"It could work," said Schulenburg. "Stalin has set up a puppet government for Poland and if he has agreed to elections, as intelligence tells us he has, why not let the Poles liberate themselves?"

"And it would create a buffer between the Russians and the German border, at least on the central front. The Soviets wouldn't be able to just roll over the Home Army if we arm them so their advance would slow, and we could fortify the border and wait for them there," said Wever. "Alright let's try it but we need to move fast."

V

By January 1945 the Russians took Bialystok. Soon the stories of rape and murder that were perpetrated by their troops in this region were well known. Home Army units that tried to communicate with the Red Army were disarmed and their officers shot. This allowed the Germans to reach out to the Polish forces and a deal was struck. The Heer retreated gradually toward the proposed German border though at this stage Danzig and a triangle of land running from the port back to the Oder was kept. The German army also defended East Prussia while its citizens were evacuated. Arms and equipment were handed over to the Poles as the Germans withdrew, including armour and artillery. When the Russians tried to disarm these Home Army units fighting erupted.

The Polish government in exile immediately argued to be flown back to Warsaw and the Germans offered an air corridor over their territory for the journey. The five hundred thousand strong Home Army began to set up local councils and battles with Russian armies became wide spread. German aircraft flew combat missions in support of the Poles as the fighting intensified. Around the city of Lubin the Soviets and the Home Army became locked in a bitter conflict, the city becoming a ruin as Russian artillery pounded buildings to rubble.

The Allies understood what Germany was doing but were shocked by Stalin's willingness to attack the Home Army and his fury at the Poles for siding with the Germans. Churchill and Truman knew what the Soviet leader was up to. The British at this time proposed that the Allies sign a cease-fire and that proper negotiations be entered into with what the Allies called the Provisional German Government. The Heer then immediately started to withdraw from Greece and sent all its resources to Romania while the 2nd New Zealand infantry Division and the Polish II Corps came ashore at Athens. The latter was a deliberate choice by Churchill and when Stalin discovered that this unit was in Greece he went into a fury. He could see how they could easily be moved, with German cooperation, to their homeland.

The final straw for the alliance was when the Polish Government in exile was flown to Warsaw. At the same time most of the 1st Independent Polish Parachute Brigade was flown across Germany by the British to provide security for the returning government. The Russians responded by bombing Warsaw and attacking the Home Army across the entire central front. Lubin fell. In East Prussia the Russians were caught in an area of swamps and frozen lakes forty kilometers from Konigsberg. The month of February brought a cease-fire in the west with the Allies now holding Paris and the Germans digging in along the Seine to Troyes and then the line bent north to Nancy and south again to Basel.

At this time Germany moved all its air assets east as well as hundreds of 88mm flak guns. The US president had in the early part of the crisis tried to negotiate a settlement between the British and the Russians but both sides were unwilling to budge. Truman finally broke with Stalin when the latter bombed Warsaw. It was then he agreed to the cease-fire and started to look at the shape of a future Europe. By then Russia had already stated that it would not declare war on Japan. It was at this time that a number of prominent Polish pilots in the US Army Air Force flew their aircraft, without permission, to Warsaw.

The Germans then freed leading ace Lieutenant Colonel Francis Stanley Gabreski from captivity, along with a number of other Polish pilots they had captured, gave them all FW 190 Ds and sent them to Poland. (Gabreski made another four kills during this campaign, lifting his total score from twenty eight German victories to thirty two in total.)

Soon Churchill allowed whole squadrons of Poles to fly home and of course Germany facilitated this. Over fourteen fighter squadrons and two bomber squadrons made the journey. This force of over one hundred and fifty top line fighters, including the latest Spitfires and Mustangs, immediately found themselves fighting Russian planes over central Poland.

The Polish II Corps was put on trains in Athens and the sent secretly to Kracow where they went into action to support the Home Army which was being forced westwards. Then the Polish 1st Armoured division was moved across Germany from France and detrained at Warsaw. Sherman Fireflies found themselves duelling with T-34-85s around Ostrow, ninety kilometers from the capital city.

The Royal Navy ship controlled by Polish crews sailed home, their passage left unmolested by the Kriegsmarine. They brought with them another Polish brigade and more civilians who had fled the country but now wanted to return home.

Despite these forces the Soviets forced back the Pole and were within eighty kilometers of the capital city. Winter fighting had caused heavy casualties on both sides with the Germans even losing the eastern half of East Prussia. The relationship between Stalin and the west was in free fall with the cancelation of Lend Lease and the suspension of all supply convoys. At least fifty US Polish pilots flew east to support their country but unless the Allies committed their own air force and ground troops to the area it was looking like the Home Army would be destroyed.

The revolt of the First and Second Polish Soviet Armies and their advance from Kaunas in Lithuania to East Prussia and there reappearance before the Red Army before Warsaw is now legendary. Stalin had doubted the loyalty of the formation and moved them away from the front in late January but the Poles in these units knew what was happening in their homeland. The Russian officers based with the armies were arrested and taken with the Poles as they stripped other surprised units of all their equipment before advancing through the German lines to attack the Soviet forces in the flank before Warsaw. The Russian 47th Army reeled back, losing many men and much of its artillery as it was chased back beyond Ostrow. German forces also counterattacked in East Prussia at this time and pushed the 11th Red Guards Army back as far as Volodino.

Stalin raged but the Russian Army was spent and needed time to resupply and rest. It had suffered huge casualties but the Soviet leader vowed to attack again in a few weeks. It was during this time that Churchill used the lull to move every Pole he could find back to their homeland. Over eight hundred thousand Poles were now under arms and they were well equipped with a variety of weapons and aircraft from both America, Britain, Germany and even Russia. Nearly one million seven hundred thousand Soviets in East Prussia faced one million three hundred thousand Germans. In Poland two million Russians faced almost half that number of Poles. The biggest change though was in the air where both the Luftwaffe and the new Polish Air Force had at least neutralised Soviet dominance of the skies.

Then Churchill managed to convince Truman that they needed to commit ground forces to the area. Both the untested US 13th Airborne division and the British 6th Airborne Division were flown to Warsaw and the US 9th Armoured Division and the British Guard's Armoured Division moved to Danzig by sea. The US president warned the Soviet leadership at this time that Poland was under the protection of the Allies and to join them at the negotiating table in order to have a say in the future shape of Europe. Stalin refused and his armies attacked.

Chapter Fourteen: Spring 1945

They had let him and a number of other pilots return to Germany at the end of winter. Kapitänleutnant Hans-Joachim Marseille was overjoyed to see his mother and his fiancée Charlotte Hermann. They met in Berlin and he explained he was part of a prisoner exchange and would be expected to go into battle again. His time at home was brief and after a short-lived stint retraining on the Fw 190 D he was sent with other new pilots into battle over the forests of East Prussia. He didn't know that the land he was defending would be eventually be handed to Poland, but if he had, it probably wouldn't have mattered.

The flight took his unit of eight aircraft over northern Poland where British paratroopers were fighting Soviet soldiers. The whole concept seemed strange to him. He didn't know that this situation had been a possibility back in 1940 when Stalin had invaded Finland. He understood that the Russians and the Allies weren't technically at war, but they were definitely killing each other. It was true that most of the fighting seemed to be between the Poles and the Russians, however the American and English paratroopers had fought a number of hard engagements, particularly near the East Prussian border.

"Skipper, enemy aircraft at ten o'clock low. Twin engined machines by the look of things," said the pilot of Anton Three.

Marseille hadn't really had time to get to know any of the pilots in his new Staffel but understood that until recently they had been defending Berlin; first at night, then as the weather deteriorated, by day. They were all naval fliers and had switched to the Fw 190D not long before he had been repatriated. He had only about three hours on the plane whereas they had probably flown it for twice as long. Still, most of these men were veterans and a number were aces, unlike the Luftwaffe formations where losses had left the ranks filled with raw recruits.

"I see them and their escort. Single engined planes at ten o'clock as well, but level with us," said Marseille. These aircraft were La-7s and were flown by very experienced pilots. Below them

432

the Russian attack planes tightened their formation so the gunners could support each other. The Tu-2s were also gradually losing altitude. Marseille realised that the formation's aim would be to hug the ground to make it difficult for his fighters to get underneath them, where they had little in the way of protection.

"Alright, Cesare flight take the bombers; everyone else, let's see if we can climb above the Russian fighters. Don't use the boost until you really have to," said Marseille. All of the Staffel flew Fw 190 D13s with water-methanol boost which increased the power of the engine for a short period of time. The planes also varied from the original version having dispensed with the machine guns and were installed with an extra cannon firing through the propeller hub.

Both formations started to climb, while four aircraft dived toward the Russian bombers. The commander of the enemy interceptors soon tired of this game of seeing who could climb faster and rolled his aircraft over, sending the La-7s screaming down to protect their bombers. This was what Marseille had been waiting for and he took his fighters down after them. The acceleration of the 'Dora' in a dive surprised him, and his formation was soon behind the enemy planes. The Russians realised the danger and turned to face the approaching threat. All Marseille's pilots could do was take quick shots at difficult angles, as the nimble enemy planes weaved away from their path. This however was enough for Marseille, and his burst shattered the engine of an La-7, the pilot quickly bailing out as flames took hold. The Russian formation scattered and the Germans used their speed to perform Immelmann loops to both gain altitude and reorientate their position with the scattered enemy. This maneuver by the Germans allowed them to pick their targets and soon, in groups of two, they latched on to different enemy machines, attempting to shoot them down.

This proved to be harder than Marseille anticipated as the La-7s were well flown and very agile. The Fw 190 D could also turn sharply and soon Marseille barrel rolled his aircraft to cut the corner on a quickly turning opponent, shooting the Russian down with another quick burst. Then he heard a yelled warning and a scream. Glancing over his shoulder he saw his wingman's aircraft explode and an enemy machine closing in from behind him. He threw his aircraft into a wingover, which allowed him to turn one hundred and eighty degrees very quickly. This maneuver caught the enemy pilot by surprise and he overshot. He then continued the turn, hit boost, and went after his attacker. Major Alexander Kabiskoy had sixteen kills at this time and had fought against the Germans since October 1941. He had battled against many great German pilots, but none as good as Joachim Marseille.

As the Russian found the German on his tail he went into a defensive spiral. Marseille understood the tactic was to make him overshoot and he cut the throttle and turned with his enemy. Kabiskoy pulled out only meters above the ground, as did Marseille. Now his opponent was low and slow, and his tactic to lose his pursuer had failed. A burst from the three 20mm cannons shattered the La-7's engine and smoke started pouring from the machine.

Marseille could have blown his opponent out of the sky but he didn't enjoy killing, so he watched as the Russian attempted to put the crippled plane down in a field. They were behind the Polish line so the man would be captured anyway, probably by the British, as they held the front in this area. The plane dipped lower and Marseille watched as the wheels retracted. The La-7 then belly landed in a field of snow and mud, skidding across the surface before crashing into an area of scrub and small trees. The enemy pilot seemed unresponsive in his cockpit and in danger of being burnt alive as flames started to grow around the aircraft.

Marseille didn't hesitate. He lowered the Fw 190's flaps and lined up on the same field. He understood he was about to heavily damage his machine but he couldn't leave a man to burn to death. His fighter hit the ground evenly and then skidded across the landscape, coming to a stop only one hundred meters from the La-7. He hurled himself from the seat and sprinted across the field to the smouldering aircraft, half expecting an explosion at any moment. Hauling himself up onto the wing he quickly pulled the canopy open, but struggled to undo the Russian pilot's harness. He could see the sandy haired man had pulled off his flying helmet and appeared dazed. Blood ran from a shallow cut on his forehead, and he stared at Marseille as though not understanding what was happening.

Flames grew and he could smell fuel. Marseille finally got the straps undone and tried to pull the Russian from the cockpit but Kabiskoy pushed him away. Then flames started to lick around the cockpit and some level of shock registered in the Russian's eyes.

Marseille put his hands under the pilot's armpits and lifted him out onto the wing. Then he helped the limping man onto the ground and the two of them staggered twenty meters before the La-7 exploded. The force of the blast threw both men to the ground and Marseille felt a wave of heat on his back. He turned and rolled over to see the mangled wreck smothered in flames. Marseille lay on his back and laughed. The Russian said something to him and started to limp toward the forest.

"You're welcome," Marseille yelled after the fleeing man.

437

British paratroopers caught Major Kabiskoy before he had travelled more than a kilometer. Kapitänleutnant Hans-Joachim Marseille was back with his unit and flying again the following day.

V

Both the American President and the British Prime Minister were now facing opposition in their home countries because of the sudden change of direction in the war. Both tried to explain they had documents revealing that the Russians wanted to convert as much of Europe as possible to communism. Evidence was released of the massacre of Polish members of the Home Army and of German willingness to sign a peace agreement. Critics asked what had happened to the declaration of unconditional surrender and Churchill stated that circumstances had changed. Hitler and his cronies had been arrested and Germany was willing to allow itself to be dismantled. This wasn't all true and these premature pronouncements caused a brief crisis between the German and British governments.

In America many called for a diversion of their troops to the Pacific. Japan was undefeated and the idea of a war against the Soviet Union wasn't popular. Hard core anti-communists called for a widening of the campaign while others suggested they just draw a line on a map and tell Stalin he couldn't move any further west. Many Democrats questioned the whole strategy and pointed out that Germany had started the war, though this argument drew people to the fact that the conflict had started over Poland, a country the soviets helped attack, and the very state they would abandon if they didn't send more troops to help In the meantime, Truman pushed for the timetable of the atomic bomb test in Los Alamos to be brought forward. Even though scientists and other experts said this was impossible, there was now an extra political imperative to test the new weapon. Stalin would think twice about engaging the west in any sort of conflict if the USA had the atomic bomb.

The Russian leader was angry that his plans for expansion westward were being thwarted. He didn't want to fight the

Americans and knew they were developing a devastating weapon which would change the face of warfare. He even understood they were very close to testing it. The question was whether he should try and push as far as he could before they finished work on the bomb, or should he not risk a war that could end with the destruction of his country. He thought the latter unlikely, but the use of nuclear weapons on his army could lead to a reversal of the gains his forces had made.

Meanwhile, the Germans concentrated on the defence of Romania and East Prussia. The geographical barrier of the Carpathian Mountains kept the Russians from crossing into Czechoslovakia and Hungary, and stopped further advances into Romania. Even an area of the Ukraine was still held by German forces. Hundreds of flak guns of all calibres made their way east with the crews receiving brief anti-armour training. Most had to take static positions but they proved to be an invaluable resource to the hard pressed German army. The cease-fire with the West also allowed some breathing space. Armour was delivered to the Poles with over two hundred Jadgpanzers IVs and many Hetzer 38s (a lighter Jadgpanzer type) arriving in Warsaw in March. The Luftwaffe flew missions over Poland from Czechoslovakia and East Prussia with Polish pilots, flying a variety of allied aircraft, covering the Warsaw front.

In March fighting slowed as both sides took stock. Stalin primed his forces for one last push, with the main drive being on the Polish capital. The offensive was postponed because of poor weather, but started on April 14th with nearly the entire effort being directed at the Home Army. At the same time a renewed drive was made in East Prussia but there was no attack in Romania due to limited Russian supplies. The end of Lend Lease was already starting to bite into the Soviet ability to make war.

The attack on the Germans in the East Prussia bogged down in the swampy country around the lakes and swamps near Angerburg and Insterbourg, though an armoured thrust did reach the Courtland Lagoon where it was stopped by the 5th SS Panzer division and Tiger IIs from the 103rd SS Heavy Panzer Battalion.

British divisions were caught in the line of the Russian advance with the Guards armoured units receiving and inflicting heavy casualties. At this time the Soviets had advanced twenty kilometers in two days, and though two Polish tank units rushed to reinforce the line, it looked as though nothing would stop the Russian steam roller.

The use of massed British bomber formations to attack the Russians had been put forward by Air Marshal Arthur Harris as far back as February. At that time Churchill didn't want to escalate the growing rift between the Allies any more than he thought was necessary. Now, with British troops dying in their hundreds, he relented. Over one thousand heavy bombers attacked Russian targets along the central front, particularly near the area where the Russians had broken the front line. Most of the planes flew all the way from England and refuelled in Denmark on the return trip (that country having been evacuated by the Germans and occupied by the Allies two weeks earlier).

The Soviet spearhead of the attack was caught in the open and pounded by the heavy bombers. Some formations simply disappeared under the weight of the bombs and though the Russian air force tried to intercept the aircraft, many of their airfields had been hit by coordinated strikes from Polish fighter bombers the same morning. The rain of fire from the sky ripped artillery and infantry units apart. In some case T-34s were thrown on their sides by the force of the bomb blasts. Men were left wandering dazed around the areas of the bombardment until medical units collected them and took them to aid stations. Most of these soldiers were deaf. The English repeated the process again two days later with less spectacular results, but the raids stopped the Russian advance temporarily. When the Soviets did try and move forward again after a pause of almost a week, the Poles were waiting for them. At the same time the American 9th Armoured Division counterattacked the flank of the Russian attack, forcing a hasty retreat back to their initial positions. Renewed Soviet pressure forced the Americans to withdraw a few kilometers and Pershing tanks duelled with Russian armour at close ranges. The T34-85s were destroyed in large numbers but then IS-2 tanks appeared and some Pershings were lost.

In the end the offensive was blunted with only marginal gains being made on all fronts. Stalin was furious but also shocked at the power of the British heavy bomber attack. On May 6th 1945 the Soviet leadership called for a cease-fire. The war in Europe was over but a very cold war was about to begin.

V

"So Germany will exist between the Oder and the Rhine," said GrossAdmiral Wever.

"In the east the border runs as far as Breslau and then it turns south to the Czech border," said Admiral Canaris

"Pomerania's gone and at least half of Silesia. And of course all of East Prussia."

Both men sat in Wever's office on the Island of Rugen. The new Poland was only one hundred kilometers away.

"It could have been a lot worse, my friend. Germany was on the path to complete destruction," said Canaris.

"I suppose you are correct. It's just the placing of these British and American bases on our soil is something I find humiliating," said Wever.

"With the Russians still unwilling to hand back any land that they took in Poland or Romania, the situation is still very tense. Think of it as insurance."

"Do you think that the Romanians will be able to swap that portion of the Carpathian Mountains we still hold in the Ukraine for some of their old territory?"

"Not at the moment. There's no trust between the two sides and there's even some talk of allowing that region of the Ukraine a semi-independent status."

"Well the Poles can't be happy with the new border only ninety kilometers from their capital."

"Yes, but they are free, and provide a very useful barrier between us and Stalin."

"On another front, how strong is our commitment to these international trials?"

"We are steadfast as a government and are facilitating a complete investigation of the camps and all Germans deeply involved in the persecution of the Jews and other groups. The Russians have of course refused to participate, and are busy putting any Germans they captured on trial. It is only due to the interim government's early commitment to ridding ourselves of Nazi influence that our country may escape some of the guilt over what Hitler initiated.'

"Those poor sods still in Russia. Won't Stalin swap them for his own soldiers we captured?"

"He is not interested and says any member of his army who was taken prisoner is a coward and a traitor."

"My god, the man is as big a monster as Hitler was."

"That may be true, but we can't ignore what our country did."

"You mean the Jews?"

"They want to set up a homeland of their own in Palestine."

"Then we must do everything we can to support their efforts."

"Good, I was hoping you would say that."

"I may have little influence over the matter. Elections are to be held in a year according to the treaty we signed, with the new United Nations overseeing the affair."

"I don't know how this new international body will fair. Without Russian participation it seems doomed to failure," said Canaris.

"I don't know either. Most of the world will join, and perhaps it may allow us to avoid unnecessary wars in the future."

"Do you think Stalin will sit on his hands?"

"Probably not, however America won't just hold back in the future. That country is now a world power and a sworn opponent of Communism. If the Russians attack they'll intervene," said Wever.

"Well maybe the USA has something else up its sleeve. Their air force is certainly giving the Japanese a pounding."

"Let's hope so my friend, let's hope so."

Notes

At the point of departure, when alternate history moves away from real history, it becomes difficult to predict what could happen. All of the equipment, ships and aircraft in this book were either on the drawing board or came into service at some point during the war. The jets have only been moved forward slightly, as removing Hitler's insistence on the Me 262 as a bomber wouldn't have affected the ability to get the plane into service much earlier. It now turns out the engines were the real issue with these revolutionary aircraft.

For me, Admiral Canaris is one of the unsung heroes of history. He opposed Hitler from 1939 onwards. He didn't wait until Germany was losing to join the plot to kill the Führer. This man's influence on Grossadmiral Wever is completely imagined.

In our timeline, Kapitänleutnant Hans-Joachim Marseille died in September 1942 (of course this wasn't his real rank). He was known for his love as jazz, wine and women. He was also known for not being a fan of the Nazi party and really was brought into the world by a Jewish doctor. The playing of a jazz number in front of Hitler actually happened.

Helmut Bruck was a bomber pilot for the Luftwaffe and died at the age of eighty-eight in 2001. In reality he actually flew Stuka dive bombers.

Fregattenkapitän Hans-Gerrit von Stockhausen was really killed in Berlin in a car accident. He served with distinction as a U-boat skipper early in the war and was thirty-five when he died.

Bernhard Jope lived through the war and died in 1995, aged 81. He flew for Lufthansa until he retired. He sank the Italian battleship Roma with a Fritz X guided bomb in 1943.

General Walther Wever died in a plane crash in 1936. It is often speculated what role he would have undertaken in World

War Two if he had lived, as he'd shown a strong interest in developing a heavy bombing force for the Luftwaffe.

Nearly every other character in the two 'Kriegsmarine Victorious' books are developed from real people, though there are some notable exceptions, such as Ober-matt Helmut Khole.

In the end, these novels are pure speculation, designed to entertain and maybe to inform, at least a little. I hope you enjoyed them.

48300379R00275

Made in the USA
San Bernardino, CA
16 August 2019